Sarah Thomas was born i—
in London. *Queen K* is her

Praise for *Queen K*

'A superb debut novel ... Any—
will love Thomas's scalpel-sharp skewering of the mores and
idiocies of the idle rich' Alex Larman, *Observer*

'Melanie is an outsider keeping her wits in a world of wealth and
privilege ... Thomas evokes these complex lives with compelling
insight' Suzi Feay, *Financial Times*, Best New Debut Fiction 2023

'Balzac in Balenciaga ... *Queen K* lures you in with escapist,
beach-read vibes, then bares its teeth with a devastating portrait
of the emotional cost of greed' *Times*

'Echoes of *The White Lotus* ... A hot holiday read to brighten up
the last few weeks of winter ... A classy thriller that will appeal
to fans of Leïla Slimani's *Lullaby*' Claire Lowdon, *Sunday Times*

'*Queen K* is as compulsive as a Netflix binge, but it also asks
timely questions about status and what constitutes a dignified
life' Sheena Patel, *Guardian*

'Trust us and order this because you won't be disappointed, and
our bet is that this is going to be on the small or big screen. A
dark and brilliant take of a Russian oligarch and his family ...
such a brilliant read' *Glamour*, Best New Books of 2023

'Neither of the two female characters are straightforward; the
relationship between them is well-drawn and they successfully
propel the plot at a rattling pace. Thomas has a flair for telling
a good story with wit and candour' Christena Appleyard,
Daily Mail

'What a compulsive read this was! A real eye-opener into a
world I h—

'Patricia Highsmith-esque ... an untrustworthy narrator judging her employer's life of excess and desperate attempts to infiltrate a glittering world' *Evening Standard*, The Debut Authors You'll Love in 2023

'A fascinating journey with lots to draw us in' *Independent*

'Tensely charged ... an intriguing and absorbing debut' *Buzz Magazine*

'Meticulously crafted' *i-D*

'An enjoyably voyeuristic drama of ambition, exploitation and betrayal, which illustrates how desire for acceptance can lead us to neglect others' *Bookseller*, Editor's Choice, Pick of the Month

'Beautifully crafted and compelling. Thomas perfectly captures the textures of entitlement and the inner workings of Russian plutocratic life lived between Moscow and Europe's glamour resorts' Caroline Knowles, author of *Serious Money*

'Thrilling, revealing and disturbing, *Queen K* dives deep into the hidden lives of the mega-rich, the dark structures of privilege and power, and the lies we tell ourselves to keep the illusion afloat. Thomas knows her subject inside out and it shows – her dazzling debut is both a gripping mystery and a relevant treatise on the dangers of wealth without limits' Emma Stonex, author of *The Lamplighters*

'A wry, unsettling take on privilege, avarice and corruption. This book pulls back the curtain on the lives of the ultra-rich and reveals a world fatally distorted by greed and arrogance; it navigates questions of class and complicity with a rare deftness' Keiran Goddard, author of *Hourglass*

'Thomas has created a world of buttercream-beige luxury, brimming with toxicity and darkness, that pulls you in, and under' Calla Henkel, author of *Other People's Clothes*

Queen K

SARAH THOMAS

This paperback edition first published in 2023

First published in Great Britain in 2023 by Serpent's Tail,
an imprint of PROFILE BOOKS LTD
29 Cloth Fair
London
EC1A 7JQ
www.serpentstail.com

10 9 8 7 6 5 4 3 2 1

Typset in Freight Text by MacGuru Ltd
Designed by Barneby Ltd
Printed and bound in Great Britain by CPI Group (UK) Ltd, Croydon CR0 4YY

A CIP record for this book can be obtained from the British Library

ISBN: 978 1 80081 491 2
eISBN: 978 1 80081 492 9

For CCB

'She thirsted for everything but the clear stream of her own life, flowing hidden in the grass.'

Honoré de Balzac, *Lost Illusions*

I went to dinner with some old school friends the other night and before I'd been there ten minutes they were asking me about that family I used to work for, the billionaires. Everyone does that. Everyone's heard the story and knows I was there that night. 'Something crazy happened, didn't it,' they say, 'with that oligarch's wife; didn't she just disappear or something?' They look at me and depending on the mood I'm in I brush them off with an arch quip or I try quite seriously to explain it all: how it came to that, how Kata got it so badly wrong.

On this particular night, I was looking at those girls from school arrayed around the dinner table, in their merino knits, comfortable in their professions: lawyer; TV producer; book editor. I caught the whiff of glibness, that I was being patronised. 'So exotic!' said Charlotte. 'Being a tutor. Makes office life seem very boring!'

Charlotte had seen I was in the country from one of my Instagram stories. I'd been packing up the last of Mum's stuff and found a big book of photographs, all these pictures from Mum's youth, on the seafront at Dartmouth with the sailing yachts behind her, hair blown about by that south-coast wind.

'Wow, you look like her!' Charlotte said. 'Come to dinner on your way back through London. I'll invite some of the others.'

When Charlotte led me down the hall to her kitchen it all came back to me: the lust I used to have for houses like this, the sounds of the street dying away as we passed a sitting room with heavy curtains, a faded sofa full of cushions, a fireplace and, on either side of the fireplace, blue and white china urns. Charlotte had seemed so helpless to me when we first met aged thirteen, both new at a girls' boarding school in the West Country. There was some incident in the library, a mouse ran over her books and she screamed, then people followed her round chanting: 'Library Mouse, Library Mouse.' It irritated me, and one night in the dinner queue I told everyone how lame they were being. 'Teasing Charlotte is mean and lazy, it also happens to be totally risk free. Now, how about *her*,' I said, pointing to this girl a few years above us, someone beautiful and fascinating and tyrannical, known to be vicious in her punishments.

Push up, not down, I suppose is what I meant. Back then, I saw Charlotte as someone in need of *my* protection. It's relentless, isn't it, our need to order ourselves, to form hierarchies? When we were kids together at that school we were ordered by our wits, it was cruel and merciless. In the end of course we are ordered by our capital: it is cruel, it is merciless.

I think I was always aware Mum was heading towards an act of mortal stupidity, but I never saw it coming with Kata. Two such weak women. I grew up wishing my mother could have tried to hide her weaknesses from me, that she could at least have pretended to be some kind of a safe haven. So I could understand very well Alex's feelings towards Kata, and I could even understand the role she played in the whole sad thing. She clung on to love for her mother for a long time, before that love turned to disgust. She was so sweet and so gentle, my little pupil. I could never quite work it out: was she someone I needed to protect or was she undeserving of my protection, simply because she was so rich?

The email notification was on my phone: my return flight to Vienna the very next day, my apartment, my new life. It really was there, waiting for me. I brought it all up before me in my mind: drinking a cup of coffee in my kitchen, dressing and getting on the underground to the kindergarten where I worked, late afternoons in the cafés, evenings with Jakob and friends. I called it to myself and felt its warmth fill me, then expand outwards. It radiated through Charlotte and the others, and Charlotte's million-pound house in Clapham that her parents had bought her. I separated Charlotte from my envy, for just a moment: I looked at her across the table, at her face as she lifted the bottle of wine and brought it towards my glass, the light freckles over her nose and the top of her cheeks, and for a moment I thought, Maybe we are all helpless, maybe we are all hostage. I think Kata was helpless and hostage from the beginning to the end of her life, and she was the richest of us all.

PART ONE

Courchevel

1

I first worked for Kata when I was twenty-two. I had done a few jobs for a tutoring agency here and there in London when they told me about a two-month home-schooling job abroad. 'Sure, sign me up,' I said, but to be honest I didn't think I would actually go. February felt ages away, we were in November and I was sure something better would come along by then. One of my brief internships would have turned into a glamorous job, on a magazine, complete with invitations to parties and fashion shows, maybe even an expense account … I said yes to the tutoring job as an insurance policy but really, it was like the certainty I have whenever I buy a lottery ticket: I'm going to win, I always think matter-of-factly, already planning where I'm going to buy my house, considering even the practicalities: hmm, I like that street because it's near a pretty park but it's quite far from the tube, but then I suppose if I've won the lottery I can take taxis … A combination of magical thinking and – we can put it more baldly if you want – entitlement made me certain *things would go my way*.

Well, they didn't. But my belief in my future burned bright, in those days. I decided to embrace the tutoring job as an interesting interlude before I returned to my real life.

Real life was in London. That's where everyone went after leaving university, and I followed. It wasn't like I had any intention of going back to Totnes, the small town in Devon where I grew up. Kicking around in Doc Martens, throwing stones into the River Dart. And I hated being in the house with Mum. I'd know it from her very first sip, that look in her eyes, glassy and belligerent. Beer or wine, never spirits. So, no to all that, and yes to London. I'd been spoiled forever, anyway, for a small town like Totnes, first through my scholarship to the boarding school, where I'd mingled for five years with the daughters of bankers and interior designers and diplomats, and then by Bristol University, where I'd sat around in high-ceilinged flats in Clifton and summered at friends' houses in the South of France. Along with my peers, I now had a horror of the 'provincial'.

London was where life waited but even so, it *was* kind of exciting, when the time for the home-schooling job came around, packing up my suitcase in my flatshare in Lewisham, black mould oozing around the mirror in the bathroom, wondering: Where am I off to? What will my bedroom be like? Imagining immaculate white linen, pillows like clouds. And two whole months of not having to think about going to the supermarket, queuing for the bus, the cleaning rota, all the daily administration – no: I'd teach this kid for a few hours, easy, and after that I'd be free. I'd lie on my cloud bed and read; I'd roll around in the luxury.

And I did feel very cosmopolitan, flying off to Geneva for a job. This will be a holiday of the senses, I remember thinking to myself, when the driver opened the door of the blacked-out Jaguar and I got in and smelled the leather, put my hand on its slick surface. We drove through the French Alps way up high to the ski resort, Courchevel 1850. I'd never been to a ski resort before. The scene presented itself through the tint of the Jag's windows: chocolate-box chalets, snow packed cosily on wooden eaves. We drove through the resort and up a short winding road and then we turned into their place. It was different from the wooden chalets, the same pine facade but larger, the lines more modern. A slim, suited man opened the door to me. He took my coat, he opened a cupboard in the hallway and I remember that first glimpse of furs: blonde furs and white furs and black furs. The man added my Uniqlo puffa into the mix, into this Narnia, then he said, with a little wink: 'Better come on up with me, Kata wants to meet you.'

'I'm Sebastian by the way,' my escort said as we walked up some pale wooden steps without a banister. I assumed Sebastian was a butler, or whatever the modern iteration of that was ('concierge', he would tell me later).

The enormous dimensions of an open-plan living area opened beneath us as we climbed. There was a vast glass sculpture of what looked like a stalagmite just to the side of the banisterless stairs and I concentrated on not falling onto it and impaling myself on its glassy spike. We reached a landing. Sebastian knocked on a door and I heard from within a voice bid us enter.

A woman was sitting behind a desk. She was statuesque, her hair a rich ebony black, a colour so sumptuous it must have been dyed. It fanned out in wings around her face. She extended an arm – slowly – and said, 'Please, take a seat.' I sat. I heard the door click behind me.

Kata looked at me for some five seconds before speaking. 'Welcome, Melanie. I hope you had a good flight.'

I opened my mouth to answer, but she held up a hand.

'It is very important, Melanie, that Alex, my daughter, gets into an English school. That is why you have been hired. I have taken Alex out of her school in Moscow because I think she will benefit from one-on-one teaching. You will prepare her for the entry exams and I expect her to get in. You know these schools?'

In front of her on the desk were some prospectuses for girls' boarding schools. Lots of glossy photographs of girls playing hockey and girls doing science experiments and girls marching across blustery grounds arm in arm and laughing into the wind.

'Yes,' I said. 'I went to a school like that.'

'Good, good. Very good. Then you can encourage Alex. In the last months, her marks have gone down. She used to be top of her class. You will make her work hard and get better.'

Kata shook her head.

'She does not want to go. It is childish, she does not realise the benefit it will give her. But I am the parent. I will decide.'

There was an American twang to her accent, overlaying the Russian.

'You speak Russian, Melanie? The agency said so.'

'I studied it as part of my university degree but I wouldn't say I'm fluent. It's been a while.'

'Please, do not speak in Russian with Alex. Only English, her English can get better.'

'Only English,' she repeated.

I assured her that I would speak only English.

She pressed her forefinger to a white plastic device sitting on the desk; within seconds, the door to the study opened and Sebastian reappeared.

'She takes some getting used to,' he chuckled, as he led me through the house.

'Yeah ...' I said.

I was looking about me, taking it all in. A modern cathedral in which the icons were pale grey suede sofas, beige carpets, glass occasional tables, willow spray arrangements and chrome, so much chrome, chrome objets everywhere, spirals and hoops and panthers, two huge fingers making the peace sign. My bedroom was at the bottom of the house, away from the main guest bedrooms, but still: it had a small, comfy bed, fresh white linen. A gleaming little ensuite bathroom. There was a large picture window that looked out onto a pristine expanse of snow. 'Welcome to the team, honey,' Sebastian said, putting my case down next to the bed. He smoothed his hand over the crown of his head and gave me another wink. He was tall and neat; he picked a piece of fluff off his pale grey suit and smoothed the fabric down. His head was shaved, he was elegant. He spoke English with a global accent; I heard shades of American, I heard French inflections. I got the sense he had travelled the length and breadth of the world, working for people like Kata. We heard his name, *Sebastian*, floating down the corridor in her carrying, magisterial tone. He saw my pack of cigarettes fall out of my hand luggage onto the bed. 'Come and have a smoke later, outside the kitchen,' he said, 'if it all gets too much.'

*

I had been pleased when Sebastian told me I'd be eating my meals with the family rather than with the staff to give Alex another occasion to practise her English. It was one more chance to observe. I was glad of my Russian, which I'd always been able to understand better than I could speak. Kata saw me glance at the empty chair next to me. 'Alex is not feeling well,' she said. 'You will meet her tomorrow.'

When Sebastian and a female staff member I hadn't met yet came out with our dinner plates I was provided with my first anthropological artefact. The order in which they distributed the plates appeared illogical at first – they darted here, then there – but as I watched I realised the order in which they were serving followed the pecking order of the people at the table. Kata was served first. Next came Kata's friend Igor. He was a plump, glossy man, seated to Kata's left and solicitous of her in a hyped-up, excitable way. As his plate was put before him, he was extolling the wine, insisting Kata have some, raising his glass to her.

'A toast!' he cried. 'To Kata. This is life!'

He picked up a remote lying beside him, turned in his chair and pointed across the room. Music blasted out from somewhere, some unidentifiable house tune. Kata frowned. 'Lower, lower,' she said, and Igor obeyed.

Sergei was served next. He was Igor's boyfriend, as discreet as Igor was voluble, self-contained in navy-blue cashmere. Olga followed. I would come to know them well, because they were often around. They were Kata's entourage. Nominally based in London, they were members of what I'd come to recognise as the nomadic super rich, wandering the globe from one identikit grey and beige interior to the next, above loyalties and localities, served the same food by the same brand of personal chef wherever they happened to find themselves. Olga's husband worked in finance and was never around. Sergei had some vague-sounding ventures in hostelry. Igor, as far as I could make out, did absolutely nothing.

11

Needless to say, I was served last.

The starter was an infinitely delicate thing; it looked like origami. I think there was a scallop in there amid some decorative sprigs of fine red stuff and dashes of pink jus. It was delicious.

Kata spoke, addressing Igor and Sergei. 'We had a night that was quite ... interesting.' She nodded at Olga, who took the cue.

'Yes!' she said. 'Yes, we did. The party of Valentin Kemerov.'

'Oh!' said Igor. 'Tell us everything. How was he? What was he like?'

'He's involved in everything,' Olga said. 'He has many projects.'

She spoke softly. There was something cow-like and placid about Olga's demeanour, in contrast to Igor's manic ebullience. She had blonde hair parched by hair straighteners. She was wearing the same kind of clothes as Kata: velour loungewear, grey. Diamanté sparkles spelled the word CHAOS across her shoulders.

Even I had heard of Valentin Kemerov, because he was often in the UK press. He was a publicity-friendly exile, a regular and outspoken critic of affairs back home in Russia. The son of a high-ranking minister, Valentin had profited from the privatisation of the nineties by gaining control of one of the country's main newspaper chains, but had fallen out of favour in the 2000s by refusing to share his spoils with the new regime. He was regularly photographed in top hats at sporting events and exiting the revolving doors of stratospherically expensive London restaurants in the company of well-known businessmen, high-profile Russian émigrés, the occasional TV personality.

I pieced together what had happened through the conversation. Valentin had thrown a private party at Calico in London to celebrate his fiftieth birthday. Kata had been surprised to receive an invitation in the post as she'd never met him, but Olga had been very excited. 'We have to go,' she'd said. 'Valentin knows everyone!'

They were still reeling from the experience. There had been lots of famous people there. They had arrived, they had milled around and then Valentin had come over, in his black silk shirt, to introduce himself; the crowds parted before them as he led them over to a corner, a roped-off area, his own private table.

'Who was at the table?' Igor asked, unable to contain himself. He turned the music up a fraction. 'I can't believe we missed this to visit your mother!' He shook his head at Sergei.

'Such glamorous people,' Kata said. 'He had a friend with him who was very nice. Such impeccable manners. He was an English lord. An earl. His name was Oliver.'

He had been so charming.

Valentin had sat her next to Oliver and he had asked her many questions. How long had she been in London? Was she enjoying it? Had she partaken of any of their rather idiosyncratic summer traditions? Had she been at Ascot, Goodwood? No? That was a shame. If he had known her then, she could have come with his party. She could come with them next year, everyone was there, in the Royal Enclosure. And her husband, did he like racing?

He had known her husband's name, without her telling him.

'No? Well, it's an acquired taste. I'd like you both to come, as my guests. What about tennis: Wimbledon, the Queen's Club?'

'Fabulous!' cried Igor. 'Will you see him again?'

'I hope so,' Kata said.

Something interesting had happened at the end of the night.

There had been this man, some nobody, who had been paying Kata undue attention throughout the evening. Coming on to her, I inferred. He had followed her and Olga out of the club as they were leaving. They were waiting on the pavement for Dmitri, Kata's driver. Wanting to get rid of him, Kata told the man she was married.

'Who is he, baby?' the man said. 'I bet he's not worth what I am.'

Kata told him her husband's name and the man laughed.

'Sure, baby.'

Luckily, Dmitri arrived at that moment. Kata moved towards the car, but the man continued to harass her.

'When Dmitri saw what was happening, he got out from the

car and spoke to the man. He said, "Do you know who this lady's husband is?" He said Ivan's name and the man realised I had been telling the truth. You should have seen his face! He went completely white and put his hands over his mouth. "Please, please," he said, "a mistake, a misunderstanding."'

Igor whistled.

Jesus, I was thinking. Who exactly was her husband?

'So maybe Ivan will join you in meeting Oliver and Valentin,' Igor said, after a silence.

Kata didn't answer Igor, but she gave him a funny look. She raised her eyebrows, she pursed her lips. It was a look he seemed to understand because he answered it in kind, he nodded and pursed his lips too, and no more was said. Igor raised his hands in the air and shouted: 'Dessert!' and I saw Sebastian come through the swing doors.

Kata had been animated when recalling the events at the nightclub; I watched her now, looking down at her dessert, as she brought her expression under control, as she subdued herself into immobility. Her lips set themselves into a pout. She reached for her spoon and her arm moved as slowly as it had done up in her study, when she had gestured to the chair opposite her, when she had looked at me for five seconds before speaking.

'It is very good,' Igor said to Kata, 'that you will be based more in London from now on. You will have a bit more freedom there. And you will see more of us. And now you know Valentin, and this lord, they can introduce you to others. We will all go to Ascot this year,' he said, raising his glass. 'Cheers!'

'I will stay in London more,' said Kata, 'if I can persuade my husband.'

At the mention of her husband the others fell silent.

Igor soon rallied. 'Of course you will persuade him! Alexandra must go to school in England. They have the best education in the world!'

He turned to me then. It was the first time anyone had spoken to me. 'You will make Alex work very hard, won't you? You will make sure she gets into one of those schools.'

'I'll do my best ...'

'See?' Igor said, turning again to Kata.

The corners of Kata's mouth pulled upwards; once again, she subdued them. She pressed her little plastic bell. Coffee was brought in.

The last thing I remember from that dinner was Igor, irrepressible after several glasses of champagne, turning the music right up. Guetta blasted out and Kata moved her head. She moved it back and forth, lips pressed out. She reminded me of a mantis in that moment, swaying her head back and forth to the beat. I watched her for quite a while, hypnotised. Then I excused myself and went to bed.

*

At breakfast the next morning Kata said to me, without looking up from a glass cylinder of yoghurt and berries and seeds: 'Melanie, lessons will start after breakfast. Alexandra is in her bedroom, please collect her and go to the study. She has been in bed long enough; it is time for her to work.'

When I knocked on the door to Alex's bedroom and went in, I saw a dark-haired girl, cute with puppy fat, sprawled on a king-sized bed, staring into her phone.

'Hey, Alex,' I said. 'I'm Mel. How are you feeling? Any better?'

She didn't answer me or look up.

'Your mum told me to tell you it's time to start lessons. We should go up to the study.'

She sighed and rolled off the bed. She trudged after me down the corridor, all the while looking at her phone. Kata and the others were still at the breakfast table. They were discussing the day's schedule. Skiing, shopping, massages.

'Can I come?'

Kata stopped talking and turned to Alex. 'What are you talking about? Of course you can't come.' She pointed at me. 'It's time for you to work.'

'I'm still ill,' Alex said.

'If you are ill, then how can you come with us? Enough excuses. Work!'

She turned back to the others, but Alex didn't move. 'Please, Mama,' she said.

'No,' Kata replied.

Alex shot me a look of hatred. She began to trail up the stairs to the study.

'Melanie,' Kata said, 'you have to be *strict* with her. You have to show her who is boss.'

'Yes,' I said meekly.

I slunk up the stairs, anxious about the furious little creature that awaited me. When I entered the room, she glared. She was slumped on the floor with her back against a bookshelf, knees hunched up to her face.

What had I got myself into? Why was I here, in this strange family's house, grappling with their livid child? For a moment I felt too nervous to speak. Children have the capacity to be more intimidating than adults. They've yet to acquire the mask of politeness with which most adults spare one another. Their brutal honesty, their unfiltered responses to your person, are terrifying to the emotionally squeamish. I thought of children as animals and I quailed at the power of their instincts. Once they smell fear, it's all over.

'So, Alex,' I said, my voice a shade too strident. 'Your mum says you might be going to boarding school, in England. Have you looked at any schools? Is there one you like more than the others?'

'I'm not going.'

'You don't want to go? It can be scary, going away to school, but it quickly becomes fun. I remember it myself.'

'I'm not going.' She shook her head and brought it down onto her knees.

'Look. Let's just take it easy today.' I made my voice gentler. 'OK? What are some of your hobbies? Like, if you could be doing anything in the world right now, what would it be?'

At first she didn't respond. Then she raised her head and gazed into the middle distance. 'Watching a movie with—' she said, and then stopped.

A burst of laughter came from the people downstairs. She strained as if to hear them.

'You can join them afterwards, Alex. Lessons won't take all day.'

She peeled herself from the floor and sat at the desk.

'OK,' I said, 'look, we're going to take it easy, we're going to go through this paper together. It's a maths paper, it's like doing a puzzle, we'll go slowly, one question at a time, easy-peasy.'

She was small in the big black swivel chair. She was only eleven. She looked at the paper in front of her. 'I can't do it,' she said. 'It's too hard.' She threw the paper onto the floor.

An hour and a half later, nothing had changed. I'd put a succession of things in front of her. Comprehension stories about baby rabbits. Reasoning exercises with fun shapes. 'It's too hard,' she said, for each new thing.

'Look,' I said, eventually. 'We are going to do one of these papers today. I'm sorry if you don't like it, but that's why I've been hired. I don't mind not taking a break. We are going to stay in this room until one of these papers is done. The moment one is finished, you are free. For the rest of the day.'

Some instinct told me what might be effective. I hesitated before saying it because I knew it was manipulative. And she was so small in her swivel chair.

'Think,' I said, 'how proud your mum will be if you work hard today, if we go downstairs together and I'm able to give you a glowing report. You don't want to make her cross with you, do you?'

She looked down at the maths paper in front of her.

She wrenched a pen out of a stand on the desk with such ferocity that the stand toppled over and pens spewed all over the floor.

'Great,' I said. I knelt down and began to pick the pens up.

When I stood, she was bent over the paper, scribbling furiously.

She was already at the end of the first page; she began speeding down the second.

'Oh, come on, Alex,' I said, 'at least try. Don't write just anything.'

She zoomed down the third.

I give up, I thought. I'll call the agency and tell them I'm not cut out for this. I don't know how to deal with this girl.

She threw down the pen and walked towards the door. She had done ten pages of maths questions in under five minutes.

'Wait a moment,' I called after her.

'You said when I'd done a test I could go.'

'I meant actually *done* a test, Alex, not just covered ten pages with pen marks.'

'The answers are right,' she said.

'We'll see about that. Sit down. You're not leaving this room until I've checked them.'

She sat down, crossed her arms over her chest and watched me.

I checked them.

Every single answer was correct.

It had taken me longer to check her answers than it had taken her to do them.

*

Kata and the others were lying supine in the living room when I left the study and went back downstairs. They had a pale grey couch each, the pale grey tones of their loungewear melded into the couches perfectly, they lay there like four lazy chameleons.

I explained why lessons had finished for the day and assured Kata we'd have a full day tomorrow. I told them about the extraordinary ability Alex had displayed.

'If she's like that in her other subjects, I reckon she'll get into any school of her choosing.'

Kata sat up. 'Alexandra!' she called.

Alex appeared in the doorway. She looked wary.

A look of beatific softness and pleasure spread across Kata's face. She opened her arms wide. 'My brilliant clever girl. Come to me.'

Alex remained in the doorway. She appeared to be processing what her mother had just said. She looked confused, and disbelieving.

'My beautiful clever girl,' Kata said. 'Come and give your mama a cuddle.'

Alex started across the room, shyly. She was trying to keep her face still. But then, unable to control herself any longer, pleasure soared into her eyes, her cheeks. She ran the last few steps into her mother's arms. She buried her face in her mum's chest and Kata tightened her arms around her. When she raised her face slightly, some long seconds later, I saw that her eyes were wet.

The other three rose from their couches and chorused exclamations of their own. They moved towards mother and daughter, they formed a circle around them.

Feeling uneasy, an intruder in this scene of intimacy, I left the room.

*

To this day, I'd say that Alex is the brightest pupil I've ever taught. She didn't need a tutor at all. After those first few hours, the job, in terms of teaching, was the easiest I've ever done. She could do any task you set in front of her. They kept me on regardless. I think they saw having a tutor as standard, a thing you just *had*, along with a chef and a housekeeper and a personal trainer and a masseuse. And it was convenient for them to have someone to look after Alex for five or so hours a day.

Later that night I came up from my room to get a bottle of water from the kitchen.

They were lying on their sofas again, watching a film on a massive flatscreen that appeared to have descended from a hidden compartment in the ceiling.

Alex was lying next to her mother, nestled right into her. She was the only one not gazing up at the screen. She was gazing up at her mother. The look of disbelief I had seen earlier had not gone completely but had softened and rounded out into what seemed to me a wondering joy.

Kata moved an arm to pull her closer. Alex looked back towards the screen and they continued to watch the movie, together.

Not so hard then, to work out what had been going on, why Alex's marks had gone down over the last few months. Now the act had been dropped, there was no going back on it. Of her two conflicting desires, her desire not to be sent away to boarding school and her desire to win her mother's approval, the latter had won.

You are cruel, I can remember thinking, looking at Kata. You are cruel, for your love of that little girl to be conditional.

2

A month and a half after my arrival, Olga, Sergei and Igor began to behave erratically. They seemed jittery. Something appeared to have startled them out of their indolent daily routine. I'd grown used to watching them move placidly from breakfast down to the gym, up to the masseuse's table, back down to the sauna, into their bedrooms to change out of their loungewear into smarter clothes – jeans and sunglasses and furs – in which to go shopping, or into their Moncler ski suits before hitting the slopes. I'd grown used to them returning in the early evenings, most often to change back into their loungewear with a sigh, to take their places at the table and await Sebastian's ministrations, Igor over by the Apple Box, shouting suggestions as to what movie they should watch that night. I had wondered, at one point, how they were able to take such an extended and seemingly indefinite holiday, had wondered that there was nothing pressing calling them back home, but then I reminded myself of the world I was moving in, that I was applying layman's rules to them that were entirely inappropriate.

That first time, in Courchevel, when they were still new to me, when I hadn't yet come to understand what really drove them, I assumed that they arranged their days in this way because it was how they wanted to live them. I assumed that, because they were rich, they were living on their own terms. Maybe there were signs of the true nature of their desires, but I didn't yet have the context to pick up on them. I do remember that I often came upon the four of them huddled extra close on one of the grey sofas, eyes glued to one of their phones, watching some Insta story, which was usually pumping out loud music and laughter. Passing by I'd catch a glimpse on the screen of tanned and surgically enhanced people embracing one another, the swirl of brightly coloured gowns, the pulse of some DJ spinning house beats. I thought of Emma Bovary in the convent, transporting herself by reading the lives of the saints. Their social media forays took them all over the world: to Cannes; to London; New York; Miami; Mykonos; Buenos Aires; Mustique; St Barths. 'Beautiful,' I heard Kata murmuring one time; I craned my neck and saw on her screen a long outdoor table at dusk, with lanterns and candles and flowers and chattering people milling about in kaftans; it was a private party at some socialite's Caribbean home; she had invited a handpicked coterie of aristos, fashion designers, former supermodels and names on *the international scene*. The hostess had a phenomenally successful lifestyle brand. I'd watched her videos on Instagram before. She radiated a self-esteem so iron-clad as to survive nuclear devastation. The world could burn to ash and this person's self-regard would remain, some hard, metallic form, pulsating undaunted.

Sometimes they did go out of an evening. They would gather in the beige and chrome living room for a drink before setting off; Sebastian would pass round glasses of champagne. They would be dressed to the nines: PVC trousers, leather jackets, spike heels and accessorising bling for Kata and Olga; jeans and suit jackets for Igor and Sergei. They would look freshly showered, they would exude perfumes and cologne. They would seem nervous and excited, they would clatter off into the night. Debriefs would be issued at next morning's breakfast: they'd managed to speak to so-and-so, he owned the most famous hotel in Dubai ... But there was always a downcast air to these morning-afters, as if the night had not fulfilled its promise, and so maybe I did begin to get the sense, as the days rolled by one into another, that their loungewear-clad flatscreen-watching did not represent all that they most dreamed of for themselves.

Alex and I came down from the study after our daily lessons one day to find the living room devoid of its usual occupants. Voices murmured from the hallway where the guest bedrooms were. Dinner that night was a clipped and muted affair. Phones were checked. They seemed distracted as they lay on their sofas after dinner watching Barbra Streisand in *A Star Is Born*.

'When will you know for sure?' I heard Igor ask Kata as I collected a book I had left lying on the coffee table.

'Tomorrow morning,' she replied.

Sergei got up purposefully, walked across the room, stopped and then returned to his seat. 'I forgot what I was going to get,' he said, laughing.

The following morning when I came upstairs to breakfast Sebastian was pacing back and forth across the living room, phone to his ear, speaking urgently in French. He put his hand across the phone's mouthpiece and spoke across the room to where the four of them sat watching him from the breakfast table. 'I have three seats confirmed,' he said, 'on the 14.20 from Geneva.' The next couple of hours saw staff bringing wheelie cases out of bedrooms and gathering them in the entryway, passports in leather passport-holders being produced, Sebastian printing out boarding passes up in the study.

As the driver idled outside, they gathered round Kata. There were kisses and squeezes and exclamations of gratitude.

'Remember, don't say anything about it!' Igor said on his way out. 'Better to keep it to ourselves.'

And then, just like that, they were gone.

I was quite sad to see them go, actually. I could see why Kata liked having them around. The soothing predictability with which they kept to their roles. Docile, dependable Olga. Igor never failing to bring the fun factor. Sergei, bulking up the numbers without being obtrusive, just there, dignified and quiet.

Alex and I sat upstairs in the study doing vocabulary exercises. She'd learned twenty new English words that day and was writing sentences for each as a way of remembering them. She read out the sentence she'd written for 'unprofessional': *The doctor began the amputation with a worried look on his face that was quite unprofessional.*

'That's amazing,' I said, laughing, and she smiled. 'Are you looking forward to seeing your dad?'

But I didn't need to ask. Every time there was a noise of a car slowing down on the road outside, she would look up in excitement. She nodded now in answer to my question, she lifted her plump little wrist to her mouth. She was wearing an edible bracelet, pastel-coloured sweets on a string. She nibbled one.

When the door finally opened around 3 p.m. and loud male voices filled the house, Alex jumped up from the desk and I didn't call her back, even though we were in the middle of a lesson. I followed her down, curious, and hung back, in the living room, looking at the people who had just come in.

There were three men, the same age – mid to late forties – and they wore the same style of clothes: jeans, trainers, leather jackets. Two of them were stockily built and one was tall and slim. Alex ran up to one of the stocky men and flung her arms around his waist. 'Papa!' He had short sandy-coloured hair and his nose was soft and rounded. His face was smooth, inexpressive. He was the least physically prepossessing of the three but the others hung back, as if awaiting direction. He smiled and put his arm around Alex, he looked at her but just for a moment; his eyes were up, around, searching, until Kata appeared in the doorway. He let go of Alex, stepped forward and kissed Kata on the mouth.

Sebastian and the housemaids, Francine and Astrid, relieved the newcomers of their coats and bags and the two other men came down the stairs into the living room. 'Hello,' they said to me. They shook my hand, one after the other.

'Anton.'

'Vova.'

Anton wheeled round and scooped Alex up. He was quite hot. Tall and sexy and lanky. He whirled Alex around in the air until she shrieked and giggled with pleasure.

'How's the cheeky monkey?' Vova said. He produced something shiny from his pocket.

'It's my favourite chocolate!' said Alex, showing it to me. 'From Moscow.'

As Anton, Vova and Alex gambolled and scuffled, I looked back up the stairs to Kata and her husband. He kissed her again. He put his hand in the small of her back, he angled his head down to her. His air was paternal. He handled her like something precious.

They came down the steps together, his hand still in the small of her back. They walked across the room towards the dining area.

'Sebastian,' murmured Kata. 'We would like to have tea, please. Would you like to eat?' she asked her husband. 'Are you tired? Would you prefer to rest?'

She seemed solicitous, deferential. It was markedly different from the dominance she displayed around her acolytes, Igor, Sergei and Olga, and it was interesting to see her like this.

Alex looked up at her dad as he walked past.

He happened to glance down. He gave her an easy wink before passing on and by, out of the room, with Kata.

*

I don't really get it, I found myself thinking, later that day. Why Igor, Sergei and Olga fled like that, like animals on the Pacific plate margin that sense an impending tsunami. He's not that intimidating, for God's sake.

It was early evening and the atmosphere in the sitting room was informal, messy, relaxed. The massive screen was down; Ivan and his mates were playing Grand Theft Auto. They'd ordered in some burgers and beers, and the usually immaculate space had given itself up to paper bags and plastic wrappers, buckets of fries, beer cans.

'Who are Anton and Vova, exactly?' I asked Alex.

She had come over to where I was sitting at the dining table to ask me the meaning of a word.

'"Cautious" means careful,' I said.

25

She had been following her dad and the other two men around ever since they arrived. She had stayed beside them in front of the games console all afternoon, reading her book. The noise of heavy artillery had not seemed to bother her. She'd been nestled into her dad's side. He'd had his arm around her even while holding the controller; she'd been jostled here and there as he manoeuvred his avatar out of the way of exploding shells and mortars.

'Anton and Vova work for my dad,' she said. 'I've known them since I was a baby. They are like my uncles.'

'Look,' I said, pointing down to a comprehension of hers that I'd just finished checking. 'Almost full marks.'

When I looked back up, I saw that Kata had appeared at the door on the other side of the room. She stood there, surveying the scene. The others, absorbed in their game, hadn't noticed her. A burst of computerised machine-gun fire filled the room; they shouted instructions to one another about the game. Kata continued to stand there. I saw her eyes move over it all. They were very thorough. They left nothing out. First, they took in the coffee table; they moved, like a game of join-the-dots, from soiled wrapper to half-eaten burger to beer can. They went to the screen, where a man in an Adidas tracksuit top was having his head beaten to a pulp. She looked at Vova, she looked at Anton and then, finally, she looked at her husband. I watched her watching them, and as I did so their gestures and grunts, their open mouths as they handled the controllers, seemed bestial. A look of cold disdain passed across Kata's face. Raising her chin, she walked across the room.

*

'I want to see what Mama will be wearing,' Alex said the next day. It was noon and we were all going out for lunch. 'She always dresses up when she's going out with Papa.'

When Kata appeared about ten minutes later, I saw what Alex meant.

She was wearing knee-length bodycon in cerulean blue. Her

hair had been blow-dried into enormous curlicues that stood out around her head. Her eyes were dramatic, huge, surrounded by an eyeshadow in glittering, gunmetal grey. No potential site for display remained bare: neck, ears, both wrists were clustered with diamonds. Ivan followed just behind her, hair slicked, in a black suit and wearing a vast and complex-looking watch. Sebastian opened the closet and took out Kata's fur. He went towards Kata, but Ivan stopped him and took the fur. He would put it on Kata's shoulders. After he had done so, his hand came to rest in the small of her back, the definitive and recurring gesture with which their two bodies seemed to connect.

'Come on,' Kata said to Alex and me.

Sebastian waited until the car could be heard outside, purring its way from the underground car park, before he opened the front door.

It was a Chinese restaurant, but not the kind of Chinese restaurant in which I was used to eating. The restaurant had been done in the Art Deco style. The carpet was plush, with its pattern of interlocking grids. Kata's heels sank down into it. We were led to our table through a dim, soft space. The walls were rosewood, inset here and there with golden panels. Even the sound was soft, the clinking of metal and glass muted into something rich and rounded, the chatter of the diners mellifluous. We were seated at our table and the waiter came forward to attend us.

I was taking it all in: the weight of the white linen tablecloth, I revelled in the feel of it, rubbing it between forefinger and thumb. We were given menus and Alex leaned forward to tell me what she was going to have, what she always had when she came here. Kata and Ivan were next to us but we might as well have been at separate tables, because there was little to no communication between us and them. That was why I was there, to tend to Alex, so that the adults might be left alone. It was always the case, when I was taken along on outings, and it suited me fine. I got to enjoy the luxury privately, without the distraction or stress of interaction. I opened my menu contentedly and began to consider what to have.

When I had made my decision and set the menu aside, I noticed that Alex was absorbed in a game on her phone. I glanced at Kata, diagonally opposite me, and I was surprised by what I saw. There was something different about her, something I hadn't seen in her before. She had a look of girlishness about her, of breathlessness. It made her look younger and lighter. She stretched a manicured hand across the table and took hold of her husband's hand. At that moment the waiter came over. She let go of Ivan and sat back.

We gave our orders and the waiter went off again. Alex disappeared back into her game. Across came Kata's hand, once again, to her husband's. She leaned forward.

'You look handsome,' she told him.

He told her she looked beautiful. I saw her look beyond him, to her reflection in the mirror on the opposite wall, and smile.

He told her he liked it when she wore blues, purples, greens. The colours he picked out for her. They were the colours that suited her best. 'We will go shopping while I'm here,' he said. 'I want to choose some dresses for you and watch you put them on.'

'I only like to wear the clothes you pick out for me, Ivan,' she said. 'You know best, what is good for me.'

There was silence. In the silence I saw their fingers, caressing and interlacing. He probed his thumb gently into her palm.

I looked down at my napkin. The atmosphere had become very intimate, erotic even, and I was embarrassed. I thought they might feel embarrassed too when they remembered I was sitting right there. It only took me a second to get real. You don't exist to these people, I reminded myself. It's laughable and deluded of you to feel embarrassed. They certainly don't.

'You know, Ivan,' Kata said, gently stroking the hairs on the back of his hand, 'when we get back to London, it might be, I was thinking, enjoyable, to see some people, to entertain occasionally. What do you think?'

He nodded. He was looking across the room, maybe checking to see if the food was on its way.

'Yes,' he said. 'Why not, if you would like it.'

She smiled. I saw her look at herself again in the mirror across the room.

He mentioned a couple of colleagues of his, she had met their wives once or twice, they'd also just come over to London from Moscow. One of them lived in Surrey; in fact, they were having a barbecue in a few weeks' time, he would be out of town but she should go, take the car.

'Yes ...' she said.

She hesitated.

Large bottles of sparkling water were brought over to our table and uncapped.

'Well ...' Kata continued. 'But I meant ... How about if we had a small dinner at home, in our house?'

'If you like.'

'I would.' She was smiling again now. 'And Ivan, we could ask Igor and Olga to help us. They would know the right sort of people to invite. They have some contacts in London.'

Plates of dim sum were put on the table, a single crab claw, dumplings in bamboo steamers.

'Olga could help us, with invitations and planning and,' she repeated herself, 'she can advise us, on the right sort of people to invite.'

I cringed a bit, when she said that for the second time. I began to see where she was going. I'm not sure this is the right tack, Kata, I was thinking to myself. You're being a bit clumsy, a bit on the nose.

Ivan picked up the crab claw and ate it.

'And who exactly,' he said, 'are the right sort of people to invite?'

'Well, you know. Society people. People in the high society there, in London.'

It was hard not to feel a sort of affection for her then. The way she put it. So guilelessly, so openly. She wasn't being manipulative in that moment. Quite simply, she was appealing to him. She was asking his permission to do something, and she seemed to want him to do it with her. She was like a little girl.

'Ah,' Ivan said. He examined a plate of particularly elaborate-looking dim sum and lifted up a piece with his chopsticks. 'Have you tried this yet, Kata?'

He lifted the chopsticks until the piece of dim sum was right in front of her face.

'Open your mouth.'

She hesitated but he kept his hand where it was. She allowed the piece of dim sum to be placed in her mouth.

She chewed it down, it took quite some time. It was a big piece, her cheeks bulged and she blushed. He watched her chew.

He began to speak of something else. Of some work that needed doing on the house in Moscow.

'Ivan,' she said.

I saw her look around, as if trying to pull the right words from the air around her. 'Wait,' she said. And she began to tell him about her night at Calico. She told it in the same way she'd told it at the dinner table my first evening, to Igor and Sergei. The fact that she was retelling it, verbatim, to her husband, reinforced my impression that she wasn't trying to manipulate him, that she wasn't engaged in anything underhand.

At first she was awkward in the retelling but then, in recalling it, enthusiasm and excitement made her words flow. She told him about the glamour of the people she had seen and met in the club, about their famous names, how she had moved among them, about all the things they did and the places they went, about how, if they tried, they too, she and him, could be a part of it. Not everyone could be a part of it, but they could, they could be.

He cut her off.

'Yes, I know you went there. Dmitri informed me.'

Dmitri, the driver.

He didn't follow up on his statement.

He looked down at his plate. He ate, stolidly.

It had been a while since Kata had touched her own food.

I saw her look at her husband's down-turned head, the chopsticks shovelling food up into his mouth.

30

'I would like,' she said, 'I would like us to entertain. I would like us to get to know people.'

He shook his head and laughed, not looking up.

Kata's fists were clenched. They lay on the table on either side of her plate. Her nails must be digging into the flesh of her palms, I thought. She had very long nails.

Her mouth opened, then closed. It opened again, it closed again. He'd finished eating, he tossed his chopsticks down onto his plate. He wiped his mouth with the back of his hand, he leaned back, he looked about for the waiter.

She hesitated for a moment and then she began to speak. The words rushed out.

She began to tell him about Valentin, and Oliver.

Valentin Kemerov. Oliver who was an earl. 'Listen, Ivan, both of them already knew of you, they knew who you were! They admire you! They go to so many things, listen.'

She named some of the places. Ascot, Cannes.

'They welcomed me that night, and they'd like to meet you, too, what do you think of that? Valentin grew up in Moscow. He described the house where he grew up, it's near our house. It's on a lake, with beautiful gardens. An old and beautiful estate. As a little boy, his father took him duck shooting.'

'So, you met Kemerov in the nightclub, did you? Yes, that is fitting, that seems to be his natural habitat.'

Alex looked up briefly from the game on her phone and glanced in her parents' direction. A worried expression flitted across her brow before the game pulled her head back down.

Ivan's face was red.

Surely, I thought, he can't be jealous? It was evident even to me that Kata wasn't referring to Valentin or her 'English earl' in that way. I had wondered, when she'd first started on the story, the night I'd arrived. Maybe she's talking about someone she's got a crush on. Everything I'd seen and heard subsequently had made it clear that this was not the case. This woman isn't conducting anything erotic outside of her marriage, I thought. That's not what drives her. I thought of the way she had twirled the hairs of her husband's hands in her long fingernails. Her next words confirmed my intuition.

'Ivan,' she said. 'Valentin can help us; he can help both of us.'

When he replied, his voice was tight, his face still red.

'Kata,' he said, 'people like me cannot meet with people like Kemerov.'

'But why not?'

'There are some things you do not need to understand. But when I tell you it is so, you should trust that it is so.'

'You are not making sense, Ivan.'

'Let me try and explain it to you. Things back home have changed. There are people who used to be important who are no longer important. They refuse to understand that things have changed. I understand. Kemerov: he doesn't understand. He is indiscreet. I cannot afford to be like that. I'm not that stupid. You like this, don't you?'

He gestured around the restaurant, at the opulence that surrounded them.

'And you like these.'

He touched the jewels on her fingers and on her wrists.

'One stupid move and—'

He wiped the palms of his hands together in a nullifying gesture.

I found it thrilling, the turn the conversation had taken, the things to which Ivan was alluding. I had never before encountered people for whom the great political events of the world played out on a personal level, came and sat down to lunch with them, infused their private relationships. I might not have two beans to rub together, I thought, but I am accruing social and cultural capital, aren't I, first through my school and university and now through this sort of thing, in foreign climes, being exposed to people so radically other from me; it would all contribute to my becoming a sophisticate, wouldn't it, everything I experienced could be stored up and then bartered, could be used for my advancement, couldn't it, once I got back to London, once I plunged again into the swim, swimming upstream? I would hustle, I would ascend. I was full of such a bankrupt optimism, in those days.

A waiter moved past our table, carrying an intricate dessert. It was a delicately spun confection, pale and orbed with tiny pearls. Kata looked at it.

'Kemerov is like a piece of shit lying in the street. I can step around it, but if I step in it, I will stink like shit too.'

She recoiled at his coarse words.

When she looked back at him it was with unmistakeable disgust. It was the look I'd seen her give the soiled coffee table, the computer game.

A waiter approached the table and asked if everything was to our liking.

'Go away,' said Ivan, with his tight red face.

Kata saw the look the waiter gave Ivan, covertly, as he retreated. A deep flush swelled out into her cheeks.

'I knew it,' she said. 'Igor was right. I should not have spoken to you about it. I should have kept it to myself. You always spoil it for me, you are threatened by people like Valentin, so you want to keep me locked up forever with nothing to do.'

Just the clinking of diners, the soft tread of waiters across the carpeted floor.

'Threatened?'

He brought the word out again, a foreign object.

'Threatened?'

'Oh ...' She shook her head, made a brushing motion with her arm.

He was clicking his fingers, summoning the waiter, dealing with the bill.

For some moments I had felt a vibration under the table. I realised it was Alex, tapping her foot against the table leg. I'd been so absorbed in the drama unfolding between her mother and father that I'd forgotten about her. Now I looked at her and saw that she was looking at them, as I had been, and that she was frightened. The whole of her little body seemed clenched.

We got up to leave.

Ivan waited for Kata to go first. 'Please,' he said, in what seemed a tone of exaggerated politesse.

We were about halfway across the restaurant when Ivan reached out a hand and closed it around the soft flesh of Kata's upper arm. It was not a hard or violent grip, but it halted her in her tracks. I found myself reaching down to put my hand on Alex's back.

We were in the busiest part of the restaurant. All around us, close enough to touch, people were chatting and enjoying their meals.

Ivan spoke, loudly so that his voice carried over the chattering diners, startling many of them into silence.

'You know that man, Kata, the one who followed you out of the club, the one Dmitri had to speak to? Do you know what he thought you were?'

His voice was calm now, and tender.

'My darling. He thought you were a whore.'

3

They seemed stunned, both of them, in the car; they seemed stunned as they stood in the hallway, allowing Sebastian and Francine to relieve them of their outerwear. Ivan walked slowly up the stairs to the study. Kata, pale, put one foot in front of the other, across the living area and down the corridor to her bedroom. She did not appear for dinner. Later, down in my bedroom, I heard reverberating explosions: Ivan watching an action movie with Anton and Vova. When the explosions stopped, I went upstairs to find them lounging on the couches while the credits rolled. I went outside through the kitchen for a last cigarette and when I returned I saw Ivan's back, retreating down the corridor, towards the bedroom he shared with Kata.

I thought of how they had been in the previous days, him solid and her pliant, and how they had been just a few hours ago in the restaurant, when we had first sat down, she the girl and he the man. I wondered if she would already be asleep. Turned away from him, eye mask on, wrapped in the duvet, just a bundled-up shape in the bed. Or if she would be awake. If she would look up at him as he came into the room, the hours of the night stretching before them.

And the next morning, as I sat down at the breakfast table I thought: Yes, the long night in their bedroom must have effected something, because there was Kata, back in her proper place at the table. She was in a pink silk robe, she hadn't yet done her hair or applied her make-up, and her whole being seemed rounded, girlish, soft. She was sitting next to Ivan and she was offering him things. The breakfast items were all there, arranged upon the table, perfectly within his reach but he did not reach for them, they came to him, all of them, by Kata's hand. His juice? She poured it. His toast? She buttered it. I watched her perform these fealties in her pink silk robe, how it draped over the swell of her breasts, and whatever it was that was going on between them, that was being enacted, seemed to me unbearably voluptuous. They hardly spoke, but every time I sensed movement – Kata's hand reaching – I would raise my head, in order to see the look that passed between them as their hands met and he took her offering. Her lips would part; he would seem to grow taller. She reached for a plate of ham and handed it to him and when she withdrew her arm the pink robe slipped off one shoulder and on that shoulder I saw the bruise.

It was blue and fresh, I saw an oval, the shape of a thumb pad; the robe had slipped right down, held up now only by the curve of her breast, and Ivan reached a hand to the pink silk to slide it gently back up. 'Oh!' said Kata, only just noticing the robe had come down. She twisted her body round to reach for the fabric herself and as she shifted I saw more of her body, the back of her shoulder and upper arm and more bruises, more ovals, where his fingers had gripped her.

I was shocked to see it. The marks so stark, they might as well have been inflicted right in front of me, right here while we ate our breakfast. She looked so replete, so contented, in her pink silk, like a ripe bruised peach. I tried to imagine what he had been doing when he gave her that bruise: was there a corresponding one on her other shoulder? Had he gripped her as she knelt before him? Had he gripped her in order to lower her? Because now he seemed so sovereign, sitting there in his chair at the head of the table, and she seemed so docile, and they seemed to like it like that, they both seemed restored.

When Alex and I left the breakfast table to go upstairs for

morning lessons I found myself looking back, to the table, for one last glance at them. From up in the study I heard the clink of breakfast things being cleared away. Alex sat in silence, writing a description of a forest. One hour, two; the sun climbed higher until it was in the square of the study window. I raised my hand to block its rays from my eyes and as I did so my phone began to buzz. It was the tutoring agency. I went outside to take it.

'Good news,' my director told me. The school Kata was most hoping to get Alex into had opened up some earlier slots for prospective pupils to take the entrance exam.

'Do you want to pass the details on to Kata? Or shall I give her a ring?'

'I will pass on the details,' I said.

I put my head round the door to the study. 'Back in a sec,' I said to Alex.

Kata wasn't in the sitting room or in the kitchen and I was pretty sure, yes, that she had gone back to her bedroom, so I walked down the corridor towards it, thinking, Well, this news is really pretty important, isn't it? I really had better tell her now, not wait until she re-emerges, so I walked down the corridor to that door, behind which some ritual had taken place through the hours of the previous night, running to its own deeply private logic, where violence was not a force to rip asunder but a force to mend and knit and restore, and I thought, This is a totally legitimate reason, to go there, to knock, to look inside.

'Yes?' I heard her say, after I tapped on the door. I turned the handle and pushed.

The curtains were drawn. The room was thick with dark. I could see, glowing within the dark, the white tangled sheets of their bed. She was in it. I breathed in deeply, to take in and taste any spiced smells, any redolence, coming to me from out of the gloom.

I told Kata the news. 'But Alex doesn't need to go over to the UK to take the test,' I said. 'They can email the assessment to me. I can supervise, I can make sure she does it in timed conditions.'

'Wonderful,' she said. There was movement. 'Well, now there

37

is a lot to be done.' She rose. She went over to the curtains. She threw them open and ordinary daylight redressed the room.

She came and found me about an hour later. I was in the sitting room, on a break between lessons. Kata looked freshly showered and put together. She was carrying a large leather diary planner. She sat down on the couch across from me and opened it.

'This is good news, isn't it?' she asked. 'Do you think Alex is ready for the test?'

'Yes. She's more than ready.'

I was gathering together my notebook and phone, to leave Kata the sitting room, to go back upstairs to the study, when Ivan came in. He came down the shallow flight of steps from the entrance hall. Kata had her back to him, but she heard him coming. 'Darling,' she said, 'some good news.' I wondered how she knew it was him and not Sebastian, or Anton, or Vova. Or Francine or Astrid, for that matter.

'Oh, yes?' He came and put his hand on her shoulder, her shoulder, covered by brisk, daytime clothes now, and she reached up her hand to his.

'Alex has a chance to sit the entrance exam to the school she most wants to go to.'

There was the briefest of pauses, and then she brought it out, the lie:

'But it means we have to travel to England for two or three days, because we can't do it here. I am sorry to miss this chance to be together, but we won't be too long.'

She continued to stroke his hand where it lay upon her shoulder.

And I guess he bought it, because he didn't seem suspicious. He just said: 'OK. OK.'

Alex looked forlorn amid the preparations for departure. Sebastian, Francine and Astrid flurried in and out of her and Kata's bedrooms the next day, with cases and smaller bags. The sense of purpose had filled Kata with vitality. She issued instructions to her minions. There was colour in her cheeks. The blood that now steeped her might have been transfused directly from Alex, who looked pale and wan. When they were gathering around the car I went outside to wave them off. I tapped my fingers on the window where Alex was sitting. She gave a small wave, then looked back down. She seemed on the verge of tears. Ivan had come outside too. Kata kissed him on the cheek. His hand was in the small of her back. She stepped forward to take her seat in the car and for the briefest moment his hand remained in the air, in the place where her back had been.

*

I didn't know how to ski, but Kata had bought me a pair of massive white Moon Boots which allowed me to take walks in the snow. I put them on the morning after Kata and Alex left. I thought I might as well use the opportunity to do some exploring while they were away. The boots were light as foam but voluminous enough to make walking awkward. I slow mo-d towards the front door like Neil Armstrong.

The gravel of the car park was grey and slushy but I could see, lapping around the sides of the house, the soft white of untouched snow. From the kitchen window came the sounds of Sebastian, of Francine, of the chef, clattering and chattering, and something made me bend my legs to pass by underneath the level of the window, in order not to be seen.

Round the front of the house I paused and leaned, looking at the terrace where Kata and the others had sometimes sat on a starlit night, invulnerable in their furs, smoking the occasional slim Vogue. Beyond the terrace the eaves of chalets dotted down the slope to a valley, and beyond the valley the specks of skiers moving, ski lifts criss-crossing the distance and then mist, rising to far-off peaks, and above the peaks the great big blue of the sky. I knew that Kata and Ivan's bedroom window was at the very end of the house.

There was a large pine just to the side of Kata and Ivan's bedroom window. It shaded the area and the shade made it easier to see in. The room looked clean, tidy, neutral. The grey bench at the end of the bed held no scattered clothes. It was just a big, tidy room, that was all, and I walked past, thinking about what I'd do down in the town, but when I passed the window and glanced back, I saw Ivan.

He was sitting near the window, facing into the room. His proximity to the glass, and the light and shadow that played across it, had occluded him, but now, watching from a different angle, I saw him clearly. He was sitting in a chair and from the way his head was angled it seemed he was looking at the bed. He was very still. I could see one arm, flat along the edge of the chair.

He sat motionless, looking at the bed.

There was a clack, clack, clack in the still air, some kind of construction work, far off across the snowy landscape. It died away and then a wind came, shifting the stillness, sighing through the branches of the pine. The shadows from the branches moved across the glass of the window and across the back of Ivan's head.

I wondered how long he had been sitting there, just looking at their bed. I wondered how long I had been standing outside the window, watching him.

There was movement. He raised himself from the chair and walked further into the room, to where there was a doorway leading to the ensuite bathroom. When he reached the doorway he turned around and I pressed myself closer to the wall, still angling my body slightly in order to see. He raised his arms over his head and grasped the door frame above him. He pulled himself up, making himself taller, looking all the time at the bed. And then he let go of the door and brought his fists up to his chest, he hit his chest with them, and then he brought them down and, with his left fist, he hit out against the frame of the door.

And then he was looking at me.

I backed towards the pine. 'Oh,' I said, even though I knew he couldn't hear me through the glass. 'Oh, I was just' – I turned around and gestured towards nothing – 'I was just ... I'll come round,' I said, and made a motion with my hand to try to communicate this.

I walked round the side of the house, heart beating, trying to think of an explanation before I reached the front door.

As I rounded the corner I saw he was already there, waiting for me.

'Hello!' I called. 'Sorry! I was just having a look round! I was looking at the windows because I did a module on architecture and—'

I didn't know what I was talking about, just spouting bullshit, but he shook his head, raised a hand and made a brushing motion.

'Fine, fine,' he said. 'Melanie, was it necessary for Alex to go to England to take her test?'

This I had not been expecting. I stopped.

'Um,' I said. 'Um, yes, I think so ...'

Why was he asking this? Had the agency contacted him?

'I think it probably had to be done over there, in controlled conditions ...'

What was he asking, exactly?

He was looking at me steadily, awaiting my answer, it made me very nervous, almost dizzy, but also, beneath these heightened feelings, I was excited, sensing that much depended on how I answered this question, *me*, here outside this spectacular villa, being questioned by this powerful man.

'Yes,' I said. 'The test had to be done over there. I'm not a qualified teacher, I wouldn't have been able to supervise.'

Something in his intensity, coupled with everything else, the bruises, the whole charged atmosphere of his relationship with Kata, made me want to disarm the situation in whatever way I could.

'Fine,' he said again. 'Fine.'

I wasn't sure whether he believed me. What did he suspect Kata of doing over there? What *was* she doing over there?

'Enjoy your day,' he said, and turned back towards the house.

'Thanks ...'

I turned out of the drive and walked slowly down the hill. So much foamy sole between my feet and the ground. It was indistinct where I connected with the earth. He hadn't been bothered, evidently, by my watching him through the window. Why should he be bothered? Mousy little governess. Not exactly the level of threat someone in his position was used to contending with, I supposed. I thought of period dramas where the principal characters volleyed bitter accusations at the dinner table – affairs, gambling debts, illegitimacy – all in front of the silent footmen.

The snowy track unfurled before me. There was the scent of pines, green and fresh, there were new sights to take in, novelties to be explored. As I got further from the villa I came back to myself. What would I do down in the town? I was looking forward to having a look around. I felt the buzz of my phone in my pocket and saw a message from a friend: *Next Tuesday, when you're back, are you still up for going to that thing at Dan's?*

I replied: *Sure. Wait till I tell you about these people.*

How many anecdotes I'd gathered! I imagined myself at Dan's party, retelling the scene in the restaurant, the scene at the breakfast table, the scene of spying through the window, the comic moment when Ivan caught me. Back then I was still just a sightseer, for the most part, still rooted in other realities – the reality of my life, my friends, my plans back home. I walked on down the hill, the cold in my hair but the sun on my cheeks, quite happy, quite buoyant.

*

The town centre of Courchevel 1850 was a load of concrete blocks that looked like the outbuildings of a Tesco car park. The ugly little cubes held riches, of a sort: restaurants where a pot of fondue cost upwards of sixty euros; cosmetic surgery rest stops; the world's most exclusive designer brands. When I reached the snow-cleared streets I put on my regular boots and transferred the Moon Boots to my backpack. In the town square I stroked a hairy little Bavarian pony, tethered for children to feed and ride.

I went into the town pharmacy. It was wood-panelled and charming. I touched the cosmetics in their pretty paper packages. I bought an extremely expensive cream.

'Honey!'

It was Sebastian, coming out of a shop, slim grey coat over his grey suit, carrying shopping bags tied with ribbons. 'Let's go, let's have something to eat.'

He took me to his favourite restaurant, somewhere slick and grey and modern, a place that served cold and un-cosy food: sushi. He ordered with abandon but I was more circumspect. I ordered just three pieces of sushi, spaced far apart on a rectangular dish. We drank sake.

We compared dating apps. He was more amenable to Courchevel men than I was. He swiped right on Konrad, a BMW dealer from Munich who favoured bathroom selfies.

'How did you get into this tutoring stuff anyway?' he asked me.

'Oh, I went to a British public school. They all want to buy into that, these international super rich people. It's easy money but it's not what I want to do forever. How about you?'

'I was a restaurant manager but the place I was working at closed down, so I registered with this concierge service, in Monaco. It's not what I want to do forever, either. I want to have my own restaurant some day. But whatever,' he said. 'This is fun for now.'

The restaurant had filled up and loud music had come on. We were radiant with sake and the food was Michelin-starred.

'Yeah,' I said. 'It's fun, for now.'

I thought of all the other servants there must be in this town, and in other towns like it, in the other billionaire enclaves, an army of people providing tuition and massages and life coaching and vitamin drips; concierges and chefs and housekeepers and trainers and consultants and personal shoppers.

It felt like a recent phenomenon, one spawned by the billionaire class, but then I thought of the first gilded age, of the Rockefellers and Astors and Carnegies as chronicled by Edith Wharton and Henry James and Fitzgerald, the coal, the rail, the steel, the oil: ugly, dirty things, but when they spent their money it was on flowers, grown in hothouses and bought to fill the conservatories of their Fifth Avenue mansions: orchids and camellias and lilies, their scent and colour spilling even in the dead of winter when the sleet froze grim on the ground, and I thought of a recent story

I'd heard, of a man at a Dolce and Gabbana Alta Moda couture show who wore a jewelled hourglass round his neck in which miniature diamonds trickled through the waist instead of sand.

'What shall we do now?' I asked Sebastian when we'd finished our food.

'I'm treating myself,' he said, 'to a couple hours at the Six Senses Spa. We all got the afternoon off cos Ivan and the guys have gone to Geneva for a meeting. Wanna come?'

'Um,' I said. 'I'm not sure. So you mean, the house is empty?'

'Yup.'

'Hmm, no,' I told him. 'I think I'll go back. I think I'll take the opportunity. While everyone's gone. I think I'll take the chance to relax.'

I don't know what I expected from Ivan and Kata's room because really it was pretty blank, pretty functional, much like the rest of the house. The tones of grey and beige, the scrupulous tidiness. I couldn't relax totally because even though Sebastian had said the rest of the staff were off and that Ivan and his mates were away for the afternoon you never knew, did you? Something unforeseen might happen, at any moment the door might open, and Ivan had already seen me staring in at him – not that he'd seemed to care. I left the bedroom door ajar so I would hear the front door should anyone come back unexpectedly.

She seemed to keep her glitziest outfits right at the end of the wardrobe. I touched them all. Bodycon. Bandage dresses in metallic hues. His clothes took up less space. They were more low key. Levis. A black Bugatti fleece. I hadn't known Bugatti made fleece.

There wasn't much to see. The bathroom was palatial. Kata had the high-end toiletries one would expect. I wondered which she would miss if they disappeared.

What had I wanted from this room? Why had I rushed to come here, risked the intrusion? Was I so steeped in soporific comfort that I'd do anything just to get my blood pumping, feel my heart beating?

Whatever the strange potency I had sensed in Kata and Ivan's dynamic, they had left nothing of it here. I opened the drawer of

Ivan's bedside table. There was a photo in there. I lifted it out. It was of him and Kata and Alex but taken a while ago. Alex wasn't more than five or six. Kata had a different haircut. Both she and Ivan looked rawer and rougher than they did today. Their clothes were bulky and dated. There was a whiff of the eighties about them even though the photo wasn't from the eighties, couldn't have been taken later than 2002. They were standing in front of an ugly house that looked like a big prefabricated box. Some sort of red carpet appeared to lead up to the house. Ivan was holding Kata in his arms, about to carry her over the threshold. She was looking up at him adoringly. Alex was in the door of the house waiting for them. Fanning out from the red carpet was a crowd of people, frozen in a collective gesture of applause.

This, I would learn later, was Chukotka, an isolated region at the easternmost tip of Russia, between the East Siberian and Bering Seas. For most of the year the whole of the landscape was white. Ivan would take Alex sledding. She would sit in front of him; he would hold her to him and keep her safe as they hurtled down steep slopes. He was a king in that town, Kata his queen.

'I would lie in between them,' Alex would tell me later. 'When I woke up in the early mornings I would run down the corridor to their room. I can still hear the sound of my feet, running down that long wooden hall. I would get in between them; I would lie there like a puppy until they woke up. Before she turned him against me, when he still loved me. When it was still the three of us, together, in Chukotka.'

4

They were due back after lunch the next day. Walking through the hallway I saw Ivan, standing in the entrance, looking out the window. I heard the sound of a car pulling up. Ivan left his position and went up the stairs to the study.

Sebastian came out from the kitchen and opened the door just in time. Kata swept in.

'Melanie!' she said.

'Hi ...' I said, somewhat surprised by the full-fronted greeting. She sailed down the steps towards me. I felt pinned to the sofa by the force of her energy. She seemed triumphant, resplendent.

'Alex has been accepted! She did brilliantly, brilliantly. Thank you, Melanie, for all your help.'

I couldn't help but blush with pleasure. Her high spirits were radiant and infectious. I wasn't used to this expansiveness from her.

'Alex!' she sang.

Alex followed through the front door. She was wearing a blue furry bucket hat – a new purchase, I hadn't seen it before. With her head tilted down the hat blocked my view of her face.

'Come here, little chook!' Kata said, patting the space on the sofa beside her.

Alex sat down. Kata whipped off the bucket hat, rumpled and mussed Alex's hair and kissed the top of her head.

'Sebastian,' she said. 'Tea.'

Instructing her subordinate seemed to recall Kata to her habitual demeanour. I saw her lips press down, in their usual way. She raised her chin. When she next glanced in my direction her hauteur had returned, the appropriate distance re-established between us.

'Where is my husband?' she asked.

'I think he's up in the study.'

'Ivan!' she called out. She called out a second time, louder: 'Ivan!'

She turned back to Alex. 'Brilliant, clever girl!' Kata smoothed back the hair she had rumpled and I saw Alex's little face for the first time: tired, she seemed, a bit drawn, her eyes wide and shiny.

Astrid and Francine were bringing stuff in from the car, the cases Kata and Alex had left with but also new suitcases, big ones; I saw Francine struggling to get one over the lip of the entrance. 'Oof,' said Kata, leaning back against the sofa cushions. 'There was so much to do over there, so much to organise. But we got everything you will need, don't you think?' she said to Alex.

Alex nodded.

'Melanie, we have all of Alex's textbooks for next term. I want you to start going through them with her tomorrow.'

And here, finally, was Ivan, coming down the stairs from the study. He was looking about him at all the stuff being brought in from the car. Cases and cases of it. Then his gaze settled on Kata, on the back of her head.

Maybe Kata saw me staring at something because she turned to look behind her. She got up from the sofa, went over to Ivan and kissed him, full on the mouth.

'My darling,' she said. 'Was everything OK for you while I was away? Did Sebastian look after you? I have missed you.'

His eyes were wary, watching. She was speaking again, moving, fussing around him, calling: 'Sebastian!' Asking Ivan: 'What would you like to drink? Sebastian, bring a Coke for Ivan, with ice.' She was filling the space with her energy and activity and presence, leaving room for nothing else. It seemed a deliberate tactic, to manage him, to handle him.

'Come, little chook.' When Alex reached her she said to Ivan: 'Congratulate your daughter. She has had a big success.'

Kata was holding on to both Ivan and Alex. Ivan and Alex were not touching one another, they were connected only through Kata.

'The maths test was quite hard, Papa,' Alex said. 'But I got 94 per cent.'

'Well done,' he said. 'Clever girl.'

She looked happy when he said that, she stepped towards him and took his hand. She made a circle of them. Ivan broke away, he went to take his Coke from Sebastian, sat with it on one of the sofas.

'Alex,' Kata said, 'try on your new uniform for Papa. It is in your bedroom. Bring everything down.'

Alex nodded excitedly and shot across the room.

Ivan finished his Coke with a burp.

Alex came down the stairs slowly, shy again when she returned, wearing a grey pleated skirt and a pale blue shirt with a pale blue V-neck jumper over the top. White socks came up to her knees and there were black tasselled loafers on her feet. She was wearing the whole thing at once, every season. She had the summer boater on her head: straw with streaming ribbons. She even had the school lacrosse stick in her hand.

'Come,' her mother beckoned. She motioned Alex to the centre of the room. 'Turn around ... Such a little lady.'

'Now, my darling,' Kata said to Ivan, 'this does mean I will have to spend a little bit more time at the London house, in term time, when Alex is at school.'

'She will be at a boarding school, won't she?'

'Yes, but it's good for her to have me near, in case she needs anything. It's important to you, isn't it, Alex, to have me near?'

'I ...' Alex said. She had stopped twirling. The lacrosse stick drooped from her hand.

'I won't be there all the time, of course. Just here and there. I will still be a lot in Moscow.'

'I still don't know,' Ivan said, 'what was wrong with the school in Moscow.'

A look of impatience flitted across Kata's face. She paused, she made it subside before answering him.

'Alex is ready to take the next step,' she said. 'She wants to grow up to be cosmopolitan, a citizen of the world.'

Ivan kept his eyes on Kata but did not respond. He leaned back against the sofa cushions.

'Alex wants to go to this school!' Kata continued. 'Please, let's not spoil her moment.'

Alex stood rigid. She was holding tightly on to the lacrosse stick with both hands. She was pressing the stick down into the ground.

'Come here,' Ivan said to her. He pulled her gently onto the sofa beside him.

'Do you want to go to the school? Be honest with your papa. It's OK.'

She looked across at her mum.

'It's OK, little one,' he said. 'No one will be angry at you. Be honest.'

'I don't want to go,' she said. Her voice was a whisper.

'You are happy in Moscow, you like being at home.'

Alex nodded. She angled her head, she cringed away from where her mother sat, opposite her and Ivan, on her own sofa.

'But you want to please your mama.'

Alex nodded, the tears spilling out.

Ivan looked up at Kata.

'*You* want her to go to the school.'

I saw Alex wilt into her father's side as he said those words. He held her.

His last words – '*You* want her to go to the school' – rang in the air. They were working upon Kata. They affected her by degrees. When first he said them, the anger was hard and immediate in her face. But she seemed to bring it under control. She closed her eyes and as she did so her face softened. She opened her eyes and when she spoke her voice was a little girl's.

'I try to do my best,' she said. 'Maybe sometimes I have the wrong idea. I thought this would be a good thing, for our daughter, but you know best, maybe I should send, should send all this back ...' She gestured shakily at all the suitcases and shopping bags; her voice trembled.

Her uncertainty, her fragility, hung in the air.

'I just try to do my best,' she repeated. 'If you want, I can send everything back, try to re-enter her in the school in Moscow, but I don't know how to do it, it's too late.'

There really were tears in her eyes now. I saw one tear slide down her cheek; she raised a manicured hand to wipe it off.

'No,' Ivan said, softly. 'No. No one is suggesting that.'

He sighed.

He looked down, to his daughter. 'You will give it a try? You will see how it goes?'

He gave Alex a cuddle. He might even have kissed her on the top of her head.

*

Later that night, I went and knocked on Alex's door. She was tucked up in bed. Sebastian had brought her a drink she liked. Warm milk with honey and vanilla. She wiped a trace of milk froth from her upper lip.

'Are you getting an early night, sweetheart?' I asked her. 'You must be tired.' I sat on the bed. It was dark in the room, the only light coming from Alex's laptop, an old comedy series she was watching.

'Did you have a good time, in London?'

She shrugged. 'It was OK.'

There was a pause.

'Mel,' she said. 'Will you stay and watch something with me? We can watch anything you like.'

'Of course I will.'

I got under the covers. Little girl. Alone in here, with her laptop and her milk.

50

Alex often spent the evenings alone. She was very sweet and very little, I wanted to reach out a hand to stroke her, but I didn't, because she wasn't my pet. Kata treated her like a pet. I remembered how Kata had whipped off Alex's bucket hat, had rumpled her hair. Alex was an extension of Kata, to be handled at will, no permission needed. She would swoop to cover her in kisses whenever Alex had submitted to her, had allowed herself to be an instrument for Kata's desires – performing well in her tests, getting into an English school. But there was no constancy to this affection, because look at Alex alone here now, as she was night after night, afternoon after afternoon, alone and staring into her laptop or her phone.

But maybe I was projecting my own experiences onto Alex.

My dad's parents had wanted me to go to boarding school, had encouraged me to go for the scholarship, had helped out with the extra costs, the school uniform, the money required for extracurricular activities. They lived in a big house outside the town, with formal gardens and dim rooms where grandfather clocks ticked. My mother would harp on about the connection, even though my dad had died when I was only two years old, even though her connection with his family had been brief. My grandparents died when I was still in my early teens, and I guess they must have been leveraged up to their eyeballs because when everything was settled, the money my mother had been banking on failed to materialise. The only remaining evidence that she had ever been connected with the upper classes was the fruit of that brief union: me.

It sometimes felt like that was the point of my existence, as far as my mother was concerned: a segue into a particular topic of conversation: 'Well, you see, Mel's father …' 'Mel takes after her father, in that …'

A strong feeling had come up in me when I had watched Kata whip the bucket hat from Alex's head. By the end of the day Mum's drunkenness would have reached its peak of slovenly sentimentality. She called me once, weeping. 'Oh my Mel,' she said, 'I went for a walk today past a field of dairy cows, they'd just

51

had their calves taken away from them and they were crying for their babies.' She was a howling mess. '*I love you*,' she wept and I thought, Fuck your love, it's not the kind of love I want, I want a love that is calm and steady and solid, that is a *place* in the world where I can go.

A character in the old comedy series made a funny remark and Alex laughed along.

'Did you get up to anything fun while you were in London? Did you and your mum meet up with anyone?'

'Papa asked me the same question. He asked me if Mama met up with anyone.'

'Oh ...'

'Just Olga and Sergei and Igor, they helped us with our shopping. Oh, and we had this really fun night where a chef came over and gave us a sushi-making class. Look.'

She reached for her phone and showed me photos: of them in a big white kitchen, making goofy faces and holding up strips of seaweed. She continued to slide through her camera roll. I saw them lolling around on sofas in the usual loungewear, Igor popping a champagne bottle – that was to celebrate when I got my result, Alex said. I saw Kata lying back against sofa cushions, glass of champagne in her hand, eyes closed in the moment the photo was taken, looking happy and at ease. Olga, Igor and Sergei all lived in London. I found them quite touching, these photos. Endearing and innocent. She wasn't skulking over there to meet up with Valentin or Oliver. She just wanted to take a breather, see her friends. A breather from what? I didn't know exactly, but I thought maybe it was the sheer intensity she had wanted to escape, for a few days. The whole scene in the restaurant, his calling her a whore, their extraordinary abundance at the breakfast table the next morning, when both had seemed so saturated, the eroticism of her bruise. By the time she had left, there had been something strained and forced in the air between them, I had sensed the same in their interaction earlier over the question of Alex going away to school. If these photos were to be believed, her trip to London had been one long pyjama party, with some shopping thrown in. I snuggled down into the pillows of Alex's bed. I was wearing the fluffy bathrobe I'd found hanging in my ensuite bathroom on my first day. I'll miss this fluffy bathrobe, I thought, and I looked at Alex, that sweet plump little wrist of hers with its bracelet of sweets, she was a good little thing to make the sweets last, not to chomp them all down in one go; she nibbled one now, I watched her do it and I felt very tender.

'I'll miss you!' I said.

'I'll miss you too, Mel.'

A character on the screen was wearing a broad-brimmed straw hat with ribbons on it.

'It looks like your school hat,' I said. 'It was cute. Let's see it again?'

I felt her body go rigid. She didn't say anything. She shut her laptop and got out of bed and walked away.

I heard what sounded like a cupboard door opening, then paper rustling.

The overhead light snapped on. She was standing there, wearing the hat.

'Are you OK, Alex? I'm sorry, I know you have mixed feelings about going away to school. Sorry if that was insensitive of me.'

She just stood there in her hat.

'Alex?'

'I can't answer you,' she said, 'because I'm not here.'

She sat down on the floor and from where I was on the bed I couldn't, in fact, see her; all I could see was the hat.

'I think you're a little overtired. I think this has all been a bit overwhelming for you. I understand, it's a big change, I know it seems scary, but you never know, you might love—'

'Mel. Can you get me my retainer case from the bathroom? I want to take my braces out.'

'You want me to bring the case in here? Shouldn't you take them out in the bathroom?'

'Please, Mel. I want to take them out now. They're hurting me.'

'OK, OK. Hold on.'

I went into her bathroom.

'It's in the cupboard,' I heard her say.

'Which cupboard?' But she didn't answer. I rummaged around, eventually I found it. When I returned to the bedroom Alex had gone. There was just the hat on the floor.

'Got it!' I called. I put the case on her bedside table.

'Alex?'

I sat on the bed to wait, scrolled through my phone.

But after five minutes she hadn't appeared. I wandered out into the corridor, looked around. I went to the living area, looked in the kitchen, looked up in the study. I went back to her bedroom. Only the hat. On the way down to my bedroom I passed Sebastian.

'Are the doors locked?' I asked him. 'I mean, the doors leading outside. You can still get out though, can't you, from the inside, without a key ...'

'Where are you thinking of going?' he said. 'Sounds exciting.'

'No ...' I hesitated. She was probably just in her parents' room or something. 'Night,' I said.

I had washed my face and was in bed when she came to my room. I had taken my contact lenses out for the night so when the door opened her form was blurry, but I knew it was her. I reached for my glasses.

She came over to the bed.

'What happened?' I asked.

'Sorry, Mel. I didn't mean to scare you.'

But she had scared me, a little.

Her eyes were red, I could tell she had been crying. I stroked the side of her arm.

'Where were you?'

'I hid in the cupboard in my room.'

'You were in the room the whole time?'

Quiet in the cupboard, while I had sat waiting for her, while I had said her name.

'Why did you do that, Alex?'

'I don't know. I felt upset.'

'Come on,' I said, lifting the duvet. 'In you hop. I'm sorry that you are going away to school. You won't be homesick forever.'

She told me again that she would miss me. I felt grateful that she didn't blame me for my role in the whole thing, in the whole exercise of sending her away. She didn't blame them, either. Their harm was subtle and only just beginning to show itself, had yet to reach its full unwitting capaciousness.

Sweet, puppylike little girl. Cuddled into my arms. I could never have imagined that she would grow up into someone so cunning and methodical. And elaborate too, so elaborate, in her choice of punishment.

PART TWO

Monaco

CHAPTER TWO

Morocco

5

Three years went by before I next saw Alex and her family. 'I worked for this family that were kind of ... intense,' I'd tell people. 'The husband and wife were sort of obsessive about each other. I don't think it was easy on their kid.'

Mostly people were interested in what their house was like, if they'd had a private jet, how much money they spent. 'Did they have diamond hubcaps?' someone asked. 'And how about cigar jewellery, have you heard of that? For £200k you can buy a ruby ring to put round your cigar while you smoke it – did the oligarch guy have one of those?'

So to some extent they faded back into cliché in my mind, too, but something did remain, some remnant of curiosity and unease, so that when I got a call from my director – I was one of her old hands by now – and was told that they wanted me to tutor Alexandra again before she began her GCSEs, I said, 'Sounds fine, OK, sign me up.'

Put something in front of me and I'll do it. Show me a burrow, into which I can crawl. That's how I felt at that time. So, I'm going off to work in the South of France for two months, am I? OK, I'll do it, and while I'm doing it, I won't think about what comes after it.

And the good thing about new places and sights, about novelties, is that they are large enough to occupy your vision for a while. Their driver picked me up at the airport in Nice and drove me along the coast road: umbrella pines, soft air filled with scents. He dropped me outside an imposing apartment block near the Fontvieille Marina in Monte Carlo and a concierge in the marble-clad lobby directed me up to the penthouse. It wasn't hard to find; it had its own button in the lift.

Sebastian opened the door to me. 'Here she is!' he said. 'Honey!' He leaned his head to one side, he opened his arms, I stepped into his hug. The remembered smell of his cologne, the same grey of his suit. 'I'm happy to see you,' I said, and meant it. I would be here for the next two months, and I would eat three good meals a day, and I would have a comfortable bedroom and a nice bathroom, and I felt a sudden expansion within myself, an unrolling. 'Come and say hi to Alex,' Sebastian said.

He gave my suitcase to a grey-haired woman in uniform and led me through an apartment that seemed to go on forever, I peered through doorways into large rooms ending in sliding glass doors that opened onto what looked like one big panoramic terrace. I saw a dining room with purple wallpaper lit by an onyx chandelier.

'Kata's up in the mountains,' Sebastian told me over his shoulder. I had a vision of her, stately and loungewear-clad in some cave, holding a staff, a mountain hermit. 'A wellness clinic,' Sebastian said. 'She'll be back in a few days.'

He stopped and knocked on a door.

'Alex, honey! Mel's here.'

I heard a key turning in a lock. The door opened and there she was.

I was a little shocked. But I knew some teenagers could go through painfully thin phases.

'Hi, sweetheart,' I said gently. 'It's nice to see you again.'

'Hi, Mel.'

I reached out my hand to seal the greeting, to touch her on her upper arm, but as soon as she noticed my hand and where it was headed she cringed away, she actually took a step backwards.

Sebastian shot me a glance and crinkled his eyes, shook his head slightly as if to say, 'Don't worry, don't take it personally.'

He stepped towards her and stroked her gently on the side of her head. She let him. He gave her a kiss on the cheek. She let him do that too.

'OK guys,' he said. 'You have some catching up to do. I'll leave you to it. I'll send Irina with some tea.'

I followed her into her bedroom. It had none of the clutter of the teenage rooms I was used to working in, none of the posters, the scattered clothes, the photos of friends. A bed, a desk, two chairs. She'd got all her textbooks out in advance of my arrival. She began to speak quietly, taking me through the work she'd been set that summer. She'd already made a start on it. I looked at her neatly arranged folders, the planner where she'd written down everything she had to do, ticking things off as she went along. It was obvious that, as before, Alex had no need of a tutor. She was bright, and she was disciplined. She could get through all this by herself. Still, it would make my job very easy, I supposed.

'You can sit down if you like,' she said.

I would have expected her to look different: she had changed, after all, from child into teen. She was fainter than when I had known her before, lying on her bed in her room in Courchevel, puppy-plump and sulky. She took up less space in the world. Her thinness was not gangly, in the manner of a teenager going through a growth spurt. Her shoulders stooped inside a thin blouse. The only word I could think of was not a word you would usually associate with someone young: *frail*.

'How was your journey? Was it OK?'

She gave a little smile, shyly eager to please, and I wondered if she felt bad for recoiling from me when I'd reached out to greet her.

'Oh, yes, it was fine,' I said. 'It's nice to see you again.'

She looked down at her books. My chair was quite close to hers. 'So, how's school been?' I asked. 'You've been there three years now?'

She didn't answer. I reached for one of her textbooks, my upper body leaning in her direction and as I did so she shifted and I heard the scrape of her chair as she moved it further away from me.

61

I felt a little hurt. More than a little, actually. She was physically recoiling from me. I knew I shouldn't take it so hard. That it had more to do with her than it had to do with me. But I couldn't help it. It seemed one more proof of a loveless world.

*

On my first morning I woke up extra early and padded down the corridor to the kitchen, got myself some coffee to take back to my bedroom – *my bedroom*, always my favourite part of a new tutoring job: the comfortable little world that was to be my home for the stretch of time ahead. I always felt relaxed then, all worries deferred until the time I had to leave, two whole months, in this case. I took my coffee and sat with it on the window seat, looking out at the wide boulevard and the apartment block opposite, the sun warming me while the coffee woke me, and it was easy to pretend in the stillness of the morning and with the rush of caffeine that this room and the ensuite that adjoined it were mine, my own little studio flat, and that the city out there was the city I lived in, that there stretched ahead a day of brunches and lunches, nipping here, nipping there, meeting friends, a gallery, a bar, buying fresh vegetables from a market and carrying them home in a straw basket in the sun.

I drank my coffee and took possession: this room was mine. I looked at the bed with its soft white sheets. The mattress was sensational. Hugely thick – it would have taken two strong people to turn it. And the linen was matching and ironed and changed once a week, by Irina. I thought of the Ikea mattresses I used to sleep on. A strip of foam laid across wooden slats.

I could hear Alex's voice in the breakfast room before I entered, asking Irina for something. I sat down and took in all the breakfast offerings before focusing my attention on a wicker bowl with a white linen cloth draped across it and, sitting on top of the cloth, croissants: plain croissants and almond croissants and chocolate croissants.

'Sebastian ... Sebastian told me ...'

She was looking at me with tenderness and concern. She hesitated before continuing.

'About your mum.'

'Oh,' I said.

Sebastian had written to me a few months ago, had seen a message someone posted on my Facebook.

'He told me this morning. Is she still in hospital? I'm really sorry, Mel. I hope you're OK.'

'No, she came out of hospital a few weeks ago,' I said. 'I'm fine. Thank you.'

I looked again at the tableau of croissants, the sugar-dusted almond croissant leaning at an angle to the regular croissant with its bronzed ridges, its whorls. I reached for the chocolate croissant. I was always going to have the chocolate croissant.

She was still looking at me, so I smiled, I blew her a kiss. 'Thank you, sweetheart,' I said. 'It's really OK.' She smiled at my kiss and blew me one back.

Lessons rolled by peacefully and I was lying on my bed after dinner, reading a magazine, when I heard a tap on my door. She was there, saying, 'Hi, Mel, I don't want to disturb you, but Sebastian and I are gonna watch a movie and I thought I'd ask you if you'd like to join us ...'

We had popcorn, in matching bowls. We drew the curtains, we each had a blanket. I looked at their profiles, flickered by the lights from the TV screen, and I thought, Yes, this is nice, the world shrunk down to just this room, with these warm presences. The corridor that would lead me afterwards to the peaceful comfort of my bedroom, where I would sleep the whole night through.

'Well, I've gotta love and leave you guys, I've gotta make some calls,' Sebastian said when the movie ended. The screensaver had come on, floating mountains and lakes and waterfalls, and Alex and I stayed where we were, at either end of the large grey sofa.

'Mel, can I ask, what happened with your mum?'

'She fell down the stairs. She'd been drinking. It was her own fault.'

I didn't try to modulate my tone. I couldn't see her face anyway, my eyes were closed, my head leaning against the sofa cushions.

The horror of that night came back to me. I shifted my head to the side but neither my closed eyes nor the sensation of my cheek against the cushion could stop it coming.

'I've never been able to rely on her,' I said. 'I've got used to being alone.'

It was inappropriate, to share this much personal information with a student. She didn't need to know that I had such a useless parent. But lying on that soft sofa, I lost all resistance. I lacked the will to cover anything up.

A few moments later I heard her little voice say, 'But you aren't all alone. You are here, with us.'

The blanket was so warm over me. I stayed where I was, eyes still closed, taking in what she had said. And then there was movement under the blanket and, for the first time since I'd arrived, we touched. She tapped my foot gently with hers. Our feet were bare. I opened my eyes and we did that thing where you lift your legs and press the soles of your feet to the other person's feet, walk them around in the air.

We let our legs collapse back onto the sofa. A vision came back to me from Courchevel. A little girl alone in a bedroom, laptop open, with a glass of milk, and here she was, three years later, in a penthouse in Monaco, without parents or friends or siblings, with a butler and a housekeeper and tutor for company. But it was OK. We were here with her and our lives were lonely too.

'What was it like for you at school?' I asked her.

'It was hard,' she said. 'And Mama made it so much harder.'

6

She could remember it vividly, the very first day, when she had been taken and deposited in that strange and foreign place.

Dmitri had driven them there. The school was in the countryside, a couple of hours outside London.

The car had progressed up a long, winding drive. Alex and her mother were sitting in the back of the car. The car had blacked-out windows so Alex knew no one could see in. But soon the car would stop and they would have to get out.

All up the drive there were girls, in groups, or in pairs, all seeming to know each other.

Her mother's eyes feasted on them. She squeezed Alex's arm. 'Look!' she said. 'All your future friends!'

They got out of the car in a quad surrounded by old stone buildings. It was even busier here. Dmitri opened the boot and began getting out Alex's stuff. They didn't know where they should take it.

'Little girl!'

Her mum was calling to a student who was walking past the car.

'Can you tell us where we should go? My daughter is new here.'

'What year is she in?' asked the girl. She had red hair and freckles.

'Year Eight,' said Kata.

'That's my year. You should go in there.' She pointed to the dark stone building behind her and started to move on.

'What is your name?' Kata called. 'Your hair is a beautiful colour and you are very lucky to have those freckles.'

An odd note had crept into her voice. Something both tentative and obsequious.

'Harriet,' the girl said, looking from Kata to Alex. She bit her lip and her eyes glinted. She was obviously suppressing a smile. She began to move away again.

'How lucky that you are in the same year,' Kata said. 'Harriet, come.' Harriet paused. She looked over to a group of girls who were watching her and who seemed to be waiting for her. Her head was turned towards them so Alex couldn't see her face but she knew she must have pulled an expression, something mocking and derogatory, because the group of girls watching her started to laugh. Harriet turned back towards Alex and her mum.

She spoke louder now, performing, obviously speaking so that the watching group of girls could hear her.

'Yes?' she said. 'How can I be of service?'

Kata beamed.

'Will you look after my daughter? I'm sure you two will be good friends. You see, Alex?' she said, pulling Alex towards her. 'It was such a good idea for you to come to this school.'

'Dmitri,' she said, 'take Alex's cases where Harriet directs you.'

Dmitri got a contraption out of the back of the car. A metal thing that unfolded, that had two wheels. He loaded Alex's suitcases onto it.

Harriet looked back to her friends. They weren't even attempting to hide their laughter.

'You are welcome to come and stay with us anytime, Harriet,' Kata said. 'In Moscow, or in Monaco, or London's maybe easier. Alex can tell you.'

Harriet led the way into the big stone building, followed by Dmitri.

Kata and Alex followed behind.

'Hey, Alex!' Alex heard behind her the next day as she was walking down a large unfamiliar hallway, wood-panelled, trailing at the edge of a group she knew were going to a maths lesson she was supposed to be in.

Their form teacher had instructed the class to make sure to guide the new girls to their lessons. There was one other new girl besides Alex. She was called Kate and she had long dark hair and a glossy fringe. Her schoolbag was covered with badges. Alex had thought they might stick together but Kate seemed to want to keep to herself.

'Hey, Alex!'

Alex turned around. She saw a blonde girl she didn't recognise. The blonde girl pushed her lips out into a grotesque pout. She turned to the girl next to her and began to speak in a thick Russian-American drawl, an uncanny imitation of Alex's mum.

'Byootiful gurl,' she said, stroking her friend's hair. 'And look, your freckles!'

*

In the dinner queue she heard a loud voice behind her. It was Harriet.

'I would just *love* to come and stay with you in the holidays, Alex. No, I'm serious! In Moscow, or in Monaco, or in London. In all three! There's nothing I would rather do!'

Alex was in a dormitory with five girls and she was very relieved that Harriet wasn't one of them. She had the sense that whenever she entered the room when the others were in there, their conversation would stop. On the first night she had walked in and seen the others standing around, unrolling their posters and propping their framed photos on the chest of drawers each girl had beside her bed. She had kept her head down, hadn't said a word, had headed straight for her own bed, which was thankfully at the far end, in its own corner.

'Well, aren't you even going to say hello?' said a girl with a blunt brown bob.

'Hi,' Alex said. And immediately turned away. Kate, the other new girl, was also in this dormitory. As she unpacked Alex looked back covertly and saw that Kate was in easy conversation with two of the other girls. She had put a poster of a band up above her bed and she was showing a girl the badges on her schoolbag, which turned out to be band badges. When they were lying in their beds later before lights out Alex glanced in Kate's direction and accidentally caught her eye. Kate smiled at her briefly but then quickly looked away.

Three nights in she came to her bed to find her duvet and pillows were gone. She didn't make a fuss, didn't say anything, didn't go and tell the matron. She lay down on her bed, on her back, and closed her eyes. She could sleep like that all night. A couple of hours later she felt something soft being dumped on her. They'd given her her duvet and pillows back.

They had to play sport at this school in a way they hadn't at her old school in Moscow. It seemed to be more important here. People took it very seriously. She noticed that the girls who were the most popular were the ones who were best at sport. Harriet was the captain of the hockey team and played a position called centre forward.

In the first hockey lesson they put Alex in defence. Alex hoped she wouldn't have too much to do back there. For the first half of the game it seemed that way. The ball was constantly at the other end of the pitch being scrambled over by some tough sturdy girls who didn't seem to have any fear of the long wooden sticks or the dangerously hard ball. But just after half-time the ball raced towards Alex and the whole pitch was screaming at her, 'GET IT GET IT GET IT!' She froze in panic, the ball swept past her and the girl propelling it went on to score a goal. A few games later Alex was knocked out when someone's hockey stick cracked her across the forehead but she knew that had genuinely been an accident, that even these girls wouldn't go that far.

Kata was disappointed when Alex didn't bring a friend home during the first holiday, that she didn't have someone over for at least one night in the house in London, that she didn't even have plans to meet one of her friends for an afternoon. Didn't any of them live in the city? They must do.

Alex tried to offer some kind of explanation on her first night home. They were staying a few days in the London house before going to Moscow.

'It's Christmas,' she said. 'Everyone has plans with their families.'

Kata seemed to accept this as a reasonable explanation.

And the next holidays, Easter:

'We have exams next term. Everyone's parents are keeping them home for the holidays to study.'

Kata seemed to accept this as well and on the pretext that she, too, had to study for the tests, had to study all holiday like everyone else, Alex was able to spend a lot of time, most of the time in fact, in her room.

She could relax when she was in her room. She could *only* relax, when she was in her room. She could only relax when she was not around other people.

She thought back to how it had been only a year ago, before she had started at that school. She had not really been aware of herself then. She had just *been*. She thought of herself running to her dad as he came through the front door after trips away and throwing her arms around his waist. She had just done things without thinking about them. But the girls at the school had made her aware of herself. She was as thin as a stick and ugly and everything she did was weird and wrong and strange. So she couldn't just do things, she had to stop and consider before she did anything, stop and consider if the thing she was about to do might not be weird, or wrong, or strange. Most often she didn't know if it would be or not, so it was safer just not to do it. Her mum was always watching her, too. Watching her to see if she was a normal girl, with friends, like normal people had. Mealtimes she had to come out of her bedroom, and when she sat at the table, she could sense her mother scrutinising her. She had only to catch her mother's eye for her mother to ask her a question and so she kept her head down and tried just to get through the meal.

Her father said, 'You are very quiet these days.' Another person looking at her and thinking she was doing something wrong. She didn't know how to reply. She wanted to reply to him, but she didn't know how. She looked down, begging herself to know what to reply. He said, 'Don't you have anything to say to us anymore?'

By the time the summer holiday came around Alex's excuses wouldn't wash. They had two months off. Surely her friends at school weren't tied up *all* that time with family plans, weren't going to spend *all* that time studying? As usual for the first few days after school broke up they were in the London house.

'There are some plans,' Alex said, 'nothing definite yet.' She made up the name of a friend. Sophie.

'And where does this Sophie live?' asked her mother. 'What do her parents do? Why don't you call her up?'

Alex managed to delay.

But four days later she was trailing after her mum round Harrods. She had to get some bras. Her mum was waiting outside the cubicle while she tried them on.

'Which of your schoolfriends live in London?' she heard her mother say from the other side of the curtain.

She didn't answer. She clipped on one bra that was more comfortable than the others.

'This one, please,' she said, holding her arm out through the curtain and handing over the bra.

They went downstairs to the oyster bar and sat on white leather stools. A silver platter of oysters was put in front of them. Kata began to speak again and Alex knew from the tone of her voice what it was going to be about.

'Mama,' she said. She looked down at the oysters. She held one by its curved and jagged edges. 'The girls at school don't like me, OK? I don't have any friends.'

'What do you mean?' Kata asked.

'Just what I said. They don't like me. I don't have any friends. No one is going to come and stay with me in the holidays, and I'm not going to go and stay with anyone.'

She forced herself to have an oyster, swallowed it quickly and slimily down her throat.

When she looked up, she saw that her mother was trembling. She was looking anywhere but at Alex. She pushed the platter of oysters away across the counter.

'Get up,' she said. 'We're leaving.'

She looked at Alex then and it was unmistakeable: her disgust.

She didn't speak to Alex on the drive home and when they got to the house she disappeared upstairs and didn't emerge for the rest of the day.

When Alex came down late after dinner, after her night-time shower, she saw her mother was in the TV room, wrapped in her grey fleecy slanket and watching *The Real Housewives of New Jersey*. She went and sat next to her on the couch. At first her mother didn't acknowledge her presence. She kept staring at the screen. Alex noticed her eyes were watery and quickly looked away. 'Lexi,' she heard her mother say. She turned to her. 'Come here.' She went to her mum and her mum held her tightly. Fiercely. Alex felt herself squeezed. She closed her eyes and buried her head into her mother's side, into the grey fleece of the slanket that smelled like a mixture of the Diptyque Roses candle that always burned in that room and Chanel No. 5, her mother's perfume.

7

I found it very surprising, given what Alex had told me, that she seemed to be looking forward to Kata coming home. 'Mama arrives tomorrow!' she said the next morning at breakfast. She went and picked two sprays of bougainvillea from the terrace and asked Irina for a vase. She put the flowers on Kata's bedside table. 'I might not be able to watch a movie with you guys tomorrow night,' she said to Sebastian and me. 'Because a lot of the time Mama and I watch movies together, in her room.'

'Do you want to come for a walk this afternoon?' she asked me. 'Along the coastal path, have you been that way yet?' She walked ahead of me, in the direction of Cap-d'Ail. The path was hewn from the side of the cliff. Decorative tiles were fixed here and there among the rocks. A terracotta-coloured langoustine. Her body was thin without being nimble. A couple of times she blundered, almost tripped. We sat on an outcrop to rest.

'You know,' she said, 'a girl who used to be at my school is coming to stay. She's arriving on Thursday. Her name is Tatiana.'

'Oh!' I said. 'OK, well, cool. That's nice. We'll make sure to get your lessons out of the way in the mornings then, so that you guys have the afternoons free to hang out together.'

She didn't say anything. She plucked a blade of seagrass and drew the end across her ankle. The skin of her ankle was dry and dusty and the tip of the seagrass left a clear line.

'I don't want her to come,' she said.

'Oh. How come you invited her then?'

She shook her head. She threw the seagrass over the cliff. 'I didn't,' she said.

*

When she'd been at the school for just over three years, posters began to appear in the main school hallway advertising something called Help Week. 'What is Help Week?' she asked one of her classmates, a sporty girl with a force field of wholesomeness around her.

'Don't you know what Help Week is?' the sporty girl said.

'No, or I wouldn't be asking you,' Alex replied. The sporty girl shook her head and explained.

It happened once every three years; it was a tradition in the school and in other boarding schools across the country. Each pupil in Alex's year and the year above would be assigned to an older student for a week. The Helper's job would be to assist them, at their direction. Maybe tidy their room, arrange their bookshelves, return books to the library for them, go to the village and bring them back a snack. They would do whatever they were told to do.

'It's practice, for when we leave school and intern, do work experience, have our first job as someone's assistant. You know,' the sporty girl said.

Alex didn't know.

'That's how I first met Tatiana. I was assigned to her. I was her Helper.'

Tatiana was in the Upper Sixth, in her last term of school.

Alex had known who Tatiana was before being assigned to her. Everyone knew who Tatiana was.

Tatiana was famous. Tatiana was a TV star.

There was this reality series, it was in its fourth season. I'd watched some of it, I had a weakness for that kind of crap. It was called *The Royal Borough* and it followed the lives of a group of twenty-somethings who lived in Kensington and Chelsea. The camera would pan along the wrought-iron railings of a row of stuccoed facades before cutting to the interior of a Notting Hill café. A group of girls would be sitting there, wearing fake fur and felt hats, consoling one of their number, invariably in tears because she'd just found out the guy she was seeing had 'hooked up' with someone else. Tatiana, younger than the rest of the cast, had made it onto the show by dating one of its prominent males. They had lasted one season before he had cheated on her. Tatiana had won the respect of the female cast members by throwing a drink in the male's face at a rooftop bar. Newly single, she'd managed to stay on the show by striking an allegiance with a flamboyant personality called Simon-Alexander, an outrageous snob and aesthete who appeared to have arrived in a time machine from the 1920s. No longer one of the main characters, with all the sordid showdowns and entanglements that would have required, she was on the show just enough that she could use it as a calling card in other areas of her life without allowing it to wholly define or circumscribe her. If this was intentional positioning, it was shrewd.

The girls in Alex's year were piqued to learn that, of all people, Alex was going to be Tatiana's Helper.

Tatiana had a reputation for being good-natured, both at school and on the show, so Alex wasn't afraid when she approached her room on the first day of the assignment – not that she'd necessarily have been afraid anyway, because she was used to the treatment she got in this school by now, and it only went so far, it only boiled down to words and looks in the end, and what could those do, really? She wasn't expecting Tatiana to be a total bitch but she was surprised by just how nice she was.

'Hey!' she'd said, smiling warmly as she opened the door. 'Come in, nice to meet you, sit down! Would you like something to drink? Tea, coffee?'

She'd shut the door, she'd made the tea, she'd sat down as well and for the next two hours she hadn't made Alex do any of the chores she'd been expecting she would do. They'd just talked.

Alex had been shy. But Tatiana had seemed so at ease, so relaxed, so sunny, that Alex had felt herself relaxing too.

She found Tatiana pretty bland, to be honest. The stuff that flowed out of her mouth was pretty basic. It's not like they'd sat there and had some deep and amazing conversation and realised they were kindred souls.

'So, you grew up in Russia? Wow, amazing. What's it like there? What do you want to do at university?' Patter patter patter.

But she had appreciated the way that Tatiana had made her feel normal. Because Tatiana's conversation had been so bland and Everyman, could have been directed at anyone, there was the sense that she, Alex, *was* anyone; that she was no different from anyone else.

*

Even after Help Week, Tatiana continued to single out Alex. Walking in the grounds, in the hallway between lessons, in the dining hall queue. 'Hi, Alex, how's it going?' she would call out, or she would stop and chat, and this public display of approval began to have a palpable effect on the girls in Alex's year, the ones who had always treated her with such disdain. Even Harriet seemed affected. Alex was sharing a room with Harriet that term. Her heart had sunk when she had seen the room lists on the boarding house noticeboard. On the first day of term Alex had been unpacking her things with her back to Harriet and the other girls when she'd heard Harriet say, 'Alex, Alex? Do you see this line?'

There was a seam in the carpet running down the room near Alex's bed.

'It's quite useful,' Harriet said. 'Think of that line as marking your area. That side of the room is yours, and this side is ours, OK?' But one night, after a particularly long chat with Tatiana in the dining hall, both of them holding their trays and in full view, Alex entered the dormitory. It was late, just before lights out – she usually left it as late as possible – and she was walking towards her bed in the far corner, head down, when she happened to look up at the wrong moment and catch Harriet's eye, but Harriet smiled at her. A bit later, when the lights went out, Harriet said, 'Night, everyone. Night, Alex.'

*

There was an open day for parents about three weeks before the end of each summer term. It was the worst day of the entire school year.

Alex would wait in the quad along with everyone else. Cars would begin to arrive around eleven o'clock. She'd wait for the blacked-out Mercedes limousine, she'd wait for it to park up and for Dmitri to get out, in full livery, and open the back door for her mother.

Her dad never came.

He was too busy. But Alex thought that wasn't the whole reason. She thought he didn't want anything to do with the school. 'You've changed since you went to that school,' he had said, some holidays ago.

She had been sitting on the sun terrace of the house in Rublyovka, reading a book. The previous night, her mum and dad had gone to Vova's mother's house to celebrate her eightieth birthday. Alex had not wanted to go. She knew Vova's nieces would be there, girls her own age, she was shy of them, she could feel the stress coming over her, wondering what she would wear, how she would look, how she ought to behave around them, whereas it would be so peaceful to stay behind, just her and Irina.

Her dad was going to insist on her coming but Kata stepped in. 'Let her stay,' Kata said. 'Why should she come? What has she in common with those girls of Vova's sister?'

'Oh, well,' her dad said. 'If you think you are too good for them now.'

That's not the reason, Alex wanted to say, you don't understand. Her mum and dad, standing in the big marble hallway, getting ready to leave. Stop making up your own stories.

It was her mother who felt this sort of occasion was beneath her. But there was no question of her not going, because Ivan expected it of her.

And then the next morning, when she was on the sun terrace, reading, her dad saying, 'If I had had all the things you have when I was your age, I would have been a bit happier, I wouldn't have sat around looking so miserable all the time.'

She had looked up at him, wanting to explain, but he looked cold and angry, and she was frightened. 'When I was a student in Moscow,' he said, 'I saw the people who grew up with everything, just like you. Just a pig from Ingushetia, that's what they thought of me.'

He turned, with a laugh, he went down the steps into the garden, he whistled to their Alsatian, Kira.

There's been a misunderstanding, she thought, as she watched him go. A misunderstanding. She felt herself become stuck on that thought, that word. A misunderstanding.

Now her mum got out of the car and Dmitri shut the door behind her. She had the same look she always had when she was anywhere near the school: that look of defensive bravado barely masking a quavering, tremulous hope. Alex went towards her.

Kata was wearing a massive purple hat that swooped all over the place; some small round baubles – were they meant to be grapes? – tumbled off one side. Her skirt suit was purple and her shoes were purple and very high.

There were all sorts of events: a tour of the classrooms, of the new chemistry lab, of the extended art block, a presentation and some speeches on the lawn. And then everyone stood around on the lawn while small girls from a lower year brought them plastic bowls filled with strawberries and cream.

Being around her family seemed to embolden Harriet and make her revert to type. She had horsey-looking parents with braying voices. Her mother always wore a battered straw hat with a silk scarf tied round it and seemed to be confidently acquainted with all the other mothers; her siblings were numerous and boisterous. When she and her clan passed Alex and Kata, she gave Kata, in her heels and tight-fitting suit, such a withering and open look of disdain, so forceful and venomous even by Harriet's standards, that Alex knew her mum, already painfully sensitive at events like this, would register it.

'Hello, Harriet,' Kata called out, and Alex heard the tremor in her voice. She still remembered Harriet's name from that encounter three years before when Alex had started at the school. Alex looked away, not wanting to witness Harriet's response. She heard laughter, but at least she didn't see the look, the look she was sure Harriet would have given her mum. When she did return her gaze she saw that her mum's hand, as she moved her plastic spoon down towards her pot of strawberries and cream, was shaking. As she brought the spoon back up towards her lips her hand shook a glob of cream and a small fat strawberry onto the purple lapel of her jacket. The jacket was suede, the worst kind of material to get stains out of. That stain would sit on her lapel for the rest of the day, even if she fussed at it with a napkin or tried to wash it out.

At that moment Alex felt a hand on her shoulder. 'Alex!'

She smelled the clean sweep of Tatiana's blonde hair, took in the sunny, untroubled countenance, the air of absolute belonging and ease; there was so much of it that if she were next to it she couldn't help but be fortified, feel it seeping into her. Her mum was now holding herself still. Her pursed lips and the vast mirrored expanse of her sunglasses gave nothing away.

'How's it going, Alex?' Tatiana was saying. 'Oh my God, I love your outfit, you look so chic.'

Alex was wearing jeans and a plain shirt.

'And you must be Alex's mother,' Tatiana reached out and shook Kata's hand, still holding Alex to her side. 'It's so nice to meet you. You look amazing too. Style obviously runs in the family.'

Alex wondered if her mother would be aware of who Tatiana was, if she'd seen the TV show. It was likely. She could tell that her mother was paying attention to Tatiana with every conscious cell; at the same time, her right hand was fidgeting, anxiously, with the lapel of her jacket that bore the stain, trying to fold it inwards. It wouldn't stay there, it kept flopping out.

'Oh, I don't know why they insist on serving this strawberry and cream thing,' Tatiana said. 'There are multiple casualties every single year. Last year I thought I'd destroyed a skirt, I spilled cream all over it. The skirt was red suede but it *did* come out, so don't worry, your beautiful suit is safe.'

Kata's hand had been on its way up to her lapel again. It paused mid-journey and then continued. Instead of fussing the lapel in on itself she used her hand to smooth it out into its normal position. She patted the stain, now fully visible, looked at Tatiana, and they both laughed.

'Yes, this would not be my usual choice of afternoon snack,' she said.

She held her pot out to Alex. 'Go and put this in a trash can.'

The bin was some way away on the other side of the lawn, next to the library block. Alex weaved her way through families. Some of them had brought picnic rugs and spread them over the grass. As she made her way back she saw that Tatiana and her mum were still talking. They were both laughing. Alex kept on walking towards them; occasionally milling people blocked them from her view. Tatiana didn't seem to have her own mother or father with her. Alex didn't remember ever having seen them at the school. It was hard to imagine Tatiana needing parents.

She glanced to the right and saw that a girl called Jess, and some others, were heading in Tatiana's direction. 'Tatiana!' she heard Jess call. Tatiana kept on smiling and chatting to Kata, appearing not to have heard. But she must have heard because – still chatting – she raised a hand and moved it back over her shoulder, palm out, a 'stop' gesture. 'Tats!' Jess called out again. Alex saw Tatiana reach out a hand and put it on her mum's upper arm, smiling, then turn briefly in the direction of Jess. The moment her face was turned away from Kata, Tatiana's smile disappeared. She shook her head, warningly, at Jess and mouthed the word 'No'. Jess stopped, said something to the others, and they walked away. Tatiana turned back to Kata, smiling once again.

Alex realised she'd stopped walking and was standing still. She was close enough to see both her mum's and Tatiana's face quite clearly and it had been striking, the swiftness of the change in Tatiana's expression from when she was facing Kata to when she was facing away, the bright sunny smile turned on, then off.

She started walking again, she went up to where they were standing, she put her arm around her mother's back and held her.

'I have invited Tatiana to come and stay with us in the summer holiday.'

Alex felt the arm holding her mum go rigid. For a moment she imagined using it to knock her mother to the ground.

*

The day was interminable. After the speeches on the lawn one of the teachers made an announcement through a megaphone and they were all herded off to the main hall, to sit through yet more hymns and presentations and skits and on and on and on.

'It will be awkward having Tatiana to stay, Mama, she's not even in my year, she's so much older than me, she's about to leave school,' Alex said.

'Don't be silly. She likes you, she told me you are great friends.'

'And you know that she's on a reality TV show?'

'Oh?' said Kata, noncommittally, not responding further. Alex knew that had she been learning this news for the first time her reaction would have been greater. Her chin was raised, her pout set.

'You know how Papa will feel about that. You know how he is about keeping things private. Tatiana is the last sort of person he wants coming to the house.'

Tatiana's Instagram followers were in the hundreds of thousands. She posted every moment of her life in her stories.

Kata shucked off Alex's concern. 'You know he's always in Moscow working. He'll be with us maybe just a few days here and there over the summer. And anyway, he wouldn't even notice about the TV show. When would he ever watch a thing like that, to know?'

Alex thought of making the point that he needn't have watched it himself in order to know, that there were people around him whose sole job was to make sure he knew everything he had to know, but a feeling of apathy overcame her. She mustered her last bit of strength to argue her point, but then Kata was saying: '*You* want Tatiana to come and stay. It is very good for you, to make friends at your school. Tatiana will be a very good friend for you.'

Alex watched her mother's mouth moving, she took in the narrative being rewritten, so boldly, with such unconcern – did her mother even know she was doing it? – as if she, Alex, were not there, as if her very being were not a fact in the world. There was something annihilating in it. She realised she was standing still and that her mother was walking on ahead.

*

They were slowly crowding into the assembly room, filing down the aisle, then turning left to inch their way along a row of wooden chairs. They reached their allotted chairs and sat down. Alex was right at the end of the row. On the other side of her mother sat a woman with a ruddy face full of broken veins beneath a thatch of hair. Alex could see dog hairs on her tweed trousers. She had the air of the military about her.

The situation her mum had got her into was not irrevocable.

Nothing need be done today. In a few days' time, she'd tell Tatiana that something had come up, something unforeseen, that made her coming to stay impossible. And on the same day she'd ring up her mum and tell her ... something: Tatiana had filming commitments, Tatiana had an internship in Washington DC for the whole of the summer.

Her mother's perfume was very strong. It always was, because she tended to apply it several times throughout the day. She did so now. An act on the stage had finished, there were claps all round, and her mum leaned forward to her handbag, got out her travel-sized perfume bottle, and daubed the pungent liquid over her neck and wrists. The smell was intense.

Alex saw the military-looking woman's nose crinkle up; she turned towards Kata, tutting and shaking her head.

'Honestly,' she was saying. She turned to the man sitting on the other side of her – now he really did look like a general, or was it a colonel? – who was equally red-faced with a disciplined moustache, and began to mutter.

Her mum was oblivious.

A new batch of students was taking to the stage. Tatiana was one of them. It was a group of leavers; they embarked, in tandem, on an earnest speech about how grateful they were for all the school had done for them.

Kata was radiant as she watched Tatiana. She put her arm around Alex again, pulled her in close. The military woman was still glancing sideways occasionally, tutting and muttering. But her mum remained oblivious. She could not be touched. She stretched her legs out in front of her as far as she could, she crossed one over the other, she leaned right back in her chair.

Alex gave the military woman a cold, cold look. She held the look until the military woman looked away.

Leave my mum alone you stupid ugly red-faced bitch, she was thinking.

When she'd forced her to look away she took her mother's moist and manicured hand, she looked at her gazing up so happily at Tatiana on the stage, the first time she'd seen her mother at ease in all the times she had ever visited the school.

She gave in.

She didn't say anything to Tatiana, she didn't make up any reason for her not to come.

*

It was starting to get chilly on the rocky outcrop. I shifted. Alex was shivering. Goosebumps stood up on her skinny calves. She pulled at the sleeves of her thin jumper. She tucked her fingers inside the fabric and hugged her arms around her knees.

'Do you want to head back?' I asked.

'Mama takes everything and makes it her own,' she said. 'I was having a shit time at school. *I* was. And now I'm letting this Tatiana girl come here, just to make *Mama* feel better.'

I thought of the vase of flowers Alex had put beside her mother's bed.

'Because you are kind,' I said. 'You want to make her happy. And what can you do? You love her, after all.'

8

When I heard the sounds of Kata's arrival the next day I left my room and went down the long hall, eager to see her. Sebastian and Irina were fussing around her. She looked as I remembered, the same glossy hair, the same glossy lips. Body statuesque, chin raised in practised hauteur. If anything, she looked slightly younger, her skin more taut. Did I sense the traces of a lower face lift? Her skin shone with chemical peels; I guessed she'd had a fair few of those up in the mountains. 'My chook,' she said to Alex; she bent down and air-kissed around Alex's head.

She was undeniably a presence, arcing her grand slow movements through the air, but as I stood there and watched her I felt something I hadn't felt back in Courchevel. I felt contempt for her, and it was because of the things Alex had told me. You are a silly, selfish, grasping woman, I thought. You live your life in bad faith.

'Irina, please bring some tea to my room. Melanie, hello, welcome, I hope lessons are going well, we will speak later. Now, I need to take a rest.'

With those words she disappeared to her room, Alex following her.

That night Alex came into the kitchen when Sebastian and I were in there; she went to the cupboard and got out a box of Ladurée macarons. 'Mama and I are going to watch stuff in her room,' she said. 'But you guys should use the TV room. What do you think you'll watch?'

'Oh no, honey,' Sebastian said, giving an exaggerated yawn. 'I'm too tired tonight. Straight to bed for me.'

'Same,' I said. Neither of us would have used the TV room without Alex's being there. Our legitimate terrain was our bedrooms and the kitchen. Use of the other rooms required the authorising presence of a bona fide member of the household. It was touchingly innocent of Alex to be unaware of this.

Over the following days Alex spent a lot of time with her mum, hibernating in the master suite with her, as she'd said she would.

I would walk past and hear murmuring coming from in there: always it was Kata's voice, talking, talking. I wondered what she was talking about, how she found so much to say to her daughter. I asked Sebastian if Kata and Alex always spent this much time together when they were in the same house.

'It depends,' he told me. 'They are very close.'

'It's funny,' I said. 'From what Alex told me, I wouldn't have got that impression at all.'

'It's ups and downs, you know,' he said. 'They go through their phases.'

Mum's casts were off. She kept me updated with photos and the occasional video call. Her image showed up on my phone a couple of days after Kata's return. The word Mum pulsing on my screen, over the picture of her, looking pretty with her hair in a messy bun, doing something to a flower bed.

The early morning light fell soft over my white sheets. I sipped on my warm coffee. She was drinking coffee too.

'What are you up to today?' I asked her. 'Are you back at work yet?'

My Aunt Janet had a Holistic Beauty and Wellness Salon in Totnes.

'Three clients this afternoon. Quite an easy day.'

'Which treatments?'

'Pedicure, Gua Sha Facial, Non-Acid Peel.'

'Gua Sha is the massage with the green jade stone?'

'Green jade roller.'

'What does it do?'

'It boosts circulation, it's good for lymphatic drainage. I thought I gave you one, darling?'

'Yes, you did,' I said.

I felt warmth in my chest, hot little coals. A prickling behind my eyes. Early morning caffeine always heightened things. But still. There were topics on which Mum was expert and when we kept to these topics she was the parent I'd always longed for. It was why I always sent her pictures of plants I didn't know the names of, even though I could easily have downloaded the app that tells you such things. *Ficus*, the answer would whizz back, authoritatively. *Rubber Fig*.

I saw that it was nearly half past eight.

'I'd better go, I've got to get ready for lessons.'

'OK darling. Speak this evening?'

'Maybe some morning later this week,' I said.

Evenings were her danger time.

We had been eating dinner together, the four of us – Alex, Sebastian, Irina and I – in the dining room. Now, Kata and Alex ate in Kata's bedroom in front of her TV and the rest of us grabbed dinner when we could. Sebastian and Irina had duties in the evenings so we ate separately, ad hoc, depending on Kata's wishes and plans. No longer the masters of our own time, we took scraps where we could, where the opportunity presented itself. 'Wanna watch an episode of something?' Sebastian might ask, coming to my room at 9 p.m. We'd settle down to watch; half an hour later Sebastian's phone would buzz. 'Kata wants me to book her a spa appointment for tomorrow,' he would say, and off he would go to his laptop. We both felt nostalgic for the communal rhythm of our nights before Kata had arrived. I imagined what it would be like if Sebastian and I owned the apartment, and Alex lived in it with us. The texture we would establish. It would not be prey to contingencies. It would be something on which we could rely. Each night would find us in the TV room, curtains drawn, watching movies together. Or maybe, if the place was ours, we'd no longer feel the need to cling to this ritual. Maybe we'd leave the curtains open and let the wind from the marina blow in. Maybe some nights we would watch movies, and some nights we would not.

If a text came through from Mum after about 5 or 6 p.m. I tended to delete it without reading it, but a couple of days after our morning call one came through just before lunch.

Why don't I take a few days off and come out to see you? Janet won't mind. It's been ages since I had a holiday.

Not a good idea, I wrote back. *I'm working. Plus Monaco a v expensive place to stay and obviously you can't stay here.*

Not Monaco, she replied. *Have found reasonable Airbnb in village up in hills. You can come when you have time.*

PS Your dad and I stayed near there on our honeymoon!! Be interesting to see that part of the world again.

You mean you've already reserved it?

No, just thinking about it. They have some availability next month.

But at ten-thirty that night messages came through and I couldn't stop myself looking at them. First there were honeymoon photos of her and my dad, photographs from her album. Him handsome in a summer suit, her girlish and excited beside him, on the terrace of a grand hotel. Him at the wheel of a vintage open-topped car. 'An Aston Martin!' Mum had told me, what felt like millions of times. I'd seen the photos millions of times too. After the photos there was typing for ages, but the message, when it came through, was just a single word:

Booked.

*

In an English lesson one morning Alex kept yawning. 'Sorry,' she said, 'Mama and I stayed up until 2 a.m. watching *American Idol*.'

'No worries,' I said, examining the page in front of me, an essay plan she'd just done.

She must have read something into my minimal response because after a silence I heard her say, 'Um, you know ...' and pause. Sensing something was on her mind, I looked up at her.

'The things I told you about Mama ...' she said, 'don't ... don't think too badly of her. She's a complicated person, she has her reasons, I'm spending time with her because—'

I interrupted her. 'Alex. Sweetheart. You don't need to explain yourself to me, OK? I understand. Alex?' I waited until she looked up at me. 'I understand totally, OK? She's your mum.'

She seemed relieved when I said that. 'OK,' she said. 'OK.' She returned her attention to the task at hand. We continued to go through her plan.

And it seemed this little moment brought her closer to me, made her feel she could trust me, because quite late that night, when I was already in bed but with my light still on, reading, I heard a tap on my door and Alex came in and sat on the edge of my bed.

'So, you know Tatiana's arriving tomorrow?' she said. 'I feel very nervous about it. We're going to the airport in the morning to pick her up. Please, Mel, will you come with me? Will you come too?'

*

I was curious to see this Tatiana person.

We stood waiting for her in the airport. On screen she looked glowy, her skin a uniform golden colour, but then so did all the people on the show. What would she look like in real life? 'Ah,' murmured Kata, 'here she is.' I followed her gaze and saw a blonde girl detaching herself from the stream of arrivals and heading in our direction. She raised a hand from her trolley, gave an unemphatic smile. She did not hurry.

She was very beautiful, more so in the flesh than on screen. Her hair was a soft, blonde cloud, like in photos of old-time Hollywood movie stars. Her features were exquisite, as if each had been sculpted into the most perfect possibility of a lip, an eye, a nose. Her whole person seemed dewy and supple. '*Hello*,' she said. She wore a delicate chain around her wrist. She kissed Kata on the cheek, and then Alex.

'This is Alex's tutor, Melanie,' Kata said.

'Hello,' said Tatiana. She did not kiss me.

Kata was queenly in the back of the limo, saying little apart from the occasional formal, stilted offering: 'Have you enjoyed your summer so far, Tatiana? Have you visited Monaco before?'

But even I could tell that beneath her lofty manner she was nervous. Alex was staring glassily ahead. Tatiana did not seem anxious at all. She responded to each of Kata's niceties perfectly, but she didn't prolong her answers, or make any attempt to fill the silences with an inconsequential patter that would have put everyone at ease. When she had finished answering she would continue to look in the direction of whoever she had been speaking to, with a steady gaze that seemed almost forensic, almost as if she wanted it known, that she was taking in, processing ...

This was not what I had been expecting; it seemed to me deliberate and bordering on cruel. I marvelled at how quickly she had established her ascendancy. I sat there in the back of the limo with them all, not saying a word, just watching. There was no need for *me* to feel nervous, because nothing was expected of me: no conversation; no contribution. I was on a completely different footing from the other people in the car, on a completely different footing from Tatiana. I was only six years older than Tatiana. We had been to the same sort of school. And yet what a gulf between us. Here we were, in the back of this limo, with these billionaires, she as their guest, I as their employee.

When we got to the apartment, I saw it afresh, through Tatiana's eyes. I'd become accustomed to the over-plush sateen heaviness, the purples and blacks and greys. Tatiana walked through to the living room. I saw her reach out and take a fold of purple taffeta curtain between her finger and thumb.

'It is due for a makeover ...' Kata said. 'We moved in here some years ago ...' Kata was statuesque and fleshy but her whole aspect seemed permeable and exposed.

I winced. Stop apologising. Stop apologising for your own home.

Tatiana turned around. 'I think it's *amazing*,' she said. 'I *love* it.

Thank you so much for having me to stay. You have such exquisite taste. It's so beautiful here. Can you show me around?'

*

The next morning, Tatiana stretched out her arms luxuriantly before lifting her morning cup of green tea to her lips. 'I slept like a *baby*,' she said.

'Yes, please,' I said, when Irina came in and asked who wanted a second coffee, but Kata said, 'Please, Melanie, take it with you to Alex's room, lessons will start early today so that Alex is ready to come with us at 12.30.'

'Oh,' said Alex. 'No, I don't need ...'

'Oh, you've got to come, Alex!' Tatiana cut in. 'A friend of mine from *The Royal Borough* is having a trunk show of her swimwear collection in a suite at the Hotel de Paris. It should be super fun. I was hoping Kata might like to come along with me.'

Would she ever.

'*Please* come with us, Alex!' Tatiana said and Alex replied, 'Well, OK.'

Alex shook her head when she heard them calling her name at 12.30. She was wearing white shorts and a grey T-shirt. She stood up and pulled on a thin grey cardigan that came down below the hem of her shorts. Kata and Tatiana were waiting by the door, wearing high heels and carrying stiff, heavy handbags. Kata looked Alex up and down and opened her mouth as if to say something, but Tatiana said, 'Cute outfit, Alex!' so Kata smiled agreement and then two pairs of heels clattered out the front door, with Alex following behind.

I was waiting in my room when they came back, my door ajar, ready for Alex to come and fill me in, ready to laugh with her about the absurdities of the day, but she didn't come, and when I went to her door an hour or so later to ask, 'Well, how was it?', she turned to me with cheeks pink with pleasure and said, 'Actually, it was kind of fun.'

*

They were out all the time. My lessons with Alex shrank from four hours a day to three and we began them one hour earlier in the mornings. They went all sorts of places. 'And where was it today?' I would ask Alex. One day it was Nikki Beach down in St Tropez. They took a helicopter and Tatiana introduced Kata to a swimwear model who was currently dating a Hollywood movie star! The model invited them to a party on a yacht hosted by a British high-street tycoon, where they met more supermodels and a French DJ of international fame. This sojourn was parlayed into an invitation to be part of a table at that year's charity gala at the Hotel du Cap. A single place at the table cost around ten thousand dollars. Tatiana was sharing her contacts and Kata was footing the bill, an old and established custom, nothing unusual in it.

One hundred years ago someone like Tatiana might have been supported by a solid and incontestable wealth, in the form of inherited family estates. Today, she was still of the ruling class but the capital that had once underpinned people like her had dwindled away, relative to the new power players on the global stage.

The elite status of people like Tatiana came from their heritage, their networks, their manner, their understanding of the codes, their insider access; they now had to hustle to parlay these things into actual wealth. Whether it was a TV show, a well-paid city job, a house bought by their parents – a lot of money compared to someone like me, who relied solely on a wage, but nothing relative to the people they would actually be mingling with and comparing themselves to: the oligarchs, the owners of oil reserves, the tech billionaires, the monopolisers of entire sectors of emerging markets. People like Kata, with their recent billions, were still insecure enough to defer to people like Tatiana, so long as people like Tatiana offered them the requisite amount of flattery. How easy it was for the Tatianas of the world to offer this flattery; whether it did or did not stick in the throat was hard to tell: the controlled veneer, the *breeding* of people like Tatiana, meant that resentment, were there any, would never be shown. Or never inadvertently, at least.

I didn't know how wealthy Tatiana was, not exactly. I knew from googling her that her dad worked in finance, and I had worked out from her Instagram that even though she was only nineteen and had only just left school, she had moved into a flat in London that she called her own. It served as her base; she didn't seem to be there very much. Her class was evident both from her person – her precocity and self-possession – and from the snapshots of her life as seen on her Instagram: the French windows and stone balustrades and oversized lamps that lurked in the background of her selfies, group photos and videos taken with her friends. The TV show, flattened and formatted, revealed less about her.

Trained from an early age to be a good house guest, Tatiana wanted to take Kata out for dinner to thank her for having her to stay. 'Anywhere you like,' she said. 'It would be my pleasure.'

I was putting a piece of smoked swordfish into my mouth, feeling my tastebuds pop, when I heard Alex saying from down the table, 'Mel, maybe you would like to come with us?'

'Oh, no, no, thanks,' I said. But she was gazing at me with a tender look of – what was it? – was it pity for me? Was she keen to the fact that we hadn't been doing as much together as we used to? 'Oh, come on, Mel,' Alex said, putting her head to one side, and as much to move the conversation on as anything I said, 'OK, thanks.'

Kata chose her favourite place, as Tatiana had said she should. It was the sort of place I'd expected she would like. High-octane, prohibitively expensive, VIP. It was early evening when we arrived but the inside of the restaurant-bar-club – whatever it was – was completely sealed to the outside elements; no natural light came in. It could have been midnight. Round tables dotted the ground floor, fanning out from a circular bar. A curving staircase, velvet-carpeted and underlit with red lights, led up to a second-floor gallery. At the top of the staircase, presiding over the whole of the club, was a vast Buddha, hewn from some kind of dark metal.

The place was a bit out of Alex's age range, but Kata didn't seem concerned.

Loud house music pulsing from a DJ up on the gallery made it hard for us to hear each other but we did our best. We sat together at one of the little round tables; a waiter came over and we shouted some orders for dinner.

Kata had wavered over where to go. 'You decide, you are the guest,' she had said several times to Tatiana. Being insecure in her own tastes, she was reluctant to take responsibility for the evening. But Tatiana had been adamant. 'No, no,' she had insisted. 'It's my treat to you. I'd like to take you to the place you like best.' So eventually Kata had had to make a decision, and here we had come. When we'd arrived, I'd seen Kata look anxiously at Tatiana; she'd opened her mouth to speak and I'd wondered what she was going to apologise for. Was she going to say she didn't remember the music being this loud, or that they must have changed the decor since she'd last been, or that she didn't remember it being this busy? But before she could say anything Tatiana had said, 'Wow, this place is amazing, great choice, Kata, what a treat.' So that by the time we were sitting at our little round table, Kata was completely relaxed.

I was anxious what would happen when it came time for the bill so I ordered the cheapest thing I could see on the menu, a pizza margerita. As the evening had been Tatiana's idea I assumed she would be paying for all of us, but I still felt the need to make as little impact as possible on the tally of the evening, for my imprint on the bill to be as faint as my imprint on the evening itself. I said nothing as I sat at the table with them. I smiled and nodded and was ready to respond if anyone looked to me for anything. It was a more negative state of being than if I hadn't come at all, and I wished that that were so, that I had not come at all.

Kata asked Tatiana when shooting on the TV show would resume, when was the new season starting? There was a feverish cast to her as she asked, a slight tinge of red, some uncanny life in her solid, product-moist cheeks. I suspected she'd been holding off from mentioning the show as an act of will, but now judged enough days to have passed to be able to bring it up in a way that seemed nonchalant. She brought her glass of champagne to her lips, then set it back down with a robotic, slicing motion.

'Oh,' said Tatiana, 'I'm taking a break from that actually. Yeah, I don't want, you know, that show to be the thing that *defines* me. It might stop people taking me seriously.'

'Oh,' said Kata. 'Yes, yes, I understand.'

'I'll be at university from September,' Tatiana continued. 'I'm going to the Courtauld Institute to study History of Art. Any time you want to come and have a look round, just give me a call, Alex.'

'OK, cool, thanks,' Alex said.

'I'm good at the subject, but Alex really has a gift for it,' Tatiana said to Kata. 'She understands how to look at art, she is really able to *see*.'

Alex smiled with pleasure.

'It is your best subject, isn't it, my darling?' Kata said to her. 'But then, you are good at everything, my sweet.'

'We should do some day trips together,' Tatiana said. 'There's the Matisse museum in Nice.'

'And the Fondation Maeght in St Paul de Vence,' Alex added. 'And the Cocteau Museum down in Menton.'

'Deal,' said Tatiana, raising her glass. She and Alex clinked, and Kata joined them. Alex put her glass down and lifted her hands to her cheeks, which were rosy.

'What is it, my girl?' asked Kata.

'Oh,' said Alex. 'Nothing. I'm just ... happy!'

Tatiana blew a kiss to her across the table. 'You and me both,' she said.

When the waiter brought the bill Kata tried to pay but Tatiana wouldn't let her. 'Absolutely not,' she said. 'My treat.'

'Um,' I said, feeling like gaucheness personified, 'can I, um, give you something ...'

'No,' Tatiana said, without looking at me. 'It's done.' She took her card back from the waiter. Her oyster nails, perfectly mani-cured. 'Shall we?' she said and at her prompting we all rose.

She was *younger* than me. I kept forgetting it. We followed her

94

towards the exit. Where will she be, I wondered, what will her life look like, in ten years' time? I knew I would never have her poise.

Back in Courchevel, I'd taken pleasure in going along with Ivan and Kata and Alex to restaurants I could never have afforded to eat in if I was paying for myself. I'd taken the experience for what it was and enjoyed what it had to offer. The pure material pleasure of it. They were far enough removed from me – they were *billion-aires* – that I was able to simply relish the novelty of it all. But with Tatiana there it was different.

She was too close to me.

I walked two paces behind her as we made our way across the restaurant. Two paces behind the perfection of her hair, her clothes, her carriage.

I was close enough to touch. I could reach out a hand to that silk-clad back. I could feel it, I could taste it, what it must be like to be her.

I slackened my pace. I let her move ahead, and I followed them at a distance out of the restaurant door.

*

It was quiet in the entrance foyer, padded doors closed behind us to mute the sound of the music inside the club. Kata was calling Dmitri on her mobile, instructing him to bring the car. 'Let's sit,' she said. Couches lined either side of the foyer. We moved towards one.

'Well, well, well,' we heard a loud male voice say. A man, somewhat rumpled in a linen jacket, was raising himself from an armchair. 'International woman of mystery,' he said.

Tatiana stopped, flew a hand to her chest. 'What the ...?' she began. 'What are you doing here?'

The man smiled, unfazed; he looked around at the rest of us. 'Hello, hello,' he said.

I put him in his mid-forties. The white shirt he wore beneath his jacket was open to the second button. 'What am I doing in Monaco, or in this nightclub?' he said to Tatiana.

'Both,' she said.

'Well,' he said, 'with regards to this particular establishment, I've had a meeting, I'm waiting for my car. I bumped together a few business meetings, thought I'd make a long weekend of it.

'Hello,' he said again, turning to the rest of us, 'hello,' and he shook Kata's hand. He paused, her hand in his, he kept his gaze on her face, he looked quizzical, he stepped back a bit, still holding on to her hand. 'Have we met before?'

'Yes,' Kata replied, shyly. 'Yes, we have met, I am not sure if you will remember. It was some years ago, in a nightclub called Calico.'

*

The coincidence, first of Tatiana and then of Kata, was too much to be borne. No matter his early start the next day: Oliver insisted we turn on our heels, that we have another drink.

'Not down here though,' he said, 'let's go upstairs. The private rooms, where we can hear ourselves think.'

A waiter let us in to room number seven, a small room with dark-leather club chairs, wood panelling, some hunting-style paintings on the walls; a sort of riff on a gentleman's club, apart from the rogue element of an enormous vase of willow spray in one corner, reaching almost to the ceiling.

I watched Tatiana and Oliver closely, wondering about the exact nature of their relationship. There must have been a twenty-year age gap between them but Tatiana assumed an air of dominance when it came to Oliver; she made fun of the room, said it was a bit funereal – there were candles – she made fun of his shoes, spanking new navy-blue boaters – 'Bit off-key, Oliver,' she joked – but through all her chaffing there was a definite sexual element, in the way she would raise her eyebrows, hold his gaze.

I wondered if this was specific to her interaction with Oliver or if Tatiana used her sexuality in this way with men in general. The men she was used to being around probably expected this from women, I thought, or at least expected it from women who looked like Tatiana.

Oliver was thrilled to see Kata again. 'What a stroke of luck,' he said, more than once. He thought it called for champagne and typed the order in to a sort of iPad thing attached to the wall.

He had the exquisite manners which are the main calling card of men of his class, manners which to the uninitiated bespeak an intoxicating attentiveness but which, to those of a more cynical bent, show a uniformity of response very close to indifference. Kata basked in Oliver's attention. She was asked question after question, her most bland and unremarkable reply celebrated by Oliver as if it were some fascinating and pithy witticism worthy of Oscar Wilde.

'And is your husband going to put in an appearance?' he asked. 'Or is he too busy stoking the home fires? Or maybe he'd cramp your style?'

Kata giggled and fluttered over this but I thought I saw Tatiana shoot Oliver what looked like a warning glance.

'Maybe,' Kata said. 'Sometimes, if he gets a break in work he comes. And where are you staying, Oliver?'

'With a good friend of mine,' Oliver said. 'In fact' – and I definitely did see him shoot a glance at Tatiana before he said this – 'with a friend ...' – and here he shook his head as if to say to himself: 'How funny!' – 'with a friend you've met. On the very same night that we first met. Do you remember your compatriot Valentin Kemerov?'

Coincidence upon coincidence upon coincidence, how very extraordinary!

This called for more drinks. Cheers! Tatiana fiddled with another of the iPad gadgets attached to the wall and the ubiquitous house beats piped into the room.

Oliver handed Kata his card. 'A relatively new venture,' he was saying, 'but it seems to be going quite well.'

I leaned my body in order to look at the card: *Spencer-Forbes: Lifestyle Consultancy*. I said it a few times in my head so as to remember it.

Alex looked tired and bored. 'Look at this,' I said, showing her my phone. An Instagram video of a hamster, to all appearances putting in a Skype call to a duck.

Eventually it was time to leave, and we all stood up. Kata, Tatiana and Oliver were filling the corridor with their excited chatter as we headed back into the main part of the club, exchanging plans to meet again very soon, very soon, in the coming days. When we were back down in the entrance foyer, where the chance meeting with Oliver had occurred, Kata veered off to put in a call to Dmitri and Alex slumped down onto one of the sofas and stared at her phone.

For the first time that evening, Oliver and Tatiana were left to themselves. They stood some way off, talking intently, looking at Kata. There were lots of people milling about in the foyer. I could slink out of Oliver and Tatiana's eyesight and circle my way closer to them. They didn't register me anyway. Had they so much as spoken to me, up in that wood-panelled room? Over the course of what, two hours?

We were quiet in the back of the car. Kata and Tatiana were all talked out and Alex was almost asleep. The car purred a wide arc around the Port Hercule, the big and brightly lit boats. The night-life of the harbour-front bars could be seen but not heard. The cold of the air con; the smell of the leather. I looked at Tatiana, at Kata and at Alex.

I might be lowest in the pecking order, I was thinking, but when it comes to information, I have the bird's eye view.

Because I had managed to overhear part of Oliver and Tatiana's conversation.

'Why didn't Valentin stay and join us?' Tatiana had asked. 'I thought that was the plan.'

'One step at a time,' Oliver had replied.

'I told her my dad shot pheasant,' Tatiana laughed. 'They love that sort of thing.'

'They certainly seem to,' Oliver said.

'Well,' Tatiana replied, 'you would know.'

What was she up to? On the clear road, the car sped up and

the motion pinned me, held me back against the seat. I looked at them – Kata, Tatiana, Alex – like I was watching characters in a reality TV series, aware, as viewer, of over-arching plot developments in a way the individual characters were not. I was used to watching reality TV series, I watched them all the time. I'd watched all four seasons of *The Royal Borough*. It hadn't yet struck me that, when it came to this particular show, I could use my viewer's omniscience to alter the course of the plot, to change the direction in which things might go.

9

Kata seemed particularly alert and expectant at breakfast the next morning. She asked Irina for a third espresso.

'OK!' she said, drumming her fingers on the table. 'Alex, Melanie, off to lessons, let's go!'

I saw her eyes flick shyly in Tatiana's direction. Tatiana looked sleepy. She yawned.

'What would you like to do this afternoon, Tatiana?' Kata asked her.

Tatiana finished her yawn. 'Oh,' she said, 'I really don't mind, I'm happy to do whatever you like, to chill.'

Kata looked disappointed. 'Well, we'll discuss,' she said.

Her hands stopped their drumming but then, a moment later, she danced them on her thighs. I saw her glance down at the empty cup of her third espresso somewhat regretfully. Where would her nervous energy go if all they were going to do that afternoon was 'chill'? I think Kata had spent many, many afternoons of her life 'chilling'. I think she was ready to do something else.

I went to the bathroom before the lesson and when I went into Alex's room she was sitting at her desk hunched over her phone. A selfie of Kata and Tatiana.

'Where's that from?' I asked, but I already knew: it was from Tatiana's Instagram. I looked at Tatiana's Instagram all the time. The photo was from the night before and the location had been tagged.

'Look,' Alex said, showing me a second photo, this time including Oliver.

I'd seen that one too. 'Is that bad?' I asked her.

She shrugged. 'She shouldn't have put my mum's name,' she said. She scrolled down. *Chilling with* — Tatiana had written out Kata's name in full.

'Why not?' I asked.

'Because my dad won't like it.'

'Is he on Instagram?'

'No, not him,' she said.

She played one of Tatiana's stories: Kata and Oliver clinking their drinks together over and over again, boomerang effect.

When we emerged for our lunch break Kata had changed out of the tracksuit she wore around the house. She was wearing an ankle-length white kaftan with slits to mid-thigh, jewelled sandals, a Pucci bandanna and very large amber-toned sunglasses. Her lips were glossily and carefully painted.

'Have some lunch quickly and then get changed, Alexandra!' she said. 'Maybe the nice white dress we bought for you. Oliver has invited us to spend the afternoon with him on a boat trip and maybe an early dinner in Antibes.'

Alex looked at me, but Kata quickly intervened. 'I'm sorry, Melanie, but there is limited space on the boat. This time it's a family trip. But please enjoy the apartment, use the pool.'

As soon as they left, I stretched myself out on one of the sunbeds. After about ten minutes I heard the glass doors sliding open and saw that it was Irina, the housekeeper, carrying a tray. There was a pitcher of what looked like fresh lemonade on it, a single glass, a bowl of fruit.

'Is that for *me*?' I asked her, but I was the only person out there, and she was setting it down beside me. 'Wow, thanks!'

I ranked lowest among the people of the household, the family and their guests, that is, but I ranked highest among the staff, floating somewhere between the two groups and not really belonging to either of them. I felt on equal terms with Sebastian, but he didn't have breakfast with the family like I did, and his bedroom was in the staff section of the apartment; he didn't have a guest bedroom like me. If it had been Tatiana lying out here sunbathing, I thought, Irina would have brought her the exact same tray. I took my first sip, leaning back, feeling good. Just the taste of the lemonade, the heat of the sun on my body and the sound of the pool pump, splash, splash.

*

When I'd got back to my room the previous night I'd googled the name of the company on Oliver's card. Spencer-Forbes: Lifestyle Consultancy.

The home page had unfurled across my laptop screen: London at night, a glittering lightscape, all the monuments: the London Eye, the Shard, the high-rises of Canary Wharf, twinkling with promise. I'd clicked enter and a menu had appeared on the left-hand side of the screen. It had sub-headings like 'The London Season'; 'Glamorous London'; 'Historic Houses'; 'The Arts'; 'Sports'. Each section brought up images. There were aerial views of stately homes and badly lit photographs of canopied, four-poster beds. There was centre court at Wimbledon, polo matches, members of the royal family at Chelsea Flower Show. There were pictures of guests in smart, summery clothes sipping champagne outside famous London cultural institutions. There were stags on Scottish mountainsides, pheasants, opera singers, ballet dancers. There was the facade of Eton College, in the section titled 'Education'. *The English elite live the most exciting, exclusive and agreeable lifestyle in the world*, the website told its readers. 'Agreeable' was a nice touch. *But English high society has its own, very specific social etiquette and tradition of 'good form'*. Spencer-Forbes could help you with this. Spencer-Forbes was all about connecting, introducing, facilitating. What were some of the services Spencer-Forbes actually offered? I browsed through. They would propose you for membership of exclusive members' clubs. They would arrange for you to stay the night in a *historic aristocratic stately home* and enjoy dinner with your distinguished hosts. They could offer introductions to some of the UK's most highly regarded business professionals in the areas of *accountancy, tax, banking and legal matters*.

So, this was the kind of racket with which Oliver, Kata's English earl, attempted to shore up his dwindling, aristocratic coffers. Well, I thought, he's struck gold with Kata. She's a sitting duck for this sort of thing.

It didn't quite add up, though. If it was in fact that simple – if Oliver was just trying to recruit new clients and had enlisted Tatiana to help scout them – then why all this subterfuge? The fabricated accidental meeting. Was this how he normally brought people on board? Surely not. Surely he'd just call up or email prospective clients? Straight-up offer them his services. Surely some posh young intern in his 'office' had access to a database of rich, non-dom London residents and it would be a simple matter to post glossy newsletters through the doors of their Knightsbridge and Belgravia mansions? Scatter some additional newsletters round the waiting rooms of Harley Street, and you were off. No, Oliver's whole approach to Kata had been too circuitous. I was convinced that something else was going on.

*

I had half drowsed off in the sun when there was a rustling on the sunbed next to me. I opened my eyes to see Sebastian sitting there, lighting one of his slim Vogues. I smiled at him and closed my eyes again. I could smell the smoke and then I couldn't. I found myself on my side, hugging my bunched-up towel, saw that Sebastian was still there, lying on his back, his eyes closed now too. Asleep in his suit, I thought, slipping back into sleep, both of us in the shade of the umbrellas. Then came voices, the sound of something sliding, the glass doors. 'Sebastian,' I heard a voice say. A pause and the heat of the sun, just on my calves and feet, the rest of me shaded by the umbrella.

'Sebastian.'

We both sat up and then Sebastian was on his feet. I whipped up my towel and wrapped it around me.

Ivan was standing there, some three steps from the glass doors. Anton and Vova were behind him.

*

'I am *not* taking the rap for this,' Sebastian said, in the kitchen. He was putting together a tray of cold drinks. 'Nice of Kata to let me know. We don't have the food he likes. And the guys' apartments haven't been prepared!' His voice was rising. 'I bet she'll make out like she told me and *I'm* the one who forgot.'

Irina was at the kitchen table writing a list. 'I'll go to Carrefour,' she said. 'I'll get everything.' Her phone lay in front of her, on loudspeaker. She tutted and shook her head as it went to the voicemail of Etienne, the chef.

I was still in my bikini and towel. I hadn't yet braved the long stretch of corridor back to my room. Sebastian shouldered open the swinging doors of the kitchen and headed to the sitting room with the drinks. While they were all gathered there, I seized my opportunity; I pulled the towel tighter around me and padded down the corridor. A door opened up ahead and Ivan came out.

'Oh, hi, hello,' I said.

'Greetings,' he replied. When I had passed him, he said, 'My wife. Do you know what time she will be back?'

'Um … I'm not sure; they've gone on a boat trip and then I think they were planning to go out for dinner afterwards, so I'd say quite late, maybe around nine, ten?'

He nodded and walked in the direction of the sitting room.

I ran a bath and sat on the edge of the tub, testing the temperature with my hand.

When the bath was full I took off my bikini and got in.

Why had they suddenly shown up here?

I thought of Alex's response to Tatiana's Instagram post: 'Papa won't like that.'

I lowered my head under the water, then brought it back up. I thought of someone I hadn't really considered before. Dmitri, the driver. I remembered the ugly scene between Ivan and Kata in the restaurant that time in Courchevel. How Ivan had known about the man coming on to Kata outside the club. 'You know that man, the one Dmitri had to tell to go away? Do you know what he thought you were? My darling, he thought you were a whore.'

Did Ivan have spies everywhere?

10

*

Anton was *hot*. He was as hot as I remembered. It was an assembly of physical features I could not help but respond to. The tall, lanky frame; the big nose and hands. A particular quality of forearm: wiry and elegant, veined.

'What's the deal with Anton and Vova?' I asked Sebastian as we stood down in the parking lot, smoking. 'Do they have lives of their own, or do they just follow Ivan around like dogs?'

Sebastian looked around, as if scared one of them might be loitering nearby. Anton, Vova, Dmitri, Ivan – it seemed suddenly camp and comical, our world populated by sinister and inscrutable men.

'They own their own apartments in the building,' he said. 'And they have their own houses in Moscow. They are in Moscow most of the time but they go with the boss when he travels, yes. They work for him but they are also old friends. They all grew up together, in the same part of Russia. These mega-rich Russian guys. The most important thing to them is to be surrounded by people they trust.'

We speculated on why they had arrived just as Valentin had made his appearance. 'God,' I said. 'Better not go near any sushi restaurants. Watch out for Polonium-210!'

I looked at Sebastian, expecting him to be careening merrily along with me down this line of conjecture, but he didn't seem interested. He was looking at his phone. 'Oh, who knows, honey,' he said. 'And to be honest, who cares. I don't think it's anything exciting like that. It will be something to do with business. It's always to do with business. I do my job but, apart from that, I try to have my own life.'

'I think Anton's really sexy,' I said.

'Not at all. He's like a scarecrow. Vova's way hotter.'

'Gross. Vova looks like a cube.'

'Coming?' he said, moving towards the lobby doors.

'I'm going to stay here for a while, in case Anton comes down for a cigarette.'

'He has his own apartment and a balcony to smoke from.'

'Oh yeah. Well, I'm going to stay anyway. It's not like I have anything else to do.'

After Sebastian had gone, I walked out further from the building, looked up and wondered which apartment belonged to—

'Fucking hell,' I said, and sped back the way I had come. Then I sidled out again. Anton was right there, two balconies up, striding up and down with his phone to his ear. He saw me standing there looking up at him and gave me a preoccupied wave. Taking courage, I raised the hand holding my cigarettes. 'Come on down!'

'You like westerns?' he asked five minutes later when he emerged from the building.

'Um, yes?'

'I like them.'

His hair was longer than when I'd first met him; a curl fell over his forehead. 'Have you settled in?' I asked him.

He shrugged. 'Sure.'

A woman from the apartments was exercising a tortoise on the circle of grass that formed the centre of the parking bay. We watched. Her hair was red. She was stout and old. The tortoise raised a wrinkled foreleg in the air, held it, held it, then began to bring it down. Anton threw his butt away and looked back at the tortoise. He shook his head. 'The people in this town are insane,' he said.

'Don't you like it here?'

'There are some good restaurants. It's a good place if you like to look at cars. But no, I don't really like it. There are too many stupid people. I like it better back home.'

'Aren't there stupid people in Moscow? Is Moscow where you mean by home?'

'Nowadays it is. There are as many stupid people in Moscow as there are in Monaco. Maybe more. But I don't see them as much. I have my own places to go.'

'By stupid you mean ...'

'Ridiculous.'

I wondered how much Anton was worth. Nowhere near as much as Ivan but he probably had multiple properties, multiple cars. He didn't look rich but then Ivan didn't either, apart from when he got dressed up to go out with Kata.

Anton turned and looked at me. He stared steadily, without self-consciousness.

'Come by my apartment sometime,' he said. 'For a drink. The next few days will be busy, but after that. We can ... do something.'

*

I was reluctant to go back inside and just sit around in my room. Anton's invitation had excited me too much. I felt full of restless life. I went upstairs and got my phone and earphones then came back outside and found a playlist of songs labelled 'euphoric and anthemic'. I sat on a bench close enough to the wall of the building that Anton wouldn't be able to see me, still down here, if he happened to glance over the lip of his balcony. I smoked cigarette after cigarette. The buildings' lights came on and the circle of grass the tortoise had walked on was illuminated. I wondered what time Alex, Kata and Tatiana would come back.

I wanted to be out here when they arrived.

I still had no idea whether they were aware that Ivan had turned up.

I was some twenty songs into my playlist when the blacked-out

Jaguar rolled up, a ubiquitous model of vehicle round here. The doors opened and yes, it was them, disembarking, looking happy and sunburnt. Even Kata had a pink tint to her cheeks. I saw Alex was laughing and saying something to her mum, and her mum laughed and rumpled her hair in response.

I took out my earphones. 'Sleepyhead,' I heard Kata say as they came closer. 'You choose the movie.'

'Hi!' Alex waved at me as they came up the steps and Kata and Tatiana looked at me.

'How was it?' I asked. 'Did you have a nice day?'

'Wonderful,' said Kata, with suddenly pursed lips and a private smile, her head held high. She sailed on up the steps; she did not appear to want to elaborate.

Tatiana did not break her stride either. 'Did you have everything you needed?' she asked me as she made her way up the steps. Who the fuck did she think she was? She spoke to me as if she was older than me.

Alex hung back to chat. 'It was such a cool afternoon!'

'I'm glad you had a good time.'

'We went on this amazing boat. It was huge!'

Limited space on the boat, huh? I didn't say it out loud.

I got up from the bench and we walked up the steps side by side. 'We met Valentin,' Alex said. 'He's so nice. He's invited us to dinner next weekend.'

'Great,' I said.

We caught up with Kata and Tatiana waiting for the lift. Kata's hair had been blown about. They weren't chatting as they stood there but their silence was not tense like it had been in the back of the car the day Tatiana arrived. It was the peaceful silence of people grown comfortable around one another. They stood there sleepily and it was clear to me that they had no idea what awaited them upstairs. I wondered how they would react when they went into the apartment and saw him there. I'd soon find out: the red numbers above the doors were steadily descending.

I looked down and Alex smiled up at me. It suddenly didn't feel right, to wilfully conceal information from her. Even if her dad arriving wasn't a big deal, even if he regularly dropped in unannounced, when last-minute breaks in his schedule permitted, it felt wrong to go up in the lift with Alex knowing something she did not.

'Um,' I said, as the lift opened, 'I forgot. Hang on a sec, Alex, I want to show you something.'

Alex stood back and the doors closed on the others.

'Were you expecting your dad? He arrived this afternoon.'

She stood very still. Then she said, 'No. We were not expecting him. Thank you for telling me.' She took my hand.

'Is it bad, that he's come?'

She stood still, holding my hand, looking down at the floor. 'I don't know,' she said.

We went up in the lift together and stepped from its doors into the apartment. We paused as the lift closed behind us, to listen. We could hear the chatter of voices from down the corridor. The voices seemed cheerful enough.

'My line hooked a sailfish,' we heard Tatiana saying as we got closer. 'But of course, I wasn't strong enough to pull it in myself, one of the crew had to do it.'

'And you, Kata?' we heard Ivan say.

'No, no,' Kata said, 'I just watched. I don't enjoy to fish. It's wonderful to have you here, my darling.' We heard glasses clinking.

When we reached the door Kata said, 'Alex! Look at this wonderful surprise: your papa is here! Come.'

'Hello, Papa,' Alex said. The way she greeted him was stilted, formal.

'Well, what are you waiting for?' Kata said. 'Come!'

Alex hesitated.

Ivan observed her hesitation. 'Yes, I am here,' he said. 'You were not expecting me, were you? I hope I have not spoiled your fun.'

11

When I came to breakfast the next morning, Kata was examining a hard-boiled egg. She peered at it. 'Is this how you wanted it? It is too hard, it is overdone, you like it softer.'

'It's fine,' Ivan said, but Kata pressed her plastic bell. She spoke to Irina sharply; the egg was taken away. A few minutes later, a more suitable one was brought in.

Kata's whole manner – the way she angled her body towards Ivan, the way she spoke pretty much only to him, in lowered tones that were demonstrably meant to exclude the rest of us – sent a clear signal: that he was the most important person at the table, that his needs came first, that he was her focus and her priority. She deigned to address the rest of the table – by which I mean Alex and Tatiana – only once, and then it was to say: 'And what do you kids have planned for the afternoon?'

She did not appear the least shamefaced about disassociating herself from them in this way, eyebrows raised imperiously.

Tatiana looked momentarily confused but played along. 'I don't know, what do you feel like doing, Lex?'

Kata had already returned her attention to her husband.

Kata and Ivan went out a lot in the days that followed. For lunch, for dinner. They would get dressed up in the way I remembered from back in Courchevel. For her outings with Tatiana, Kata had worn leggings and leather jackets, kaftans, high-waisted trousers and tank tops, pencil skirts, a whole assortment of outfits – but with Ivan, she wore only dresses. Dresses and high heels. I would see them arranging themselves for departure in the hallway and remember similar scenes from Courchevel. How fascinating I'd found them back then, and yes, I still did, there was nothing simple or straightforward about the way they interacted. When they were in the room, or at the breakfast table, I couldn't help but want to study them and their complex dance, but this time my interest felt different, cerebral where it had been sensual, their bedroom door, for instance, no longer such a locus, no longer so redolent.

Their movements felt rote and I wasn't sure if this marked some change in them or in me.

I would watch them, at the breakfast table, in the hallway and living room, and I would watch Tatiana watching them too.

'Girls, we are leaving!' Kata called from down the corridor one evening and I went to watch the twilight chorus, as I had done every night that week: Tatiana and Alex gathered in the hallway, waving them off, Ivan with his hand in the small of Kata's back as they stood waiting for the lift doors to open.

Once they had gone, Alex trailed down the corridor to her bedroom, giving me a wan smile as she passed. The sleeves of her grey merino cardigan were so long they drooped past her fingertips.

The successive arrivals of Tatiana and Ivan had put a stop to Alex's alone time with her mum. I no longer walked past Kata's bedroom door to hear the mingled sounds of reality TV and Kata's voice, talking, talking.

Ivan's coldness towards Alex on the night of his arrival had been striking. And it hadn't gone, not completely.

'Papa,' she would say, hesitantly, at the table, 'would you like to try some of this chutney, it goes well with what you are eating ...'

'Papa, Vova told me in Moscow there was a deer in the garden ...'

He would respond politely. I sensed a wariness. His eyes would linger on her for a few seconds after he had answered, as if he was assessing her, trying to work something out. He didn't seem to like her looking at him during meals. 'There is nothing wrong with my food how it is,' he had replied, the time she'd suggested the chutney.

I returned to my room and sat on the window seat. I got out my phone and reread the message.

I was just drafting a reply when I heard a knock at the door and I looked up, knowing even before the door opened that it would be Alex.

The wan smile was still there. She had changed out of her cardigan and leggings into pyjamas and a faded pink sweatshirt.

'Are you busy?' she asked.

I laughed, put down my phone gladly.

'No.'

She held up her book. 'I was thinking, maybe I could ...'

'Sure, come in,' I said. 'Make yourself at home.'

She sat in my armchair, smiled at me and opened her book. Curled down into the chair like a little animal, she rested her head on the cushion and began to read. I went over to the bed and picked up a magazine from the bedside table. It was nice to be in this room with someone else in it too. Reading a book, or a magazine, these solitary activities, so much warmer with another human body in the room, doing the same.

Alex had spent a lot of time on her own with Tatiana since her dad's arrival. 'You kids' as Kata had designated them. Ivan and Kata had commandeered Dmitri for their purposes but Sebastian had set up an account with a premier Monte Carlo chauffeur service and a silver Range Rover had conveyed Alex and Tatiana to museums and galleries, their shared interest. They would return bearing bags of glossy art books and gift shop catalogues. Alex would seem animated but within about ten minutes of being back she would make an excuse and disappear off to her room. I got the sense that she found her time alone with Tatiana a bit of a strain. It gave me a twinge of triumph to think that it was *me* she chose to come to now; that *I* was where her comfort and solace lay.

After an hour of quiet and peaceful companionship, her with her book and me with my magazine, Alex said, 'Shall we go to the kitchen and get a tray of things, some tea, some snacks?' We brought the tray back and put it on my bed and then we searched on my laptop for something to watch, a reality TV show with an elimination format, *Project Runway*. It dawned on me that what we had recreated here, together, was the intimacy Alex had enjoyed in those long evenings with her mother, before the others had arrived. First her mother had been absent, then she had been overwhelmingly present, pressing Alex to her, talking, talking. Now she was absent again. There is no constancy to that sort of love, I thought, and I remembered having the same thought, back in Courchevel. Selfish mothers. Self-absorbed mothers. Mothers bloated and sodden with their own dramas.

The opening credits of *Project Runway* rolled. Alex snuggled down into the bed and I retrieved my phone from where I had slid it, face down under a pillow.

Mum had sent through a video tour of her Airbnb. It looked a bit unkempt. The kitchen fittings were harsh and ugly. The view from her terrace was undeniably gorgeous, however. Sea meeting sky in hazy extravagance.

Here!

I hadn't yet told her that I had the day after tomorrow – Sunday – off.

When I'd been away from Mum long enough, the image I had saved of her on my phone, the one that came up when she called, prevailed through sheer repetition. I had sent her a copy and she used it as her WhatsApp profile picture. This *was* her, it could therefore come to seem: this wholesome, smiling woman, kneeling in the sun with a trowel.

It really was a lovely picture. It had captured her at her absolute best. The open and happy features, the messy hair piled high. The skill she demonstrated, plants and flowers blooming to life through her care.

I thought of Kata's mannered posing as she took her leave each evening. I thought of her pursed lips and averted gaze when she had returned from the boat trip and I had dared to ask her how her day had been.

I'll reply, I decided. I'll tell her I'm off on Sunday.

I returned my attention to Alex, huddled in the armchair.

'You must miss your chats with your mum,' I said.

'Kind of,' she said. 'Except, I don't know ...'

'What? You can tell me.'

'Except that sometimes it felt like – it's hard to explain. Like she was talking to me as if I wasn't there.'

'You weren't there?'

'Because she tells me everything. No filter. I know she wouldn't talk to anyone else like that. So maybe she talks to me like that because it doesn't matter what I think. Do you understand? It doesn't matter to her what I think or what I know. She might as well be talking to herself. She's always talked to me like that.'

She was a sweet and uncertain girl. Her long limbs had been dusty that day, weeks ago, when we had first sat on our rocky outcrop and she had scratched a seagrass stem across one leg and made a white mark. She was gawky and gangly as a new deer and it gave me a pain in my chest to look at her, like I was looking at myself when I was her age.

'I know what you're trying to say. But you could look at it another way, couldn't you? Maybe she tells you everything because she trusts you. Maybe it's because she's closer to you than to anyone else in the world.'

Thinking to myself: *What* does she tell you? What? How does that woman have so much to say?

*

Ivan told Kata, as she buttered his toast for him the next morning, that he would be going out for the day. He and Vova were testing a new fishing boat. They would eat on the boat, and he would be back in the evening, around nine or ten o'clock.

'What do you want to take with you?' Kata asked. 'Tell me what you want and I will arrange it with Sebastian and Irina. They will pack a cool box for you.'

Ivan hadn't mentioned Anton. I wondered if he was staying

behind. I hadn't seen him since his invitation, apart from a brief glimpse of him now and then on his balcony, phone to his ear.

When Ivan took his leave we were lying out on the sunbeds. 'Come out to the pool!' Alex had said to me and I had gladly taken her up on the offer.

'Check it with your mum first though,' I'd said. She had checked and told me it was fine.

Kata rose from her sunbed and went to kiss Ivan goodbye, to do a last-minute check that he had everything he needed. We heard, distantly, the front door close. Kata came back outside and at once the act of the past few days was dropped, the demarcation of adults and 'kids'. Kata was saying, before she had even resumed her place on her sunbed: 'I think we will wait, Tatiana, until Ivan has gone, to accept Valentin's dinner invitation. I have been thinking about it. I know we are supposed to be there tomorrow but I think it is best to postpone. I hope Valentin does not mind.'

She lay back down, completely in the shade, her hair immaculate, her legs pale and solid and moisturised. She never went in the pool.

'Really?' said Tatiana. 'How come? I'm sure Valentin would love to meet Ivan.'

Kata did not reply immediately. She allowed a few moments of ponderous silence, as was her wont. 'It will be more relaxed, for me, if we wait until he has gone,' she said. 'He is not always the best guest at this type of thing. He will change the mood.'

I was watching Kata through my dark glasses. She was two sunbeds away from me; Alex lay in between us. 'He will probably leave in two or three days, anyway,' said Kata. 'He never stays for long. And we have many more weeks of the summer. I hope Valentin will not mind, to postpone. He won't, I'm sure?'

Tatiana didn't answer her straight away. Kata turned her head towards Tatiana. Perhaps she had been expecting immediate agreement. Perhaps her question had been rhetorical.

'I'm not ... sure,' Tatiana said. 'He may have made preparations already.'

The habitual injection of nerve-freezing toxins made Kata's forehead less than mobile; nonetheless, I saw the shadowy echo of a frown arrange itself across her brow. Tatiana's response had not been satisfactory.

'I do not want to offend Valentin ...' Kata was saying. 'Maybe we should let him know now, before he goes to any trouble. If we could move the dinner from tomorrow night even just a few days, it would be better.' She gave a long sigh. 'It is very stressful, for me ...'

She turned her head to look through the glass windows into the living room. I followed her gaze; through the glass I could see Anton. He picked some papers up from a table, then disappeared from the room.

'These people Ivan has to have with him, all the time,' Kata said. 'Anton and Vova. To spend time on the boat with Vova, drinking beer, eating sausage, catching fish, as if they were still poor teenage boys in' – she said a Russian-sounding name– 'as if nothing has changed since then.'

She shook her head. The glass doors were opening but it wasn't Anton coming through them, it was Irina, bringing us some fruit. 'Thank you, Irina,' Kata said, before turning back to Tatiana. 'Ivan needs to behave in a way that is more appropriate for his position,' she continued. 'If he always just keeps on like he is, he will never be anything more than how he began.'

'Mama.' It was Alex, looking at her mum. She indicated Irina, now lifting the plate of fruit from the tray and putting it down on the table, absolutely within earshot.

Kata waved her hand in a gesture of dismissal. '*Prostoludin!*' She said the Russian word loudly. I had no idea what it meant. But Irina did. At the word her eyebrows shot up. She went back inside, holding the empty tray.

'*Mama!*' It was Alex again. Her face was white, and I was alarmed by her clear distress. 'Mama ...' She could hardly get the words out. 'Why do you say things like that? What if it gets back to him? Why can't you be more careful?!'

Kata responded by waving her hand again, another gesture

of dismissal, this time of Irina, of Irina's perceptions and reactions, of Irina's cognitive independence, her capacity to take in an action or statement of Kata's and respond to it – perhaps even act on it – in an independent way, a way that might have an *effect* ... The possibility of all this Kata negated with one sweep of her dimpled hand. She lay there, big and stupid, just a slab of ignorance, and I wondered what it would be like to slap her, or prod her hard, or tickle her, scrunch up her hair, do something, anything, to surprise her into a state of shock and disarray.

'I think,' said Kata, 'if it would be OK with you, if you would not mind ... to give Oliver a call, maybe, to ask him if he would mind asking Valentin if it is possible to postpone. Now, I think, would be best.'

'OK,' said Tatiana. 'I'll go in and call him now.'

'Thank you,' Kata said.

I lay there for a few moments after Tatiana had gone inside. The sliding doors had closed behind her, I watched her form recede through the living room. I thought around for an excuse. I didn't really need an excuse. 'I'm going to go in for a bit, I've got to make a call,' I said to Alex.

Dark spots danced in front of my eyes as I made my way through the living room. I heard my name as I reached the corridor.

'Mel.' It was Anton.

'Hi there,' I said. I heard a door close further down the hall. I wanted to get there before Tatiana made her call.

'How about that drink tomorrow night?' I asked him.

'Sure,' he said. 'How about my place, at seven?'

As my vision adjusted he assumed a clear form before me, tall and sexy. I felt my stomach flutter and in the same moment I recalled that tomorrow was the day I was due to see my mum.

His lips parted into a slow smile. They were shapely and delicate lips for someone who was, in my imagination at least, so rugged, so tough.

'Yes,' I said. 'I'll be there.'

By the time I reached the door of Tatiana's bedroom she was talking. 'She wants to wait until he's gone,' I heard her say.

[...]
'I know,' she said. 'I know.'
[...]
'I'm not sure. I can't really intervene.'
[...]
'I don't know, Oliver. Think of something.'

12

It was her clothes I took in first. I'd been curious about her get-up for this trip. She was waiting for me near an ornamental hedge in the Princess Grace Japanese Gardens. I saw the ruffled blouse. A ball of greenery obscured her lower half; it wasn't until I was right up next to her that I saw the bootcut jeans, the word *Milano* splashed in white beneath a heart.

'Hello, Mouse. My beautiful girl.'

She hugged me. The smell of her so familiar, her perfume, I was back in the kitchen of the house in Totnes as she took delivery of her very first bottle. I remembered her spraying it around the kitchen, shooting a spritz at me when I said it was time I was getting to school. 'Oh, shush,' I remembered her saying, picking up the leaflet, 'and listen to this: *The unique molecular structure of this scent draws people irresistibly to its wearer!*'

'It's nice here,' I said. 'I've never been before. Shall we have a wander around?'

'Yes, indeed!'

She hummed a little, in that nervous way of hers. We paused under a tree covered in purple flowers.

She cleared her throat and spoke in mustering tones. 'These are mainly Mediterranean plants, you know, but they've been pruned to give them a Japanese appearance.'

I didn't reply straight away and, unable to bear her own words hanging in the air, she effaced them and herself with a little giggle.

'I don't *really* know, I just read it in the visitor info.'

'So, what have you been up to,' I asked, 'in the past couple of days?'

'Oh, I've had a lovely time, all this gorgeous sun, such a change from rainy old England!'

We climbed the curve of a red lacquered bridge.

'I've been pottering about, going to the market, sitting in the square, watching the funny old men play boules.'

'Look at all the koi carp.'

'Oh, yes,' she said.

The water was clear. They drifted through it, golden.

'Beautiful,' we said, at the same time.

'They really are beautiful, aren't they?' I said.

'Yes. They really are.'

We wandered off the red bridge and went down closer to the pond, walking over white pebbles. The water was cool on my fingers. In the middle of the pond there was a tiny island with a tree on it.

'Pine cloud,' she said, softly.

'I'm sorry I haven't been able to spend more time with you while you've been out here, Mum.'

I could easily have asked for a few days off. Maybe it would have been nice, sitting in the square, watching the funny old men play boules.

'Oh, don't worry, darling, I know you have to work.'

She hadn't pressed me to come up and see her. There had been the video tours, the photos and commentary – *Look how red this tomato is!!* followed by the sunglasses emoji – but she hadn't once badgered me to put in an appearance and the tone of her messages had been gently chipper.

We left the garden and crossed the road and sat outside an innocuous-looking Italian café.

'We're not far from the border, are we?'

She ordered sparkling water. Then she called the waiter back, but it was only to ask for a cappuccino.

She got out her sunglasses, cleaned them with a pristine little cloth.

'Are they new?' I asked, already knowing the answer.

'Oh, yes, I saw them when I nipped in to say hi to Linda in her shop. They caught my fancy.'

Everything she was wearing was new, bought especially for this trip. I knew it as surely as I knew her. Her clothes sat ceremoniously on her flesh, unhabituated. The flouncy blouse that still smelled slightly of shop. *Milano*. Her glittery toenails peeping out of shiny, imitation leather sandals. I imagined her trying it all on in Linda's shop, Linda cooing, Mum asking, 'Does it say *French Riviera*?', Linda cracking open the third bottle of bubbly.

'I'm glad I'm here! You know, it really hasn't changed that much since your father and I were here.'

'I thought you and Dad went to Biarritz.'

'That's right.'

'That's a totally different part of France. It's right on the other side.'

'Yes, but by the sea!'

She was wearing lots of make-up. I could see the orange of her foundation caking into her pores and clinging on to her wispy little facial hairs.

'You never tell me anything about Dad, do you? Not really.'

'You are a funny girl! I tell you lots!'

'No, you don't. You tell me the same few things over and over again. How you met at that barn dance. That weekend in London when he bought you a Cartier watch. This must be the hundredth time I've heard about the honeymoon.'

I looked at her sitting across from me, the lie of her fastidiousness, the lurch I'd felt in my whole body when she had called the waiter back, the pathetic relief when she'd asked for a cappuccino.

Her left arm that was still slightly thinner and paler than her right, after weeks of being in a cast. Her walking wasn't completely back to normal. Her physio would not approve of the glittery sandals.

'The same stories, over and over again,' I said. 'Are they all you can remember about him? I have no idea what kind of person he was. Really, what was he like? And I mean apart from being glamorous and posh, Mum. What was he like, apart from buying you watches and taking you to Biarritz?'

The waiter placed the cappuccino before her.

He retreated and she opened her mouth to speak but a motorbike roared by.

Dust blew towards us in the quiet of its wake.

She picked a bit of dust gently from the spray-painted Milano jeans.

'He was lots of things.'

'Was he? How illuminating. He was lots of things.'

'He loved you.'

'Cool. He loved me.'

'He was larger than life.'

'Larger than life. Great. Anything else?'

'He was a bit of a snob.'

She cast her eyes down immediately. There was a horrible scraping as the couple sitting next to us pushed back their chairs.

They left and there was quiet again and just the remnants of dust from cars and motorbikes floating in the air between us.

'I don't think I ever quite looked the part,' she said.

When she finally looked up her eyes were fearful, submissive. She crossed her arms as if to protect herself. From his gaze. From mine.

Her hands were thick and wrinkled and spotted from sunbeds.

She gave her little giggle. 'Oh, well,' she said. 'It's such a lovely day, what shall we ... we should ...'

'Please can we watch the video of your Airbnb again?'

I moved close, to watch it with her. My shoulder touching hers.

We paused it room by room, discussing how we'd renovate it if the place was ours. 'Some whitewash? Put a small sofa there?'

'Rip out the kitchen, that's the first thing I'd do,' she said.

'Yes,' I said, and my voice sounded faint to me, whispery.

Yes, I thought. Let's rip out that ugly kitchen.

Sometime later, knowing how much she always wanted me to

confide in her, I said, 'You know what, I have a date this evening.' I told her all about the family, all about Anton. 'Should I go? Or should I stay the night with you?'

But we both knew what her evenings held.

'Oh you should go, darling, how exciting, I'll come with you now, let's go shopping, I'll help you decide what to wear.'

*

The light in Monaco always seemed soft and golden and the surfaces it fell upon, the well-tended gardens, the cliff-top palace, the street signs, the plants in the casino grounds, looked rounded and replete, unnaturally clean and cartoonishly cute. The workers of Monaco – the people who staffed the shops and restaurants and bars and medical establishments – would leave once their working hours were over and go back into France, to the more affordable regions of Beausoleil and La Turbie, leaving this place to its international assortment of tax-shy denizens. Little moneyed bonsai of a principality. I remembered something, I'd found it amusing, it was something Prince Albert had said on his accession in July 2005, that he no longer wished Monaco to be known, in the words of Somerset Maugham, as 'a sunny place for shady people'.

We went into a shopping centre with a creamy facade, vines trailing over its curves. The floor was marbled, globes of light hung down. Teenage girls sat outside an ice-cream parlour holding plastic cups, glossed lips sucking down on plastic straws. The artificial lights shone over their perfect faces. They wore brightly coloured designer trainers. I had put on make-up, I was wearing my favourite trousers and my most expensive loafers, but still I felt dowdy, other, and I could tell Mum felt the same. She walked beside me with trembling bravado, bright rictus smile, eyes wide and frightened. We went into the ice-cream parlour, but, standing in front of the glass-domed bar, she was unable to make a decision – 'Oh,' she said, 'Oh,' first when I prompted her and then when the vendor did the same. I had just taken delivery of a small cone of stracciatella and was turning to tend to her when she said, 'Darling, I'm just bursting for a pee, I'm going to find the loos, I won't be long, you go on and have a wander, see you in a sec!'

The ice cream was cold in my throat. She skittered out of the café. I stood with my cone watching her recede through the crowds. Cut loose from me, a solo agent. I noted the purpose in her step.

I sat down at a table outside the café.

Sometime later, when I saw the stracciatella drooling down the cone onto my fingers, I got up and threw the whole flaccid mess into the bin.

I walked in the opposite direction to her, turning my attention to the fronts of the shops, their bright radiance, the crisp items displayed within. A familiar feeling began to effervesce and today I welcomed the absorption, gave myself to it gladly.

Maybe, I thought, I'll buy something. Maybe I will.

Something exquisite and expensive. I gave in to this impulse, occasionally, on tutoring trips. It was becoming harder and harder to resist. The word occasionally was not admitting the whole truth.

'You must have saved loads,' people would say, knowing that when I was on these jobs I had no living costs to cover, no rent, didn't even have to buy my own food. But still, I always managed to blow it, I never returned with any kind of a nest egg.

It would come over me, the desire, usually around three-quarters of the way into my stay, when the end of the job was approaching and with it the return of all the existential worries I had managed to temporarily defer. I would mourn, in advance, the ease of my surroundings; I would crave something potent and immediate and gorgeous, to swell through me and push all anxiety away.

I would long to buy something.

I would resist the impulse for a while, but, ultimately, I would succumb.

I would talk myself into it. Having enough money to buy a flat, something that would give me actual permanence and security, I would tell myself, that isn't on the cards, you'll never have enough for that, so don't beat yourself up for comforting yourself with the occasional smaller treat. In the absence of a rooted life, I was accumulating a moveable feast, one that could be taken with me from temporary lodging to temporary lodging. On one job, in Dubai, a Prada handbag had stalked me for weeks, I'd surrendered to it in the Mall of the Emirates. On a job in Montreux, Switzerland, it had been a Céline coat. The collection I took with me from bedroom to bedroom was becoming more and more perfect, more and more refined. It was becoming increasingly pleasurable to unpack my clothes and hang them neatly in the empty cupboard, to retrieve my toiletries and arrange them around the bathroom sink. My beautiful flacon of white magnolia Decléor oil, resting on a marble countertop.

I would arrive in international airports, the driver of my new employers waiting for me, my name on a sign, and as I walked towards them, hair lustrous – Dr Barbara Sturm's molecular serum – Céline coat on, Gucci loafers, wheeling my sleek black Montblanc polycarbonate suitcase, I would look like the kind of woman who might very well have her own driver, who was about to be conveyed to her own home, as opposed to the home of her boss.

Now, in the shopping centre, I felt the familiar desire come to fill me, I let it suffuse me, and as it did I thought, OK, OK, yes, I will, and in that submission I felt a rush of optimism for my future.

I looked to my left and saw her returning, I saw the glassy look in her eyes, and I knew.

Turning from her, I walked towards one of the shops. The display window was a cube of glass encased in a softly shining metal. Inside, it was hushed like a cathedral. I ran my fingers gently over the beautiful items, displayed singly like pieces in an exhibition. I tried to imagine what I would buy if I had as much money as Kata. What would I take away with me from this shop if I could take anything? And if you had as much money as Kata, that's what it would be like: taking as opposed to buying. It would be, in fact, to live in a world where money did not exist, where things just sat there, and you could take them or you could not.

'What are you going to try on, then?'

She was by my side, a new person now, the hardness that came over her after even a few sips.

The shop manager was watching me. I put on my boldest smile: 'I'd like to try on these, please.'

Alone in the changing room I shed my ordinary clothes and began to remake myself. I put on a blouse in a pale pistachio green and a slim sheath of skirt that looked like it was crafted from Inca feathers. I slipped my feet into pointed pumps edged with something that glinted, ethereal. I looked at myself. I was perfect and beautiful. The lights in the changing room were soft and flattering and even the material of the curtain was superior, full and heavy as it flowed to meet the carpeted floor. I was above ordinary people and I deserved exemption: scarcity could not come to a person who looked like this. The beautiful things of the world were on their way to me. I would trust in the universe to deliver them.

I could hear her, beyond the curtain, a font of sharp confidence, her voice bold and loud, unembarrassed.

'Ready yet? Show me what you've got on. You're good enough for any of those people. You wow that Anton tonight. Hook him. Be sexy. Go for it. Why not? He must be worth a few quid.'

The heavy jacquard fabric that lined the walls of the changing room, the silken wool of the curtain, the carpeted floors. They muffled her. I could build a fortress around me and within it I would no longer be an orphan.

Held by wealth. No more moving around, keeping my belongings to two suitcases' worth so that I could move easily from sublet bedroom to tutoring bedroom and back to sublet bedroom. I'll buy a home in London and I'll plant things in its garden. I'll get a job in the culture industry that pays peanuts but has status. I'll install shelves from floor to ceiling and I'll fill them with books. I'll have ill-advised relationships, I'll have heartbreaks, existential crises, doubts and lonelinesses but I'll live them out held all the while by that fundamental security so they will be manage-able, I will embrace them, in fact, as the stuff and adventure of life. There was no longer anything to fear. For a moment it was so tangible, that place of safety, I could see it, just a few steps down the line. It was written in my destiny.

13

I'd pretended to the others I was going out for a night-time stroll around the town; when I got out of the elevator on Anton's floor I took off my trench and flat shoes and took my beautiful new heels out of my backpack. I wasn't good at walking in heels at the best of times and now the combination of nervous excitement and a shaky feeling from lack of food made me particularly unsteady on my feet. I tried to check my reflection in the metallic surface of the lift doors, now closed, but it was inadequate for my purposes; my face was a blur. I looked down and stroked the exquisite sheath of skirt encasing me from my waist down to the middle of my calves. I paused outside Anton's door. My thighs slid against one another under the skirt, freshly shaved, rubbed with oil. Where would we go? What would we do? I could go anywhere, dressed like this. I rang the bell. There was quite a lag before the door opened. 'Oh, hi,' he said, 'come in.' He was on the phone. After gesturing me in with his hand he resumed his conversation. He was wearing a tracksuit, unshaven and bleary-eyed, like he'd just woken up from a nap.

He was on the phone for fucking ages.

At one point I raised a hand to my lips and mimed the action of drinking. He waved me after him into the kitchen, still on the phone, where he opened a cupboard of glasses, then pointed to the fridge. I drank a glass of white wine and smoked a cigarette inside. He was smoking one. By the time he got off the phone I was no longer nervous.

'Let's go outside,' he said, and led me out onto the balcony, where there was a small table and two chairs. He got a lighter out of his pocket and walked off to get something from further down the balcony, a candle in a small glass holder. He lit it and put it on the table between us and then I forgave him slightly for the long phone call, and for his tracksuit, and some of my excitement for the evening returned. He brought out some wine and put it on the table, then he tapped something on his phone and music came from somewhere, a euphoric kind of beat. I had the first sip from the new bottle of wine, the lights of Monaco down below were spreading and sparkling, I crossed my legs, not under the table but out, where he could see them, where he could see my new shoes. The skirt rode up and I saw him looking at my legs.

'Nice view,' I said, looking beyond the balcony.

'Sure.'

It was barely seven-thirty. The night stretched ahead.

'Where do you like to go?' I asked him. 'Maybe we should go somewhere?'

'Could do,' he said.

I imagined dancing, making eye contact across a table in a noisy crowded room, wondering where the night would go, inhibition loosening with each drink, hands brushing, eyes meeting on the dance floor, leaning in for the first kiss. We could go for dinner first, maybe in the harbour, an outdoor table, the twinkling of the boats.

He was looking at me intently. I looked back at him. He moved his chair closer. His lips were beautifully shaped, his nose incredibly sexy. We kissed.

'Shall we ...' I began, looking down again at the lights of the town. I liked the thought of a long evening out there with the anticipation of how the night would end pulsing under it all, adding to the excitement of the places we went, my new clothes, all the sights and sounds, but before I could continue, he put his hand between my legs and I knew we weren't going anywhere.

He pulled my chair closer to him, parted my legs, pulled my pants aside and pushed two fingers into me, looking me in the eyes, and I arched my back and clamped him to me, I wanted it so much I no longer cared, not in that moment, that the whole evening, the whole encounter, was obviously about nothing more than sex; the lights below receded. He used his other hand to pull down his tracksuit bottoms and I saw his dick, thick and erect, and I shuddered. He took out his fingers, put me on the table, pushed my skirt up round my hips, pulled my pants off; I lay there and I felt my legs couldn't open any wider, they were open as wide as they had ever been, waiting for it. He pulled me closer to his dick and pushed it inside me, a huge, amazing pressure, it filled me completely, he moved it in and out three times, slowly, and I squirmed against it, I felt like it would burst me. He took it out and pulled me up off the table and took me into his bedroom.

The bedroom was sparse, the bed was unmade, I saw weights and a gun holster; it was truly ludicrous, like I'd entered some kind of crude fantasy. Anton's tracksuit was Louis Vuitton, the black top had the huge L and V crossed over, an elegant design I'd always liked, he kept it on even though his trousers were now off. For a moment I saw Mum in the corner, watching avidly, goading me on, and I wished I'd drunk even more wine out there on Anton's balcony, but in the next moment a different kind of oblivion came to wash all thoughts of her away because he put me onto his bed and pushed inside me again, and all sensation, all sensation, was down there, in my pussy, where his dick was, he moved it in and out of me, and when he also put his thumb down on my clit and rubbed it I was helpless, I came immediately, and it was so intense that I cried out in one drawn-out sound. My orgasm took a long time to subside; when it had, he pulled out and came all over my belly.

*

I lay looking up at the ceiling of Anton's bedroom, covered now in his sheets, shivery from the air con, and I thought about how they were up there, five flights up, Ivan and Kata and Alex and Tatiana, and what they would think if they knew where I was and what I had just done.

I could hear Anton in the bathroom, moving around, coughing occasionally. I didn't think he was having a shower, I hadn't heard water running.

It did all feel very surreal, in that moment. I remember it quite strongly, lying there in that bed, feeling suddenly bereft, wanting to cry. I felt a bit scared too, at having done it, at having got carried away. I felt very naive, but somehow protective of my own naivety, wanting to burrow even deeper into it, I wanted to go upstairs and get into my bed and read something soothing. I thought of the books that had been read to me as a child, vegetable patches, the Flopsy bunnies. They had been read to me as I lay clean and cosy in a little bed, with the special handkerchief I liked to curl around my fingers while I sucked my thumb. I would stroke my nose with the soft handkerchief, the curtains in my little room closed, just a soft voice reading to me, a wayward puddle-duck wandering through foxgloves, a bonnet on her puddle-duck head ...

I cringed over the clothes I'd bought that afternoon and wondered if I'd be able to return them the next day.

Sometime later I did go back upstairs. I packed my new shoes into my backpack and walked down the corridor to the lift barefooted. I had to text Sebastian to let me in because I didn't have my own key. 'How did it go?' he whispered.

I shook my head. 'I'll tell you another time,' I said. 'I just want to go to sleep.'

The hard grey tones of their decor. The hall carpet was silver leather, nailed into the floor.

I opened the door and saw Alex, lying asleep on my bed.

She was curled up. She hadn't got under the covers. She probably hadn't wanted to mess up the bed.

I stood looking at her. Her brown hair. Her thin arms hugging a pillow.

I closed the door gently, not wanting to wake her.

The room was lit by only one lamp, on the bedside table. The curtains had been drawn. Here was a soft space. A sweet and gentle place.

I put my backpack down, began to open drawers, getting out my nightclothes, still trying to be quiet, but her eyes opened. 'Hi,' she smiled. 'Sorry, I hope you don't mind ...'

'Not at all,' I said in a whisper. 'Go back to sleep if you like, there's plenty of room.'

'Thank you,' she said, and her eyes filled with tears.

'Alex! What is it?'

I went to her, sat on the edge of the bed.

She rolled onto her back and stared up at the ceiling. She shook her head.

'Is it something to do with your mum? Your dad?'

She didn't reply.

I thought of her white and strained face earlier that day, out by the pool.

'You were a bit cross, weren't you, with your mum, for saying that about your dad, in front of Irina? What did she say?'

Alex still lay on her back, looking up at the ceiling. 'She called him a peasant.'

'Oh. Charming.'

She turned to me then. I had spoken quickly, harshly. She had heard my contempt. 'It's more complicated than you think!'

She sat up, still holding the pillow.

'I'm sorry,' I said. 'I'm sure it is. I don't know anything. I'm just sad to see you upset. Let me go and have a shower quickly, OK? Then we can be cosy together. Get under the covers, sweetheart, get comfy.'

I wanted to get the smell of sex off me before I got into the bed with her. I would be warm in the shower and then I would put on fresh clean pyjamas.

I turned the tap on very hot and rubbed soap all over my shower mitt and began to scrub myself.

A few weeks previously I'd been in a pub in London with some

133

people when the guy next to me had asked what I did for a living. I told him about the kind of families I worked for, that I was about to go off to Monaco for the summer. 'You do realise that anyone who got billionaire-rich in Russia in the nineties is a criminal?' he said. 'They pocketed the state's natural resources and left the rest of the population to starve. Fuck knows the things they did to get there, especially the ones who didn't already have connections. Seventeen of them became billionaires in a decade – your guys included, I'm guessing. Meanwhile, there was a 40 per cent drop in GDP and a drop in average male life expectancy to the levels of sub-Saharan Africa. And the ones who managed to hang on to all their money through the 2000s, the ones who've still got it today, they only kept it by staying on the right side of politics, if you know what I mean. At least, I'd hope you know what I mean.'

The pub was in Euston, this guy was some SOAS PhD-type, bearded and vehement, lecturing me across his pint. 'They're not "my guys",' I said. 'I just work for them. It's not exactly the dream I always had for myself. I need to earn money somehow.'

'Well, that's all very tragic,' he said. 'I'm sure that does justify facilitating people like that, spoon-feeding their already over-privileged kids, giving them an educational advantage, doing your tiny little part to uphold the international hegemony of Mammon.'

He shrugged, he turned his attention elsewhere. There was a conversation going on further down the table about mining cooperatives in Venezuela and he wanted in on it. He was an insufferable prick, even if he was right. Fuck your structural concerns, fuck your bleeding heart, fuck your ethical pieties. I'm trying to keep my own head above water, I can't think about anyone else, I'll take whatever I can fucking get.

But then why, why was I doing this? It wasn't the only way I could earn money. I could try to get a job in a school. Then at least I'd be in one place and could think about making a home for myself. I could move out of London, that would make things easier. But I didn't want to move to a smaller town, hold up my hands and admit that the finer things were not for me. The hot water stung my body. I dropped the shower head and it clattered to the floor, I stubbed my toe as I moved to pick it up and the pain and the heat and the clumsy inefficiency of my movements banged together in an ugly rage.

I wanted the rage to come fully, to sate and then cleanse me. I kicked my bruised toe against the tiles of the shower, stepped under the boiling water, clenched my fists and pushed them as hard as I could into the wall.

She'd bought a local artisanal Brie in honour of my friends, who were visiting on their way to St Ives. She'd thought it would strike the right note. 'Mum, please,' I'd asked, 'just for this one night, OK? Just until they've gone to bed.' But we never made it to the cheese course. 'Oh, will your fancy friends mind, then?' she'd said, when I'd found her sitting on the kitchen floor, not even trying to hide the wine, drinking it straight from the bottle. Putting her to bed only to hear her incoherent mumblings some ten minutes later, trying to say something to us all from the top of the stairs before falling all the way down them to the sitting room floor.

When I emerged from the changing room, her saying to me, 'Go on, just buy it, you can afford it, you've got to look the part if you want a place at the table.'

I kicked my toe one final time against the tiles and the agony was so intense, there was no longer room for thought or memory, there was just the darkness of my closed eyes, the heat of the water and the radiating, ecstatic pain.

When I got out of the shower I moisturised my whole body with my Clarins moisture-rich body lotion, I loved the packaging, the red lettering: *Baums Corps Super Hydratant, Clarins, Paris.*

I put on my pure white cotton pyjamas and then I padded onto the carpet of the bedroom, drew the heavy curtains, got into the bed beside Alex and it was so comfortable, the springs of the mattress and the Siberian goose down duvet were a parent's loving arms, cradling me.

I looked at Alex and the thinness of her limbs was mine, and I wanted to take every little girl in the world in my arms.

Lifting the duvet, I brought it over her shoulders, tucked it around her neck and chin.

'When I had to tell my mum, in Harrods that day, that I had no friends at school ...' Alex began.

She paused. She closed her eyes.

'She got very upset about it. Later when I went downstairs to her in the TV room she told me that the reason she got so upset is because the same thing happened to her when she was at school and seeing it happen to me – it was like she experienced it herself all over again. It's usually when she's had a few glasses of wine that she talks about things.'

I reached out my hand and rubbed her bony back through the softness of the quilt. 'My darling,' I said. 'You can tell me.'

14

In the TV room, wrapped in her slanket and with the air full of dusky roses from the candle burning on the table, Kata had hugged Alex to her and said, 'The years when I was at school were the worst years of my life.'

She could walk the five blocks to school by herself. When they first moved to Brooklyn from Ust Labinsk, her mother, or her father, would walk her there and when school finished, one or the other would be waiting for her, outside the school gates. After a few years they finally let her make the walk by herself, though neither of them really trusted Americans, or the things these people got up to on their streets, their noise, the sirens that never stopped, the music neighbours sometimes blasted out long into the night, with no consideration for anyone else.

It was the girls at school who made it the worst time.

On her first day the teacher had made her stand up in front of the class and had told everyone her name, the name which was as ordinary to Kata as a bowl of soup or the shoes she put on every morning. But it must not have been ordinary to the girls she could see in the back row because they were giggling and repeating it among themselves.

The girls of the back row.

'That's Deborah, Rachel and Margaret,' a classmate whispered to her at breaktime. 'The most popular girls in the year.' Kata looked at them sitting on the low wall near the swings. Deborah had blonde hair and Margaret had red hair and Rachel's was brown. They wore it the same length, down to the middle of their backs. At the end of that first day her mother was waiting for her at the school gates, standing to one side, looking small and set-faced. She always stood to one side. When they did the rounds of the neighbourhood shops, butcher, pharmacy, she would never jostle her way to the front to demand the shopkeeper's attention; when asked for her order she would speak so quietly the shopkeeper would get impatient and tell her to speak up. Kata hung back, because she didn't want her mother to see her yet, because she wanted to wait, to watch Deborah and Margaret and Rachel come out, to see what *their* parents were like.

The girls came out, walking proud down the centre of the small yard, red hair blonde hair brown hair, like the My Little Pony dolls Kata swooned over in shop windows and which her mother refused to buy. The girls hung around the school gates popping big bubbles of pink gum. Soon a red-haired woman appeared beyond the gates, in a brightly printed dress and large sunglasses. She waved at the girls and they waved back. Kata thought she must be Margaret's mother because of the red hair. But it was Rachel who went towards her. Rachel and her mother, there in the very centre of the area around the school gates, big and bright and colourful, while her own mother stood, small and set-faced, off to the side.

Some weeks later her mother came to her with scissors to cut her hair but she said no, no, she pushed her mother out of the room. She was growing her hair to be the same length as Deborah and Rachel and Margaret's hair, but her father would not have it, her disobeying her mother, and when he came up to the bedroom she had no choice but to sit there and let her mother cut it. 'What do you need such long hair for?' he said, just like her mother would say, 'What do *you* need those for?' when she looked at dresses and shoes in shop windows.

Her attention was always on the girls. They each wore a pink friendship bracelet around their right wrist. They belonged in the classroom, they belonged on the asphalt in front of the school gates, they belonged in what she imagined were their big bright homes. They belonged anywhere she pictured them. On the beach, in a school disco. Whatever the scene – if they were in it, they would *be* it, they would be its centre.

There was a boy at the desk next to hers with tufty hair and glasses whose mother's cousins were from Russia; he was interested to hear what it was like there. There was a skinny girl who said she lived on the street next to Kata and maybe Kata would like to come with her to the public swimming pool some time. But the boy with tufty hair went red when the teacher singled him out, just like her mother went red when the pharmacist called her name to say her prescription was ready, and the skinny girl got shy and tongue-tied even around Kata, and would do whatever she told her to do and so Kata saw that the skinny girl had no power, and after that being around the skinny girl was no different from being alone, or with her parents, who, even though they had the power to force her to cut her hair, had no power anywhere else in the world, sitting fearful and self-effacing in the little house her mother worked night and day to keep so clean.

To have power was to belong. It was to own. Deborah and Rachel and Margaret owned the classroom when they were in it. The back row was the centre. To be anywhere else was to be aware of the centre but not be in it. And then it was like one part of you was in your own seat, and another part of you was outside your body and yearning towards the back row. She wanted to be in the back row because then she would be in one place, the two halves of her would be fused, and she would be whole.

She couldn't help but look at them. The other kids started to notice. 'You can't be in their group,' the skinny girl told her. 'Rachel was only allowed to join their group when she was a new girl because she's so pretty and everyone loves her.' Kata knew the skinny girl was right and that she did not belong in Deborah and Rachel and Margaret's group. But still, she couldn't help watching them. Wherever she was – in her bed at night, making visits on Saturday afternoons to the two women her mother knew in the neighbourhood – she was aware of other places existing in that same moment, places where she was not.

'It's weird how you are always staring at them,' the skinny girl said. Even the boy with tufty hair started to avoid her.

As part of their end of term tests they each had to stand up in front of the class and give a presentation. The subject was *What I Want to Be When I Grow Up*. Kata didn't know what she wanted to be when she grew up. She only knew she wanted to be different from how she was now. But she had to talk about something. What might Margaret, Deborah, Rachel want to be? What might they think was cool? Kata decided to say TV presenter. As her turn approached she got more and more nervous. Her, TV presenter. They would laugh at her. They would all laugh at her. Deborah had said lawyer. Rachel had said journalist. She felt sick. But in the five-minute break before her turn Margaret and Rachel passed her on their way back from the bathroom and Rachel said, 'Oh, you're up next, Kata,' and Margaret stepped forward and said, 'Don't worry, you'll be great,' and stroked her on her back, just beneath her shoulder blade.

She stood where she was and watched them return to their desks, the air around her bright with something and a warmth and tingling still on her back and then it came, waves of ease and rightness rolling through her body and out from her, and there was no longer any fear about standing up and talking about being a TV presenter. When she stood up they were looking at her from the back row, smiling at her, giving her all of their attention, and as she said the things she had prepared to say about being a TV presenter they nodded and smiled even more and it all felt so right, yes, she would grow up to be a TV presenter if that's what they thought she should do, maybe it had changed the way they felt about her, maybe they would talk to her in the next break. They were allowed to write notes for their speech on the blackboard and when she turned to look at hers she heard a swell behind her, she turned back round and the faces of all her classmates were twitching and smiling, the boy with the tufty hair was frowning and looking concerned.

She continued, talking about how when she was a TV presenter she would live in a big house and have her hair and make-up done every day and tell people about all the important things happening in the world. She turned back to the blackboard and this time the swell rolled out until it was the sound of lots of people laughing, and then the teacher was looking very angry and saying, 'Stop it, you should be ashamed of yourselves.' The teacher came towards her and put her hand on her back, where Margaret's hand had been; she pulled something off and threw it in the bin, she rubbed Kata on her back and looked at her kindly and Kata wanted the teacher to stop rubbing her there, her touch was erasing Margaret's touch, she wanted the memory of Margaret's touch.

After the lesson when everyone had gone she picked the crumpled piece of paper out of the bin.

Russian Freak, it said.

*

Winters in Brooklyn weren't as cold as winters in Ust Labinsk. She forgot the winters in Ust Labinsk. Summers in Brooklyn were hotter. Several summers came and went. Her mother wouldn't allow her to wear short skirts in summer once she turned twelve and lost her skinny childishness.

They never forgave her open and hungry fixation on them.

Russian Freak. The name stuck. After a while they dropped the Russian and she was just Freak.

Her mother had never told her about it and she didn't have any girlfriends to tell her about it and so of course, on the day she got her first period, when she pulled down her pants and saw all the blood, she thought she was going to die.

Help me, she said to herself, sitting in the toilet cubicle and staring down at her pants. She pulled her pants up and ran out into the schoolyard. Deborah was there. Deborah was the first person she saw so she said, 'Help me,' to Deborah.

'I'm bleeding.' She pulled up her skirt. It was spreading through her white pants and down her legs.

'Oh my God,' Deborah said, and took a step backwards, a look of disgust on her face. Kata sank onto the floor, pulling up her knees, too terrified to care about Deborah's look of disgust. She raised her head and said, 'Help me,' and saw that something in Deborah's face had changed. Deborah came towards her, sat down beside her; she felt Deborah's arm around her, she heard Deborah calling to Rachel and Margaret.

'Look!' Deborah said when they came over. 'She has it!'

Margaret got down on the floor as well and put her arms around her; they sent Rachel off to call an ambulance.

It was a rare disease, it struck here and there, in the neighbourhood and the nearby boroughs. Deborah had known a girl on the next street who'd had it, Patricia Silverman. She'd died within twenty-four hours. 'You have to be brave, Kata,' Deborah said. 'Shh, shh, it's OK. Once you get to the hospital it will be OK. Because they'll put you on morphine and then at least you won't feel the pain. You'll just go into a deep sleep. And your family will be with you. Don't worry, I'll make sure your family are with you.'

Kata closed her eyes and leaned her head into Deborah's chest as Deborah held and stroked her. She felt her body against Deborah's body, Deborah's hand caressing her hair, her cheek. Through her terror – she was dying – came a joy that was visceral, all-encompassing and complete. In her death, all the barriers that kept her from the Deborahs and the Rachels and the Margarets of the world had fallen away. The great fact of her death had in one swift moment swept away their disgust, and she was with them. They were holding her, they were gentle and tender, she was floating in the milk of their kindness and pity and love. It was worth dying for.

*

The scent of roses hung in the room and the candle sent flickers across the wall. Kata sat huddled in her slanket, staring at nothing.

Alex knew she was supposed to comfort her mother and so she did, she said, 'I'm sorry those things happened to you, Mama.'

She held her mum in her arms as if she were the mother and Kata the child.

But there was an awful feeling in her chest as she did it, an awful feeling in the whole room, in fact, mixed in with the smoke of the candle now gone out. It was the feeling that she should not have heard these things about her own mother, that Kata could have told them to anyone else in the world but that she should not have told them to her. Her mother's experience at school and her own experience at school combined to make the world too dangerous a place. She felt her mother's helplessness as if it were penetrating her, pushing itself inside her against her will.

Alex was still comforting her mother but she wasn't sure if it was helping or if her mother even noticed it because she still had that blank look on her face, staring into space.

'That's why I wanted so much for you to make friends,' Kata said.

She turned to Alex and her facial features rearranged themselves out of blankness into something more definite.

'That's why it *upsets* me so much, to hear that *you* have no friends. You will try harder, won't you, to make friends? For my sake?'

Some of the anger and disgust she had read in her mother's face when she had raised herself from her stool in the Harrods oyster bar had returned. It was an anger and disgust whose helplessness matched the helplessness of everything Kata had just told her. Alex saw a woman held hostage, but that didn't make it any less horrible, or any less unfair.

*

When Kata was nineteen the family went back to Ust Labinsk, where they were from and where Kata had been born, to visit relatives. The trip was possible because Kata's uncle Alexei, her father's brother, had in the last couple of years become rich.

She barely even knew what to expect from Russia. She'd been so little when they'd left.

Alexei was waiting for them at the airport. He was older than her dad, by about two or three years; he looked older, much older in fact, but also more robust. He was bigger. He hugged his brother. He hugged his sister-in-law, he hugged Kata. He bundled them into his car, an ugly box of a car that stank of cigarettes but of which he seemed very proud. It was a long drive from the airport. They'd changed planes in Moscow and flown into this little airport. She was very tired, in the back of the car. She half drowsed and listened to her dad and Alexei talk. Alexei was saying something about an aluminium plant – she had no idea what that was – and some business, some consulting, recycling wires, how much things had changed in the last two years, all the new opportunities.

'I was studying,' he said, 'for a while, even though I'm an old man like you. I was in Moscow.'

The car jolted as it turned off the main road, manoeuvred over bumps and ruts.

Her dad and Alexei lowered their voices; Alexei glanced back at the women in the back seat. 'Don't worry,' Kata heard him say, 'Ivan takes care of all that.'

*

She noticed Ivan because he was the only other person her sort of age. Her grandparents' kitchen was often filled with people: her father's cousins; Alexei; Alexei's friends. Ivan was only four years older than her.

She felt as much of an outsider here in Russia as she had in America. The older people in the kitchen teased her about her American accent just like the people over there had teased her about her Russian accent. She was unfamiliar with the chores her grandmother expected a girl of her age to be able to do. The way she prepared the food, it seemed very complicated. 'American girl!' her grandmother and the other women would say, shaking their heads and tutting whenever she chopped something the wrong way. But Deborah and Rachel and Margaret had not thought she was an American girl. They had despised her foreignness. She had been Russian to them. So, which was she? She did not seem to be able to do anything without making someone shake their head and laugh, to say something to the person next to them in a code she did not understand. It was like the world was made up of clubs and secret societies and everyone was a member of one, everyone except her.

When Ivan was in the kitchen, she noticed that when he said something, everyone would go quiet and listen, even though the other men were older than him, much. It was Alexei who had brought him to Ust Labinsk, after they finished their studies at the Institute of Steel and Alloys in Moscow. 'He helped me,' he said one time in the kitchen, to the women slicing and chopping for the evening meal. He had brought him to Ust Labinsk to introduce him to the people he knew at the aluminium plant. Kata wasn't sure exactly what it was they did because a couple of months later from what she overheard it seemed like they were buying metal and selling it abroad.

When they'd been there three months her father told her that they wouldn't be going back to America. Alexei had offered him a job, helping him; there were more opportunities here now than there were back there.

She was used to doing what she was told. She was told there was a secretarial position for her at the plant. She went and did it. She was told they'd be moving, she and her mum and her dad, into their own house nearby, and that's what they did.

The other girls at the plant asked her lots of questions about America but at the same time they quite openly talked about her in a dialect she didn't understand. One of them, especially, the one who seemed to be the loudest and most confident, would often look in her direction and say something to make the others laugh.

Same as it ever was.

She would walk through the streets on her way home from the plant, past scrubland and the old houses and the place where cranes were moving and new buildings were being built, through the town centre, and every now and then she would see Ivan and she noticed that he was never alone. There were men with him always, surrounding him, following him through doorways. She knew the name of one of them because he'd come by the house once. Vova he was called, Ivan had brought him to Ust Labinsk from the faraway place they were both from. Vova had not come into the house with Ivan, he had stood outside by Ivan's car. She wondered sometimes if Ivan would go back to that place right in the south of Russia – she could never remember the name of it – or if he would go back to Moscow. She hoped he would not go.

She had felt it from the first time she had seen him in her grandmother's kitchen, and every time she had seen him since had reinforced that initial impression: if he was in a room, he was its centre. He didn't have to *do* anything in order to be the centre. He just was. He didn't have to raise his voice, or jostle. There was an Easter lunch. He came in quietly. Everyone turned to him: 'Ivan, what will you drink, where will you sit?'

She always hoped on these occasions that it would be her, sitting next to him. His dominance radiated in a circle from him and she felt that anyone within that circle was protected. 'How is your job?' he would ask her, or, 'Did you make this?' and even if her grandmother was within earshot she would not butt in and make some joke about how Kata had made a mistake, put in too many onions which had made more work for her, had meant she'd had to add more stock and water. Her grandmother would stay silent and listen to Kata's answer without any of her usual sharpness or sarcasm. In fact, there had been much less sharpness and sarcasm from her recently, and Kata knew it was because her grandmother had observed how she and Ivan often sat next to each other at gatherings; she had seen her grandmother watching them and it gave her a feeling of great satisfaction and triumph to see her grandmother watching them like that.

Everyone respected him.

And because she knew that everyone respected him it was as if he was their representative: he *was* everyone, so when he turned his attention to her it was not just his attention on her, it was everyone's, the whole world's, validating her and accepting her, and she was resting in that place, the only place she had wanted to be in, more than anything, for as long as she could remember.

She began to long to run into him on her way back from the plant, to long for his visits to the house. And when she did run into him he would always come and greet her, and the men surrounding him treated her like he did, they were tender and polite and she felt them like a shield. 'What is it like, working for Alexei and my father?' she asked Ivan once, as they walked the length of the street from the town centre to the outer houses, the people they passed nodding to him as they always did. He laughed at her question, but when he replied his voice was gentle as always and forgiving of – pleased by, even – her girlish ignorance. 'Alexei and your father work for me,' he said.

After she had been in Russia for two years the plant was thrown into chaos. People were buying up all the things that had been owned by the state, just like Alexei had said was going to happen, everyone was talking about it, the girls at the plant were worried and excited at the same time, but nothing would happen to *their* jobs, would it?

'What are you looking so worried for?' one of them said. 'Go back to America if you're so worried. No one asked you to come here.'

It was an icy morning, absolutely frozen, when he came round to show her his new Mercedes. There was a solid sheet of ice on the steps leading down from the front of the house. She was hesitating, uncertain how to navigate them. He came around to the side of the steps, opened his arms and told her to jump. She jumped and felt his arms catch her, she was pressed against his chest and her face was in the exposed skin of his neck. She walked all around the car, touching it, and then she got inside and touched the leather, asked him to show her all the different gadgets, unlike any car she'd ever seen. It seemed natural to her that he owned this car, and so she had not shrieked or clapped her hands to her mouth when she saw it. She just went and touched it and smelled it and walked all around it and got inside it. She sat in the Mercedes in the fullness of the moment, with no other realities pulling her towards them or competing for her attention. She saw Ivan looking at her and she told him, 'Smell the leather,' and he bent his head down to smell it.

The moment with the car had become family myth. Ivan himself had told it to Alex many times when she was little. As a child she loved to ask, 'How did you and Mama meet?' and he'd always tell this story of the car. He told it to her when she sat in his lap in the house in Chukotka. 'She actually made me smell the leather of the car seat. I did and then I sat up and I'll never forget the way she was looking at me, your mama.'

'I think,' Alex said, 'that was the first time he really, properly, realised that he was rich.'

Because he was rich by that point, very. It had happened in just the last year.

With the capital from his metal export business he had bought a record number of vouchers.

The girls at the plant in Kata's secretarial pool said: 'Well, did you hear, it's been confirmed, the plant's really been bought, we have a new boss.'

And Kata had looked at them, without saying anything, just savouring inside, very privately, what she knew to be the most satisfying moment of her life. They would find out in time.

Their new boss was Ivan. He'd had enough privatisation vouchers to buy a massive stake in the plant. He was one of the biggest individual shareholders after the Russian state, and a dollar millionaire. And she was lifted, forever, above the laughter of those girls at the plant, above the laughter of anyone, because on the evening after Ivan had shown her his new car, he had asked her to be his wife.

15

Oliver made his appearance the following morning. He came at 9.30, which just happened to be when Ivan could be found in the apartment each day, before he headed downstairs to Anton's or Vova's apartment to work.

Alex and I had settled down to lessons when we heard the doorbell ring. When she heard Oliver's voice, she put down her pen, stood up and went over to the bedroom door. I didn't try to stop her. I wanted to hear what was going on as much as she did. She opened the door and stepped out into the corridor. I followed her to the door. We could hear Tatiana's voice in the hall. 'It's OK,' she was saying, to Irina or to Sebastian. 'He's expected.'

Irina came down the corridor. 'Where's Mama?' Alex asked. She was in town for her pedicure, Irina told her.

We could hear voices coming from the sitting room. 'They've gone to Papa!' Alex said. She took a step in the direction of the sitting room, then stopped. She took my hand. She walked in the direction of the sitting room again, pulling me behind her. As we got closer their voices became more distinct. The voices we heard were Oliver's and Tatiana's. We didn't hear Ivan saying anything. Alex hesitated again, and then she went into the room, taking me with her.

Ivan was sitting in an easy chair. He had some papers in his lap, he was holding his phone. Oliver was sitting on the sofa and

Tatiana was in an armchair on the other side of Ivan. They flanked him. 'It was quite extraordinary,' Oliver was saying, looking at Tatiana; he was recounting the story, the *quite unbelievable coincidence*, of running into Tatiana, of how he'd then had the pleasure of meeting – becoming reacquainted with – Ivan's wife. Alex tugged on my hand again and we sat down on the far end of the sofa. I saw Ivan look up towards Irina in the doorway: he spoke to her in Russian, telling her to bring coffee, tea. He put the papers in his lap face down on the end table next to him. He typed something into his phone, then put it on top of the papers.

'Kata and Alex have really been amazing to me, amazing, I'm so thankful,' Tatiana murmured, as Oliver came to the end of his spiel. 'This place has really been a sanctuary to me.' I'd already heard her say something similar to Ivan, the morning after he'd arrived.

'Fine, fine,' Ivan said, after a pause. He picked up his phone and looked at the screen, then put it back down. Oliver and Tatiana, veteran chatterers, unaccustomed to awkward silences, no doubt having grown up with and internalised the Debrett's maxim, 'No gentleman is rude unintentionally', exchanged a glance of consternation. Was Ivan being rude intentionally? I wasn't sure either. I was still full of the vision of Ivan as conveyed to me by the things Alex had said. Did Oliver and Tatiana understand who they were dealing with? If they did understand, how dared they come here and patronise him so audaciously?

'I've come on behalf of Valentin,' Oliver was saying. 'He won't take no for an answer. He *insists* you join us for dinner.'

There was an air of ineptitude, of aristocratic mediocrity, about Oliver. When he was near a light fixture you could see the puffiness of his face, especially around the eyes. It spoke of late nights at Annabel's, at private members' clubs, at Mayfair casinos. It spoke of susceptibility.

I heard the front door open and footsteps approach down the corridor. Anton stood in the doorway. Ivan nodded and briefly shut his eyes. Anton turned to go, his muscles and sinews moved to turn him. I had seen his skin, his muscles, his naked limbs, they had been on me, they had been in me.

When he'd finally come out from the bathroom, the night before, I'd continued to lie there on his bed, unsure of what to do. Was I supposed to go back upstairs, now that we'd had sex? Was that it? He'd taken his Louis Vuitton track top off when he was in the bathroom, for some reason – to douse himself? I saw droplets of water in the hairs just beneath his collarbone. 'Shall we go outside for a cigarette?' I'd asked. He came out with me but then his phone came into play again, he was tapping things into it.

He was so permanently fucking distracted! I was glad I hadn't known, in advance, what the evening would be like. At least I'd got to enjoy the pleasure of anticipation. What the fuck did I have to do to get his attention? 'Did you know that Tatiana is on a TV series in the UK?' I'd asked him. 'She's kind of famous. She posts everything she does on her Instagram; she has tens of thousands of followers.'

'Famous?' he'd said. He'd raised his eyebrows but he hadn't seemed particularly roused by the information; maybe he knew it already. And so: 'And did you know,' I said, 'that Oliver, the guy Tatiana knows over here, the guy she and Kata have been meeting up with, did you know that he's working for Valentin Kemerov? Did you know that they are deliberately trying to get Ivan to meet with him? I don't know why. Do you know why?'

Now, in the sitting room with them all, I looked from Ivan, to Tatiana, to Oliver, and I wondered if Anton had passed on my information, I wondered if Ivan was looking at them in full knowledge. I thought again of the words I'd heard Tatiana speaking into the phone to Oliver, when Kata had asked her to delay the dinner with Valentin until after Ivan left. 'Think of something,' she'd told Oliver.

'I always see this place,' Oliver said – he swept his arm in a semicircle that seemed to indicate the view from the window – 'as neutral ground, somehow. A place to kick back, enjoy a bit of a holiday for once. When Valentin comes here, he's on holiday. He has a villa about half an hour down the coast. Good food, good wine, barbecue going. He loves his barbecues. No business.'

I did well to follow my nose, to trust my instinct. And it *had* got Anton's attention, the night before, when I'd told him. The phone in his hand had been forgotten. 'Continue,' he had said. So I had told him about Oliver's 'job'; I'd told him to look up Oliver's website; I'd even looked at the site over his shoulder and pointed out the words *connecting ... facilitating ... introducing*, I'd told him about the run-in at the club in Monte Carlo and the things I'd heard Tatiana say to Oliver when she'd thought no one was listening. I wasn't sure whether the things I was telling him were confirming what he already knew or if they constituted new intelligence; either way, it came to me now, sitting in the living room among them all, that if Anton had passed on my information to Ivan – and I was sure he would have, because that was his job, wasn't it? To protect Ivan? – then, just perhaps, the whole dynamic of this situation had been altered from what it would otherwise have been because of *me*. Ivan was now in a supreme position of power with regards to Oliver and Tatiana, because he knew what they were up to, and they didn't know that he knew; this was the power of information, strategically deployed. What would Ivan do with his knowledge? I remembered the gun holster I'd seen in Anton's room. I knew so little about the high-stakes world people like Anton moved in, the danger of it; it all mixed in with my other memories of the night: my pleasure, his body, his dick, his moan when he came. I felt myself shudder again with an almost painful excitement, I could feel it between my legs.

'Oh, *please* come, Ivan,' Tatiana was saying. 'We'd love it if you and Kata would join us. I think it would be fun. It won't be the same if you aren't there. The evening will be *dull* without you.'

It was hard to believe she was talking to him like this. Chair pulled up close to him, leaning forward, big grey-blue eyes wide open, brow untroubled, face tilted to one side. Her disingenuousness was so palpable, but she wore it with a complete lack of fear. 'Oh, *please* say you'll come,' she said again.

I waited for the put-down, for the cold, clipped word that would communicate to her that he knew exactly what she was up to, but it didn't come, something entirely other happened, something unexpected, I watched as it spread over his face: a softening, an indulgence.

'OK,' he said. 'I will come.'

She clapped her hands in delight. 'Oh, wonderful!'

Well. That was disappointing. Was he really so vulnerable to female flattery? Was that the reason he had accepted? I'd put Oliver down as the susceptible one.

He picked his phone up from the table beside him and as he did so I saw Tatiana look across to Oliver in triumph. Oliver puckered his mouth and nodded slightly in a gesture that suggested he was impressed.

I would have expected Oliver to launch into a volley of 'Well that's marvellous, great stuff, looking forward to it' but as he stood to take his leave he was markedly silent, as if conscious that a word from him might undo the strange magic that Tatiana had brought about.

His leave-taking was low-key. 'I'll just see Oliver out,' Tatiana said. They went down the hall and Alex and I were left alone in the room with Ivan.

Ivan looked at Alex.

'Well, we had better get back to work,' Alex said, in the stilted, formal manner she had whenever she felt awkward and nervous. She got up, not looking her dad in the eye.

Ivan considered the chairs in which Oliver and Tatiana had been sitting. He shook his head.

Tatiana's empty seat. She was gone, as was her golden beauty and charm. All that was left was the bald fact that Ivan had said yes to Valentin's invitation.

'Funny people you meet at your school,' he said to Alex. 'I don't think I've ever had people like that in my house before.'

'I didn't ...' Alex began. 'It wasn't ...'

In my mind I finished the sentences for her. *I didn't invite them. And it wasn't my choice to go to that school.* But she just stood there, and I felt almost irritated by how defenceless she was. She was so painfully shy as to seem rude.

He got up from the chair and went out onto the balcony. He

lit a cigarette. He stood there, smoking and looking out over the marina.

I went to say something to Alex, but she was disappearing, out the living room door and into the corridor. I went after her and as I stepped through the door I bumped into Anton. Before I left his flat I had said, hesitating: 'So I guess we shouldn't mention this to anyone ...'

His response had been quite brutal. 'Of course *not*,' he'd said. 'Of course *not*.' He had looked at me in a way that seemed almost threatening.

There was nothing but neutrality in his eyes, now. 'Good morning,' he said and I watched as he went through the living room and out to the balcony to join his boss.

Alex was lying on my bed. I'd thought she might be. I was the one she came to now. She turned to me and there were tears in her eyes. 'Alex, sweetheart,' I said. I went and sat next to her. 'Why are you so nervous around your dad?'

'I'm not nervous,' she said. She stuffed her face down into the pillow. She said something but I couldn't hear it. 'I can't hear you, darling,' I said, stroking her back so she lifted her head up and said: 'He doesn't like me.'

'No,' I said, 'that can't be true. Alex?' I got her to turn onto her side, to look at me. 'Of course that's not true. He's your dad. Everyone says things they don't mean when they're in a bad mood. Why don't you just go out there and talk to him? You weren't the one who brought Tatiana here.'

She looked as if she might be considering it but then she said, 'No!' and she actually got under the duvet to emphasise her point.

'I wish we could go back to Chukotka,' she said.

'Chukotka?' I asked. 'What is Chukotka?'

'He would take me sledding.'

I lay down on the bed beside her. I lay on top of the duvet while she lay underneath it. I took one of the many pillows and held it in my arms. I made myself comfortable.

She didn't look at me while she talked. She lay on her back and she looked straight up, at the ceiling. It was like she was talking to herself. Maybe this is what she meant when she said her mum talks to her as if she isn't there, I thought. Alex was invisible to her mother. I was invisible to them all. What might it be like to suddenly assert the reality of yourself, in a way that could no longer be ignored?

16

They had moved to Chukotka in Siberia because her dad had been told to. He was to be the governor. He was to invest his own money in the region, which in return would pledge its loyalty to the central government.

There were many months of the year when it was possible to go sledding. The houses in the main town of Anadyr looked like storage containers.

Her dad always liked to repeat that stock phrase: *There's no such thing as bad weather; there are only bad clothes.* He'd say it before they went sledding, as they prepared themselves, in the room just inside the front door, where the snow boots and gloves and jackets lived. She had a red boilersuit that she would put on over her indoor clothes. He had a big grey jacket with fur inside.

When they had arrived in Chukotka, there had been an actual red carpet. There had been an official welcome ceremony. Her dad had to go all over the region to meet with factory bosses, plant managers and hospital directors, and her mother went with him. With his own money her dad had supplied the poorest people of the region with food packages, sacks of flour, kilos of sugar, butter, dried fruits. Roads were built. Sometimes, when they drove through the streets, the three of them, and people caught sight of them, they would actually start to cheer.

Once he had put in the four years he would be allowed to return to Moscow.

When her dad took her sledding they would hurtle down steep slopes. Everything was white. The streets were white, the hills were white, the fields were white. It wasn't snow, it was just that everything was white. That's how it was. On Tuesday nights wrestling was on TV, the WWF, she'd watch it, with her dad. He liked Hulk Hogan, she liked Brett the Hitman Hart. They even made costumes. There was a photo of the three of them, on the sofa, her dad as Hulk Hogan, her as Brett the Hitman Hart. Her mum wasn't dressed up, but she was smiling.

Their house was an ugly box like all the other houses but she loved the cosiness of it, the pale wood of the walls, the double-glazed windows through which you could see the cold, stretching snow. Sometimes in the mornings she'd wake early and then she'd run down the stairs and along the corridor and barge into her parents' room and join them in their bed.

She would ask her mum, 'Do you remember how I used to come and join you and Papa in bed in the mornings, in Chukotka? We'd eat breakfast in there and sometimes fall asleep again, I'd fall asleep in between you, like a puppy.'

*

Alex's dad had been unhappy as a child. He told Kata about it. Only once, he told her about it.

When he was nine years old his mother died and it was only five months later – five months! – that his father remarried. Ivan already knew the woman, knew her only too well. She was his schoolteacher. When he first saw her, one evening, sitting there in the room beside the kitchen with his father it was like some weird dimensional slip had occurred in the universe, things had fallen out of their places, all of a sudden nothing was where it was supposed to be. She was thin and sharp, made of angles. Then he thought, Maybe she's here because I'm in trouble. Because, after all, he was the one she hated most in the school. 'A long walk again, Ivan?' she would say when he arrived in the classroom. Her voice was quiet, she spoke almost as if she was shy, but listen closely and you would hear the sting. 'There are all sorts of things lying on those roads,' she would say. 'We should write a letter, class, asking for the roads to be cleaned.' She would open the window, fan it back and forth. And now here she was in the room beside the kitchen with his papa, in the chair where his mother used to sit.

His mother had been so gentle. She had been the most beautiful being ever to walk on the earth.

Even when he was little, he could tell that his own mother was a bit helpless, a bit dreamy. She would ask him how to do things. 'Ivan!' she would call from outside the kitchen window. He'd run out. 'How do you do this?' she would ask. There was a problem with the pipe that carried the waste water out from the kitchen to the vegetable garden. He'd seen his father fix a pipe before. He only had to see something once to know how to do it himself. He showed her. 'You are so clever,' she would say. 'How would I manage without you?' She would look at him with shining and proud respect. He would feel his chest puff out. He would strut back into the house. He was always watching over her, ready to protect her, ready to do whatever she needed.

And now his father had replaced her with this bitch.

Two months after he'd first found her sitting in his mother's chair, she and his father had married. He couldn't believe it. He would never believe it. He looked at his father standing in the church and thought he must be mad. His mother had been soft. When she had said goodnight to him she had smelled of a special soap. It was fresh and gentle-smelling. As he grew older he realised he had probably idealised her but it was too beautiful and perfect a dream to let go of. His mother had been soft, round. And as for this angular bitch, always seeming to look down her long nose at him, as much at home as she had done in the classroom, even though it was his house, his house, he had been there long before her – who the fuck did she think she was?

His father didn't notice but she would find any excuse to subtly belittle him. She was cunning. In her quiet little voice. Her watchful looks. She did it so his father didn't notice. By the time he left he had nothing but contempt for his father too, ignorant old prick. Noticing nothing. Always her sly digging comments. At the dinner table, just watching the way he held his fork. 'What?' he would say. 'Oh, nothing.' She would shake her head, give her shy laugh. 'I just enjoy to study ... things I haven't seen before.'

Day by day by day, she erased the memory of his mother, his gentle and sweet mother, who had been proud of him, who had looked up to him. She touched the things his mother had touched, she sat in the chair his mother had sat in. He would come into the kitchen and see her back at the sink where his mother's back had been, and it didn't take long for her to erase that sweetness from the world, to usurp it everywhere with her cold distaste.

What if he did something? Something to assert his true position. Something to put her forever in her place.

When he was eighteen, he decided to leave. He packed his scant things. He left Ingushetia. He went to Moscow.

His dormitory at the School of Steel and Alloys was big and damp. Cigarette smoke clung to the walls. You could tell the Moscow boys, the ones whose parents were high-up bureaucrats. Through their connections they were allocated better rooms, for one thing, and they stuck together. They seemed elongated, they would lounge elegantly, and their conversation, from what he overheard, was endlessly abstract. They could live in the world of ideas, they didn't need to devote any of their time and energy to the hustle; plum posts had already been lined up for them. They had their own table in the canteen. As he passed, they looked at his coarse trousers, his jacket that was too small for him. 'Wait,' one of them said. 'Let's see, let's see ...' He looked Ivan up and down, lingering on his face. 'Ingushetia! Yes, Ingushetia. I'm getting good at this,' he said, looking back at his friends.

He told himself it didn't matter what those dandies thought of him. He told himself that. But their sneers and the subtle sneers of his father's wife collected into a hard ball inside him. He felt the ball, poked and prodded at it with a hard and painful pleasure.

Alexei, he got on with. Alexei had no time for the personal. Alexei had bigger things on his mind. He had come to the institute to study but his mind was already back in Ust Labinsk and the opportunities there, at the plant where he'd formerly worked. He told Ivan all about the plant one night when they sat up late in the dormitory. 'But I don't know if I'll be able to finish here,' Alexei said. 'I need to get back to work.' Ivan did not want Alexei to leave, he wanted Alexei to finish the course and, when they had both finished, to take him back to Ust Labinsk with him, to his connections at the plant. So he brought Alexei into a scheme he was involved in, through a cousin of someone he knew from back home, buying and selling theatre tickets on the black market.

If you gathered enough outsiders, he was learning, and got them to work together, you could form a challenge to the insiders, the ones who had always had everything.

It was 1986 and the grip was already loosening. 'Everything is about to change,' Alexei said. He looked towards the table where the Soviet elite's offspring lounged. 'They won't know what's hit them.' A few years later, when the old system had been obliterated and Ivan owned the plant at Ust Labinsk, he thought back to the mincing, complacent Moscow boys and he wondered what had happened to them. He hoped none of them had weathered the transition. He hoped every single one of them had been crushed.

He had told all of this to Kata the night after he called her a whore in front of all the people in the restaurant. He had been trying to explain himself, his overreaction to what was after all just silly female excitement over Valentin Kemerov and his glamorous-seeming life.

It had been a mistake to tell her.

*

For their honeymoon, they had gone to New York.

'To where I lived as a girl,' Kata told Alex. 'He wanted to see.'

She'd lived in this great big city but her life there had been tiny. She realised it. So did Ivan and she got the sense he liked it. She took him to see the tenement building where she'd grown up. He liked that she had lived here all those years but still, it was him, planning their itinerary, deciding where they should go and what they should do and yes, that was how it should be, she thought. She loved it that way and she let him know, with every look and gesture, how much she loved it and how much she loved him. He was the biggest thing there was in the world, taller than the Statue of Liberty. She deferred to him in a way that made her body dilate. With his confidence and authority he protected her from everything, he made other people irrelevant. When she'd shown him the tenement building in Brooklyn they had walked a little and even though they hadn't actually walked to her old school she had sensed it there, two or three blocks away, and she wished a Deborah or a Rachel or a Margaret would somehow appear, there in the street, and see her with this man. Let them see that they were no longer the centre, no, they were not. Let them see that they no longer had any power over her.

He liked that she knew nothing beyond the few Brooklyn blocks she had lived in, knew nothing of Manhattan. He put his big hand in the small of her back and they got back inside the limo. They stayed in the best suites at the best hotels, they moved hotel every few days and as they entered each new lobby, even though it was as new to him as it was to her, still: he gave it to her, and she received it, from him.

There was just one moment on the honeymoon that was out of keeping with the dynamic they had established and that was when they went to a jewellery shop. The man in there seemed very arrogant, had not seemed even to want to let them in, to buzz open the grilled door. He had sighed slightly when they had asked to see the diamond bracelets, as if they were wasting his time, as if he could tell by looking at them that they couldn't afford to buy anything. His whole demeanour communicated that he did not think they belonged in the jewellery shop, that they were not the type of customer he was used to dealing with, that they were grossly out of place, and she felt it acutely, because it was such a familiar feeling, it had been with her for as long as she could remember.

But she was with Ivan now, she was with Ivan, and he was impervious to such treatment, wasn't he, because he was so strong and authoritative, so secure in himself. He would show this man that they did not care what he thought of them, that he meant nothing to them, that they could buy the whole shop if they wanted to. But when she pressed herself closer to Ivan – her protector – and then looked up at him she saw the redness in his face and instead of putting the stupid man in his place he said, 'We're leaving.' For a moment he seemed just like a little boy and she saw that he was just as intimidated as she was.

He had been very quiet when they got back to the hotel room. He had gone and stood at the window and looked out at the city below, the tops of the trees in the park and the people down on the sidewalks. She had sat on their bed, and for a moment the luxury of their suite was as nothing, their money and chauffeurs and limos and all the new things they had bought here in this city were as nothing, because in their joint insecurity all the Deborahs and Margarets and Rachels of the world rushed back in, the money and the luxury and the limos no bulwark against them, and that is why she had married him and why she loved him, much more than his money, a hundred, a thousand times more than his money: it was because he had saved her from all that, had finally and forever lifted her above it.

What was this? This silence, this redness of face. His back to her, as he looked through the glass of the long window. Did he feel angry? Did he feel small? How had he failed to handle himself around a person like that? Was it because he didn't have those men around him, Anton and Vova and the others? Was Ust Labinsk the only place in the world where he had authority? How had he failed to lift his chin, bring out the few smooth phrases that would have put the man in his place? Instead, he had been red-faced and silent, and they had left, and so the man had been right when he had deemed them not good enough for the shop. If they were not good enough for that shop, how many other places would they not be good enough for?

And with that thought, all the back rows came back. A world

full of back rows, where some were admitted and some were not, where she was among those who were not, trapped in her body but with her attention elsewhere, yearning, divided, excluded.

His back to her, the long glass window, evening approaching, light leaving the sky.

Maybe she was just imagining it.

It had been just one tiny incident, after all. An isolated incident that was out of keeping with everything else she had ever seen of him, back in Russia.

Maybe there was another reason for Ivan's red face and his silence now, as he stood by the window. It couldn't be that he was intimidated by the man in the jewellery shop.

It couldn't be. She wouldn't believe it.

She thought of him at the kitchen table in her grandmother's house, on the streets of Ust Labinsk. His whole being radiating belonging.

So she got up from the bed and went over to him where he stood by the window. She rested her head on his chest and looked up at him and he looked down, and he must have seen something in her expression because he soon forgot about the incident in the shop and was his big towering self again, leading her all over the place. She looked up to him and he knew she did and so together they were inside a shining golden circle, this was the circle they had made together, both giving the other something essential, something deeply needed, and it continued to be like that, when they returned to Ust Labinsk, and then when they moved briefly to Moscow and then in the four years they spent in Chukotka where he was a king, he really was, she could still remember that red carpet, and the way the people had cheered them. She had formal duties there, too, she had to visit hospitals and schools and she had to entertain the most important people in the region, the factory bosses and administrators and their families, and everywhere she went she was treated with respect. He knew exactly what to do and say in every situation. In the meetings in the town hall, in the gatherings of the district leaders, she would watch him, in the centre of the room, all the most important people surrounding him, listening to him. She had never known such happiness.

When they returned to Moscow after their years in Chukotka she had been content at first to stay home in their big house in Rublyovka. It was such a novelty, her own big house on the forested banks of the Moscow river where nobles had once enjoyed falcon-hunting. There were many new houses like theirs, there was dust on the main road from all the construction, but there were also houses that had been there for fifty years, one hundred years. Two of the neighbouring houses were old dachas and the women came to greet her.

Mrs K's husband was a high-ranking minister, his father had been a high-ranking minister, son and father, even grandfather, it seemed, had weathered all political changes and stayed at the top, were natural insiders, and it was the same with Mrs L's husband, his family had lived in the timbered house two plots down for close to one hundred years. They seemed so worldly and sophisticated, these women, she was thrilled when Mrs K invited her and Ivan to a party she was having but when she told Ivan and showed him the invitation he said, 'Oh, yes, I know his type, I remember his type.'

There it was, the tight red face that she remembered from the jewellery shop, the face that had reappeared very occasionally over the years, usually when they were in Moscow. 'I would like to go, Ivan, they are our neighbours, it would be rude to refuse.' He had been silent, chewing down his breakfast, moving his jaws in a way that seemed exaggerated. When he finished his mouthful he said, 'Fine. Fine.'

The party was full of the most elegant and glamorous people she had ever seen. Within ten minutes of being at that party she couldn't believe she had ever taken pleasure in the Chukotka years of being around those rough-hewn people, skin red from the blistering cold, ugly rooms bright with overhead lights, laughing too loudly and downing shot after shot of crude strong alcohol. Everything here was tinkling and mellow and the women were so perfectly dressed. She had seen the hostess in a corner surrounded by a small circle of the most glittering women in the room. They had turned to look at her and for a moment the world had stood still as she had awaited their judgement but then: smiles on their faces and the hostess had beckoned her; they stepped aside to make room for her, began to ask her about the renovations on her house. She turned her head to see Ivan surrounded by some of the men and her whole being told her: Yes. Yes, this is it. This is how it is supposed to be. But just twenty minutes later she felt a hand closing around her upper arm and she looked round to see Ivan. He leaned close to her ear and said, 'I've had enough of this.'

Had enough of it? She looked at him, uncomprehending. 'I don't want to go, Ivan,' she said. She felt the sinking. What had been dancing and twinkling, turning to lead, sinking down through her chest and into her stomach. 'Please, Ivan,' she said. 'Fine,' he replied. He went and sat in an armchair in the middle of the room. And the evening was ruined because wherever she stood and whoever she talked to, she was aware of him just sitting there. She saw a couple of people approach him, saw him barely move his head as he replied in what looked like monosyllables. She saw the glittering group of women who had surrounded her earlier look over at him, talk among themselves, then look in her direction. She heard a voice by her side: it was Mrs K's husband. Maybe he had noticed that she looked uncomfortable, troubled, because he spoke to her smoothly and kindly; she didn't really listen to what he said but she felt reassured by his tone – now here was a real gentleman – and she felt his hand on her arm, her shoulder, in the small of her back. She was grateful to him for rescuing her from standing alone but her attention was on that magic circle, that glittering group, that shining knot of women who had welcomed her when she first arrived, she was wondering how to get back there, she did not want to leave before she had made some plan with them, for the following days, to see them again, a coffee date or maybe they could go shopping together, but then Ivan was back, and she saw the fear in Mr K's eyes, he was backing off with his palms raised as Ivan said, 'Don't touch my wife, thank you, we are leaving now, goodnight.'

They were driven home even though they lived right next door. Their heavy steel gates took a long time to open. The guards in the gatehouse nodded to Ivan as the car moved past. He said the name of the man who had touched her. 'He hasn't done a day's real work in his life. I have to warn you, Kata, if you ever did anything to betray me ...'

'He was just being polite,' she said. 'And all I wanted was to be friends with Ludmilla and her friends.' She was so filled with mortification that she was able to speak clearly. She heard her own words as separate things from her, ringing with clarity in the interior of the car.

The next day he took her shopping, he bought her a rare and large diamond, they had it set into a necklace, the people knew him in there, they were given champagne, and then they went to the restaurant at the top of the Federation Tower, they knew him in there too, they were given the most exclusive table, cordoned off and hidden away from all the other tables so that they might as well have been in a private room, eating dinner just the two of them, all alone. Mrs K had other parties but on those nights Kata sat alone in her enormous house, Alex asleep and watched over by the nanny, Ivan in the games room with Anton and Vova. She sat alone in the dining room, eating meals the chef had prepared for her, under the black Baccarat chandelier her decorator had installed.

Most people she knew of in Rublyovka also had houses in London, it was the place where you could buy anything, everything was for sale and it was good to have property in the United Kingdom because it was a stable place, nothing had really changed there for hundreds of years, and in Russia they had been through such big changes and you could never be sure when the next one might come, when those who had everything might suddenly have nothing. In London she met Olga through a Facebook group and Olga introduced her to Igor and Sergei, and Ivan seemed to tolerate them because they were obviously impressed and intimidated by him and they were much less rich, too, they depended to an extent on Ivan and Kata's largesse and Ivan was comfortable with that. She could have predicted how Ivan would react when she suggested they get to know Valentin. For so long she had wanted to give him the benefit of the doubt and allow him the chance to be the man she had once thought he was. But he only belonged around people who had grown up poor like he had, the simple people in Ust Labinsk and Chukotka, people like Anton and Vova. The moment he was around people like Valentin he was rude and resentful and red-faced.

There had been a time when she thought he was the centre of everything and it had been so beautiful. She could still remember it. More than remember it: she could still feel it, how it had felt sitting next to him in the kitchen at Ust Labinsk, and driving with him through the streets of New York, and then, at his side, in Chukotka. She knew it was important to him that she looked up to him and for such a long time she had done so, naturally and voluptuously, willingly and with every cell.

Once she had fantasised about running into the girls of the back row while she was with him. Now she knew that she would be embarrassed for them to see her with him.

She wanted so much to go back to how it had once been, and there were ways to bring it back, if only for a moment. After he called her a whore in front of a restaurant full of people he had tried to explain to her that night the reasons for his bitterness towards people like Valentin but she didn't want to hear it, she didn't want to hear it, she wanted him to be as he once was, she wanted it back, the dream she'd been sold, someone towering and impervious, she wanted to be freed, if only for a few hours, from all room to doubt him, she wanted to defer to him as she once had, truly defer to him, in her very marrow, not just playact her deference because that's what he expected from her, and so she had egged him on, hardly knowing what she was doing, and eventually, in the small hours of the night, something had clicked because he had become strong and unyielding, he had dominated her, he had used his superior physical force and gripped her by her shoulders and lowered her onto her knees in front of him ...

Alex felt disgusted to hear it, disgusted, she'd told her mother to stop, had reminded her mum who it was, lying there, listening to her speak. 'I am here, listening to you, you aren't talking to yourself!' I looked at Alex as she said this. She herself had been talking for over an hour.

'I wanted to puke, it was so disgusting when she said those things, how could she say them in front of me, she's so blind, she's so stupid.'

But still.

She too had her dreams, her memories of a perfect time.

'Me,' Alex said. She pointed a finger at herself. She moved the finger so it pressed onto the skin of her chest.

'Me.'

Their happiest time had been her happiest time.

She would ask her mum if she remembered.

'Do you remember, Mama, when there was a power cut, people came and made fires in every room, we had lanterns, we sat in the kitchen by the fire and played that game of cards?

'Do you remember we'd eat dinner in the kitchen most of the time because it was so warm and cosy?

'Do you remember every Tuesday night, WWF was on the TV, I did the Hitman Heart entry walk, Papa did the Hulk Hogan entry walk, we memorised them?

'Do you remember how much it snowed in Chukotka? Papa would take me sledding. We went fast together down steep white slopes.

'Do you remember when I would run down the long passageway in the morning and come into your bed? I would lie in between you, like a puppy.

'Do you remember, how much it used to snow, when we were together, the three of us, in Chukotka?'

17

Kata seemed nervous in the car. 'Are you sure, my darling, you want to come?' I'd heard her say to Ivan earlier in the afternoon. 'Are you sure it won't be boring for you?' She reached out a hand now and smoothed his hair into place, did up one more button of his shirt. 'Now please, darling,' she said. 'Not too much talk of business tonight, let's just try to be light, OK? It's a social occasion.'

We followed Oliver and Tatiana's car along dusky coastal roads, Mediterranean cacti flashing up in our headlights. Looking out the window, I saw the moon coming up over the sea. The driveway was long and winding.

Valentin was waiting for us, dressed all in black, standing between two of the pillars that spanned the facade of his large, white, neo-Palladian villa. He greeted Kata first, and with reverence. 'Welcome,' he said, encircling one arm behind her – without touching her – spreading his other arm wide, encompassing with it all that we could currently see – the house, the porticoed entrance – in a gesture communicating that all she saw before her, all that was his, was also hers, as his honoured guest. His greeting of Ivan was a more sober affair. He shook his hand. 'Welcome. I am honoured,' he said, as he had said to Kata, but in a tone far more grave. When he shook my hand I caught the scent of refined cologne, I saw buttons on his shirt like black pearls. Once he'd greeted everyone, he returned his attention to Kata: she should head the procession, she should enter his house first.

We followed Valentin and Kata down a long corridor that ran all the way from the front of the villa to the back. The corridor was lit only by candles, the air was cool and smelled of stone. We reached the end of the corridor and then we were out, on the other side of the house, on a large terrace.

'Beautiful,' I heard Kata say.

There was a large stone table on the terrace. It was laid for dinner and covered in more candles. There was the smell of jasmine. Ahead of the terrace the garden continued and ended in a curve. There was the tiniest bit of light left in the sky and I saw that the garden was on a promontory and that the property, at this end, was surrounded on all three sides by the sea. I could hear it, the waves lapping all around us. I could smell it. A jacaranda tree at the edge of the promontory shifted its arms in a gentle wind. I saw something pass beneath the jacaranda tree. A security guard in a bulletproof vest, carrying a machine gun. There was a second security guard on the other side of the promontory. They were circling towards one another, patrolling the property's perimeter.

'To this evening!' Valentin said. He said it loudly and gaily, ushering us away from our contemplation of the security guards. Place names indicated where we should sit.

'Ivan, here,' Valentin said. He pulled out a chair.

Ivan looked at the chair but did not move to sit in it.

Valentin's hand danced up in the air for a moment, a counter to Ivan's stillness, before coming back down, to grip once more onto the chair.

'Please,' he said.

Ivan shook his head slightly, but it must not have been a gesture of refusal, or at least not refusal of Valentin's appeal to him to sit down, because in the same moment he stepped in front of the chair Valentin was offering him and he allowed Valentin to slide it beneath him.

*

Oliver had been right when he had said, 'Valentin loves his barbecues.'

When we'd all sat down at the table Valentin said: 'If you will indulge me, a little surprise.' He raised his hands in the air. Kata and Tatiana looked at one another and giggled in excitement. Valentin clapped his hands together, twice, and in the next moment a loud gushing noise filled the air and an extraordinary-looking thing came rushing round the side of the house, moving very fast, a sort of souped-up barbecue on wheels. Sparklers were attached to all four corners of it, they fizzed up into the air; a chef in whites was manoeuvring the barbecue, he was moving it along while at the same time flipping a large number of steaks into the air. In a moment, it was all over; in one swift gesture the chef extinguished all four sparklers, removed his high white hat, stepped back and bowed. The table erupted into clapping. 'Fantastic,' Oliver said. Kata and Tatiana were letting out little whoops. Valentin bowed his head and extended an arm towards the chef. Only Ivan remained silent.

'Wonderful,' Kata said, shaking her head.

When we were about halfway through our drinks, Valentin finished filling us in on the history of the property – it had once belonged to Lord Lucan, he told us – and lifted his glass.

The steaks were being served.

'To old friends. Once in every three years, I have the honour, it seems,' he said, addressing Kata. 'It is not enough, no? Not in my opinion. And with Ivan, it is even less. What is it, once in every five years? Six years?'

'You have met each other?' Kata said. 'Ivan?'

He had just been given his steak. He was cutting it up. It seemed he was going to cut the entire steak into pieces before eating it.

'I did not know you had met Valentin before,' Kata said again.

Ivan put the first piece of steak into his mouth. He wiped his mouth off with his napkin. 'Oh yes,' he said, then took a drink of water. He wasn't drinking alcohol. 'Yes, we have met.'

He didn't follow this up with any kind of nicety and I saw Kata's lips tighten.

'Where did you meet?'

Valentin answered for him. 'Our paths crossed a few times in Moscow,' he said. 'Not a thing I have forgotten. I have always been a great admirer of your husband.'

'Good steak,' Ivan said, with his mouth full. He finished chewing.

Kata was still looking at him expectantly.

'We met earlier than that,' he said to her. 'We met many years ago. We were students together.'

'Oh,' she said. 'A long time ago.'

'Yes, a long time ago,' Valentin agreed. 'We were just boys then. Eighteen-year-old boys. Is there any animal on the earth more stupid than an eighteen-year-old boy?'

'Not to my knowledge,' said Oliver.

'I have not been in Moscow all this time, of course, unfortunately,' Valentin said. 'I made the move to London some years ago, or I'm sure we would all have met more. And of course, a man as successful as Ivan – naturally, he is very busy. Do you have enough salad there?' he said, glancing solicitously at Kata's plate.

He made a discreet gesture to the waiting staff, who were standing near a trestle table some distance away. They brought over two large bowls of salad, they went around the table offering the guests some more, then they left the bowls in the middle of the table and retreated. Valentin nodded to them and topped up Kata's wine. He was impeccable.

Kata frowned at Ivan. 'We will make up for the lost time, in London,' she said to Valentin. 'We will all meet together in London.'

I thought I saw Valentin's eyes dart to Ivan for a millisecond, as if to gauge his response before he replied to Kata. 'Yes,' he said; and there was an element of reticence in his voice. 'And tell me, how have you been spending your time in Monaco?' Kata clocked the change of subject; perhaps she also clocked the reticence, because she looked once more at Ivan.

'Ivan won't have an objection,' she said. 'It would be good for both me and Ivan, finally, to become more involved in English life. It's where our daughter is growing up, after all. Did you know that she and Tatiana were at school together?'

'Wonderful,' Valentin said.

'Yes,' said Kata. 'Alexandra invited Tatiana to visit us this holiday, and I am so happy she did. We have had such fun.'

'And how much longer do you have at school, Alexandra?' Valentin asked.

'Three years,' Alex answered. She blushed.

'And you're going to hang out with me, in London, in your holidays, aren't you, Alex?' said Tatiana.

Kata beamed.

'Yes ...' said Alex. She looked quickly across the table at her father.

'Of course, she is,' Kata said. 'Alexandra is very interested in art history,' she said, turning to Valentin. 'Oliver is going to help to find her an internship for one summer. At, where did you say, Oliver?'

'Christie's,' Oliver replied.

'That's great, isn't it, Alex?'

'Yes.' Alex looked once again to her dad as she replied. She gave her answer warily. He looked up, piece of steak speared to his fork, and saw her watching him.

'What?' he said to her.

'Christie's,' nodded Valentin. 'Very good. I have some good friends there. The director is a friend.'

'Oh,' said Kata, 'did you hear that, Alex? Maybe we can all meet, when Alex starts there.'

Tatiana raised her glass in Alex's direction. 'I'm in!'

'And which are your favourite paintings, Alex?' Valentin asked.

Alex reddened at the question but Kata and Tatiana were happy to answer for her. 'Where have you been together this summer, Tatiana?' Kata said, and Tatiana supplied the names of the museums dotted along the coast. Valentin spoke of the sailing yachts moored at Antibes, the different models he had seen, the pleasures of sailing as a counterpart to motoring, but despite the change in subject Ivan did not join in, for some ten minutes he did not say anything at all and his silence grew louder than the conversation of the others. Now and then Kata would look at him but then immediately look away and re-enter the conversation, eyes glassy, voice bright. 'How do you enjoy London in the autumn months, Valentin? When will you go back there?'

'In the autumn months, yes, it's true, London is very different depending on the time of year. I will go back in September. And you? Will I have the pleasure? Well, really, now is when we should be there. The summer is the time. Normally, I would be there for the summer months. But I like to be here from time to time. You don't get this in England, no?'

He indicated the sea, the promontory, lights dotted here and there in the trees.

'But in September, yes, there are still things. My good friend, Olga Romanov, she always has her ball, in September. You will come,' he said to Kata.

'It would be great to have *you* in London more, Ivan,' Tatiana said.

Ivan shook his head at the waiter who was offering him yet more steak.

'It would,' Oliver said.

The comments seemed to please Kata.

'We do miss him. He is working so hard all the time.'

She reached and stroked the top of his hand. She was wearing a gown in a bright emerald green. Her hair was piled up in an elaborate way on the top of her head. A hairdresser had come from a salon in Monaco to do it, at the apartment. There were diamonds in her ears. Her gown was low-cut, displaying her ample cleavage. One could see how she would seem splendid to the one who loved her: regal, delectable, the very embodiment of desire.

She drew gentle circles on the top of Ivan's hand with her nail.
'We miss him,' she said.

'Well, we'll have to put paid to that,' said Oliver.

'You guys are too sweet!' Tatiana gushed.

Ivan touched Kata gently on the side of her arm. The waiter was next to her but she hadn't noticed. 'Do you want more?' Ivan asked her. He went to pour some water in her glass.

'Well, I'm very excited about pudding, Valentin,' Tatiana said, 'if our main course was anything to go by.'

'I cannot promise such a display this time,' he said. 'I am sorry to disappoint you.'

Waiters were emerging from the house bearing plates of sugar-dusted choux pastry, with red and white cream.

'I never find anything to beat millefeuille from the man who in my opinion is France's finest pastry chef, at the Maison Lande-maine, right here in St Jean Cap Ferrat.'

Thick fresh cream, the taste of wild raspberry.

'Well, if this is a working trip, then I never want to go on holiday,' said Oliver, leaning back in his chair. I saw Tatiana glance at him sharply.

'Thank you,' he said, as a waiter gave him an espresso.

'I've loved every moment of my holiday,' Tatiana said. She raised her own cup of espresso. 'To Kata and Ivan.'

'Do you enjoy a cigar, Ivan?' Valentin said.

'Sometimes.'

'I have some, recently arrived, Don Arturo. They are in my study. Come.' He patted Ivan on the arm. 'Come and help me select. We will bring one for Oliver as well.'

He stood up. 'Come, please,' he said.

When Ivan remained where he was, Valentin lost some of the smooth demeanour that men of the world, men like him and Oliver, habitually wore. 'Please, Ivan,' he said again.

Ivan looked up to where Valentin stood begging.

'No business, Valentin?' he said. He laughed and shook his head. He looked at Oliver, still laughing. 'No business, Oliver?'

He stood up and tossed his napkin down onto the table.

'OK, Valentin,' he said, still laughing. 'I'll come and help you to select a cigar.'

*

Tatiana was wearing a tight black dress with a V-neck that plunged to her navel, the gently swelling sides of her golden breasts just visible. She wore it confidently, back straight, chin raised. She raised her glass of wine to her lips and sipped; she put the glass back down and then looked, with that calm, forensic look I'd noticed before, at Kata. I thought back to how Alex had described Tatiana, when she'd told me about their first conversations in Tatiana's room at school at the beginning of Help Week. She had described Tatiana, and her conversation, as 'basic'. 'Everyman'. There was nothing basic or Everyman about Tatiana.

She really did look incredible in that dress. Oliver kept looking at her with barely disguised lust. His eyes would linger on the sides of her breasts. 'I left my handbag in the car, Oliver,' I'd heard her say when we had first arrived on the terrace, and he had trotted off obediently to get it for her, like a well-trained dog. She was more poised, more coolly in control than he was, despite being twenty years younger.

The relationship between Oliver and Tatiana was still unclear to me. Were they sexually involved? Clearly, he would like to be. Kata kept trying to guess, too. 'You and Oliver make such a nice couple!' She'd said it several times over the course of the holiday, Tatiana smiling back enigmatically. 'You look so beautiful together!' Did they? I found it a bit strange, Kata encouraging Tatiana to be with a man twice her age. In her deference, Kata seemed repeatedly to forget that Tatiana was only nineteen.

Tatiana could make things happen. Ivan had told Kata explicitly, those years ago, in the restaurant in Courchevel, that he could not and would not meet with Valentin. And yet here they all were. Had Kata forgotten how emphatic he had been? How could she have forgotten it when even I had not forgotten it? Or was it that she didn't believe his reasons? Or had she simply swept aside his reasons because they were inconvenient to her own desires? She had a habit of doing that, after all, didn't she? How long could she go on bulldozing over things, rewriting the narrative in her own interests, before there were consequences to be faced?

I looked across the table at Alex. She looked back at me and smiled. 'Do you want to watch something when we get back?' she asked. 'We can check Netflix. I put some stuff on my list. Do you like Ryan Gosling?'

What would happen, I wondered, if I were to tell them? If I were to let them know just what Tatiana was?

*

When they returned, the last traces of Valentin's smooth geniality, of his expansiveness as host, had gone. He came out of the house a few paces behind Ivan. I found it hard to look at him. His face was white, his eyes large and staring. He lowered himself into his chair. He stared at the table.

Ivan was contemplating the cigar in his hand. He raised it slightly. 'Thank you, Valentin,' he said.

Valentin indicated a mahogany fumidor, on a silver tray in the middle of the table. Ivan reached for the clippers. He lit his cigar. 'Very good,' he said. 'So, Valentin. The ball of Olga Romanov. Are you still planning to invite Kata?'

As he spoke, he reached out a hand to his wife, to touch her on the arm. It looked tender to me, the way he touched her. It was as if he was trying to convey something, some private channel of communication. Something soft and intimate, a reassurance of his loyalties, something that overrode what was otherwise going on at the table.

'Will you still take her with you? Now that I've said no to you? Now that I've told you I will not speak to him, for you?'

*

Polite to the end, Valentin stood in front of his house, flanked by his white pillars, waving us off. The entry lights in the portico picked out his tidy figure, clad in its elegant black silk. When we were some metres down the driveway, he lowered his arm, stood still for a moment, then turned around and disappeared inside the house.

I could feel Kata's fury. It was like a physical thing, there with us in the car.

We rolled slowly down the long driveway. Oliver and Tatiana's headlights moved up and down ahead of us as they negotiated the small crests and inclines that, some ten seconds later, our own car would experience.

There was a sharp bump and Kata put a hand up to steady herself, clasping it around the handle above the window. She seemed to pull herself up with it, to make herself taller.

'I'm sorry, Kata. But he was asking of me something I couldn't do.'

She held herself rigid, her arm still raised and gripping the handle. 'Could not, Ivan? Could not? Or would not?'

'Could not, Kata.'

She didn't answer. All her emotions seemed to express themselves in that arm, raised above her and gripping on to the handle, every muscle, vein and tendon taut.

'I am not going to endanger my family and myself for the sake of Valentin.'

She turned to him. 'So, it's for my sake?'

'Yes, it is.'

'I think you loved saying no to him.'

'Actually,' he said, 'I didn't.'

'You didn't?'

'No. I did not.'

'I don't believe you, Ivan.'

She turned her back on him. She was shaking.

'I wish you had not come with us,' she said. 'I knew you should not have been there. I knew you did not belong.'

18

I watched the sea beyond the window. There it was: huge, blue, quiet. Occasionally, things moved across it. A jet ski. Two jet skis. A medium-sized sailing yacht. Alex sat beside me at the desk, working through some problems in trigonometry.

Tatiana had left the previous morning, as planned. It was three days after Valentin's dinner.

Kata had hovered as Tatiana made her preparations, packed her things. She had moved restlessly from the dining room, to the kitchen, to the sitting room. She had seemed unable to settle. Twice I'd seen her go down the corridor to Tatiana's room and linger there, in the doorway, asking her if there was anything she needed. There was a hesitation in her voice, as if she wanted to say something more, seek some kind of reassurance from Tatiana, a guarantee of some kind of continuation, once this holiday was over, despite – perhaps she wasn't quite sure what despite.

After Tatiana left, the apartment seemed very quiet. Alex and I had our lessons, as usual, and even we talked quietly, sitting side by side at her desk. We'd spend an hour, on average, on each subject. In between each subject we'd have a ten-minute break. I'd stay in my seat, check my phone for messages, stare out at the sea. Alex would lie on her bed. She wouldn't pass the time with a book, a magazine, her phone. 'I'm having a rest,' she would say. But she wouldn't shut her eyes. She would stare up, at the ceiling.

*

On the day we found out about Valentin, Kata was wearing her dark glasses, even though we were sitting inside. She had taken to wearing her dark glasses quite a bit since Tatiana had left. Ivan was downstairs in Vova's apartment, it was just after lunch, it was sunny outside, I was due to leave in two days' time. Kata lay on the grey sofa. She had half drawn the curtains, she had the air con running and the grey blanket was over her. She flipped on the TV. Alex picked up the remote for the air con. 'Do you mind if I make it less cold?' she asked.

I heard the chop-chop-chop of a helicopter, and I looked towards the screen.

Chop-chop-chop: aerial footage of a large white villa, on a rocky promontory.

Russian Dissident Found Dead.

The newsreader spoke in English. It was Sky News.

'Valentin Kemerov … former oligarch … outspoken critic of … in exile … assets confiscated … suspicious circumstances … dead in his own bathroom.'

Blackness surged to my head. I was standing next to an armchair, I reached for it through the blackness, I lowered myself until I was sitting beside it on the floor.

Kata laid the TV remote down on the sofa beside her. She did not change her posture. She watched the screen. There was absolutely no expression on her face, and she kept her dark glasses on.

Looking up, I saw that Alex had kept her arm where it was, half-raised in the air, still holding out the air con remote.

*

Alex huddled into me. We were sitting side by side, in her bedroom, on her single bed. Our backs were against the wall.

I had my arm around her. We could hear them, in the sitting room.

Kata was hysterical. 'You'll do anything. You'll do anything to stop me!'

We heard something smash. Alex put her head into my chest. I tightened my arms around her.

'What was it? He had more friends than you? Except for the *one* friend. He knew how to be polite? He knew how to show people a nice time?'

'Kata.' His voice was flat, carrying. 'You really think that this was about you?'

We heard the sound of loud, angry sobbing.

'Kata,' he said again. 'What could I have done? Do you think my speaking to him would have made any difference? Valentin overestimated my influence. Look at me, Kata.'

We heard the sound of a door sliding open and someone moving on the terrace just beyond the French windows of Alex's bedroom.

'Don't follow me out here.'

'Kata. He was using you. Don't you understand? He was using you to ask a favour of me.'

'Shall we go and hang out in the kitchen?' I whispered to Alex. 'We can go and see Sebastian and Irina, maybe we could go out and get pizza.'

'Kata. I had nothing to do with it,' Ivan was saying. 'Nothing to do with it.'

Kata did not reply. The light curtains over the French windows blew in gently. We heard a male cough, followed by the click of a lighter, and then the smell of smoke drifted into the room, for a while. Until the smell of smoke went away.

'Are you dangerous, Ivan? A dangerous man?' Her voice had lowered. It was husky, thick.

The curtains blew in, out.

We heard movement and then a sharp gasp.

And then a moan.

'Oh, no,' Alex said. 'No, no, no!' She threw herself onto the

181

bed and scrabbled for pillows, put them over her head.

I heard movement again, and a door slam and then, from the room on the other side of us, from their bedroom, I heard them start to fuck.

The sound of two animals.

Groans and grunts, furniture being bashed around. Oh God. I felt myself get wet. I was so turned on, it felt like pain.

But there was movement beside me: it was Alex, twisting and turning under her pillows.

'Alex,' I said, 'Alex! Come on, let's go to my room.'

We ran past their room and down the corridor. We closed my bedroom door and went into my bathroom and closed that door as well and once we were in there, we couldn't hear anything.

19

'Hang on,' I said, at around two in the morning. I paused the YouTube video we were watching. 'I'm going to do a raid on the kitchen.' I got some Ben and Jerry's Phishfood ice cream, leftover breakfast pastries, a bag of truffle-flavoured crisps and a large bottle of fizzy water to quench our thirst after the salt of the crisps. On my way back I passed Kata and Ivan's room but there was no need to pause, to listen, to lurk. We were no longer in the realm of titillating hints. There was no erotic mystery, not anymore. I paused in the doorway to my room, arms full of snacks and looked at Alex, sprawled in my bed. I would be leaving this room in just a few days' time. It no longer offered me any protection. The bed, the quilt, the carpet, the curtains – they could not hold me as they once had. Alex was nowhere near asleep. I put the snacks on the bedside table and sat beside her. I put my own desires aside and imagined that, for that night, I was Alex's mother, replacing the mother who trod so roughshod over her being. If I were Alex, what would I want from my replacement mother? I would want someone who saw me and who, from this place of seeing, quietly honoured me. I lay on the bed beside her. The day and night had been gross with drama. My stomach turned suddenly at the thought of the ice cream, of the heavy aftertaste of truffle crisps. I poured out some water for her, made her drink it. Sometime towards dawn she fell asleep. She lay at a slant right across the bed, so I gathered up the spare blanket and went to sleep in the armchair.

*

I had a cracking headache the next morning.

'Ufff,' I said, as I sat down at the breakfast table. 'I think we ate too much junk food last night.' I said it quietly, to Alex. 'Feeling a bit rough this morning.'

She didn't appear to have heard. She was buttering her toast very carefully, she took a bite. Her eyes were on her mum, then her dad. She had brought a schoolbook with her to the breakfast table. She had pinned it open with a pot of jam. She would look down at the book whenever her mum's or dad's eyes moved in her direction. She used it as a prop.

'Alexandra,' Kata said, 'is the breakfast table really the place for reading a book?'

Her voice was flat and depressed. She was wearing a grey track-suit. There was a pastry on the plate in front of her. The kind of stodgy thing she would not usually eat. 'No, no,' she said, wearily, as Irina offered her another cup of coffee.

Alex blushed and put her book on the floor.

'On the floor?' said Kata. 'Who leaves a book lying on the floor? Go and put it in your room.'

I watched Alex leave the room, and then I brought my gaze back to the table, to Kata, sulky in front of her croissant, and to Ivan, doggedly forking up ham, and I remembered that yesterday a man had died.

Valentin had actually died.

It was hard to take it in. The news had come to me through a TV screen, so it was difficult to feel it as something real. I wanted to feel it, it seemed important to. The black satin of the curtains. The whirr of the Nespresso machine sounding from the kitchen, as it did every morning, as it had done in the chalet in Courche-vel. The texture of the sofa cushions, crushed velvet as they had been in Courchevel, plumped hourly by staff, here as there. The same chrome, the same size flatscreen, the same box by the front door containing house slippers, to don with their loungewear, so comfortable, so endlessly comfortable. I felt the relentlessness of these objects, of this setting they took with them across the globe. Unchanging and absolute, denying all other realities.

Alex came back in.

'Did you know that Tatiana has not even messaged me to thank me for having her to stay?' Kata addressed this question to Alex. She said it as if it was Alex's fault.

Her voice was full of bitterness and disappointment.

'You will choose your friends better, next time,' she said.

'Your mother is right,' Ivan said. 'From now on, you will be very careful about who you bring into our house.'

*

She was standing in the middle of her room when I came in for the morning lesson. I said her name softly. 'Alex,' I said. 'Are you OK?' She stood for some moments in silence and I stood in silence, too. She sat down. She laid her hands on the desk in front of her.

'I don't exist,' she said, and it was true. They had murdered her at the breakfast table. I went closer to her and put my hand on the top of her head, to show her, through my touch, that she did exist, that she was a fact in the world. I stood behind her for some moments, with my hand on the top of her soft hair, not knowing what I could say.

We were both ghosts.

'It's awful, Alex,' I said. 'It's awful.'

'I don't think I can do lessons today, Mel. I don't feel well enough.'

'Of course. I understand.'

I wanted to say something further, to try to comfort her.

Her hands were clenched into balls. She pressed them down onto the table. They shook with the effort.

The clenched balls of her fists relaxed, she brought them up to cover her face. No tears came, at least I didn't hear her cry or see her body shaking.

'Alex, darling,' I began, but she brought her hands down from her face, shook her head, made a waving motion of her hand in the air.

'I'm tired,' she said.

I was thinking what else to say but she looked at me as if irritated to see I was still there.

'OK, thank you, Mel,' she said. 'That's all for now. Enjoy your day off. Feel free to make the most of the facilities in your spare time.'

*

I lay on the bed that no longer meant anything to me. It was just a big bed in someone else's house. There was something I'd been meaning to do that I'd been putting off. I needed to look on SpareRoom for a room to rent for the couple of months I had in London before my next job. I had thought I might find a live-in job in London for that stretch of time. A live-in job hadn't come through, so I needed a place. I could stay on a friend's sofa for the first week or two, but I should find somewhere for the month after that. I brought the website up on my screen and put in my search criteria. A few of the ads said they wanted someone who would be out most of the day, someone who was a 'professional' and who worked regular hours and had a healthy social life. I wondered why they wanted someone who only came to the house to sleep. Was it to keep down the utility bills? There were some places that looked quite nice. That place looks quite nice, I said to myself. Cheer up, that place looks quite nice.

I lay on the bed, killing time. I went onto the search page on my Instagram. The algorithm knew me well: houses, houses, millions and millions of pounds' worth of real estate there on my screen in little cubes, House and Garden, Design Notes, some recently divorced aristocratic mother of three decorating her new townhouse with help from Colefax and Fowler. I lay there and glutted myself on it as I had done many times before, exposing myself to it all, whipping up my self-pity, my skewed feelings of scarcity, the constant gnawing hunger, ideas above my station: why should I have to look on SpareRoom when some people have it like *this*?

At around 8 p.m. I remembered that there was a short-term remedy, a deliciously effective way of soothing myself.

Feeling warm and pleasant, I went down the corridor, I found Sebastian and I asked him, 'Hey, Sebastian, could I have a couple of your sleeping pills?'

'Sure, honey,' he said, and the moment I saw them in the palm of my hand I felt happy.

In the shower I scrubbed them all off me, I scrubbed off Anton, I scrubbed off Kata and Ivan, I scrubbed off Alex.

I drew the curtains and because of the sleeping pills and the certainty they contained, the room became mine again, if just for this one evening.

Earplugs in, curtains drawn, bedside light on, sheets clean. It was lying there on my bedside table, *The World of Interiors* magazine bought earlier that day from the newsstand across the street. The weight of it in my hands, an object of beauty, the most expensive paper of any Condé Nast title. I opened it, trailed my fingers across the pages. A mid-century modern house in Amagansett, East Hampton, a slatted wooden dock at the end of the garden, a wooden boat knocking against it, the water of the Sound. An eighteenth-century English country house rising out of a misted green park, great trees in front of it with white deer in their shadows. A London house with an architect-designed kitchen at the back, Japanese, with its pale woods, it looks onto a leafy little garden, drinking tea here in the morning. The bliss of knowing that sleep is coming, inevitable, inexorable, because of the pills, the certainty of it, lying here in this bed, and as my body relaxes this bed becomes my bed, as comfortable as any of the beds in the magazine, and my own sheets are soft and clean, and nothing will get in the way of sleep, of this oblivion gently starting to roll at my edges now the pills start to take effect, one pill or two or three, and as they do, the details in the glossy beautiful treasure in my hands begin to wash over me, penetrate me, fill me, sate me, suffuse me with pleasure, the house is a hybrid of Pacific coastal design and Dutch modernism, trompe l'oeil clouds and deer and cypresses and ripe-hanging fruit, rose quartz, tongue and groove panelling for a beach-cabin feel, blue and white delft tiles in low fireplaces surrounded by broad leaved plants, verdure and greensward, a pair of finely carved Swedish limewood panels, an inner door of rosewood, stucco with pastel shades of pale green, pink, ivory and gold, stylised flowers floating above the cornice, and then I can't see the magazine in front of me anymore and the houses in it are melding with the other houses, the houses of my pupils in Mayfair and Belgravia and Chelsea, I'm walking through them, I'm in all their bathrooms at once and they are all marble, the most beautiful soft white veined with grey, Calacatta, marble edges around the bathtubs, which are heavy and solid with heavy solid silver taps, I'm lying in the hot water in all these marble bathrooms and I'm so clean and pure, lying in this warm endless sensual ease, the safety, the solidity, the security, it's mine, this house, it's mine, I can lie down and sleep in it, I don't have to worry about anything, the bed is so soft and perfect, the curtains are so heavy, it's so quiet, it is here, in this voluptuous material luxury, more satisfying than any person any orgasm any love, that I fall asleep.

*

She came and found me the next day because she wanted to go for a walk.

'Alright,' I said. I was lying on the bed. I lay and just looked at her, standing there in my doorway. In her doorway. 'Your wish is my command.'

I got up and put on my shoes.

I walked behind her along the coastal path.

When we took a rest on our usual rocky outcrop she sat very close to me, our upper arms touching.

'I got a message from Tatiana today,' she said. 'I wonder if she texted Mama too. I'm happy she wants to keep in touch.'

She read the message out to me.

'Let me know when you are back! Let's go to a gallery or something!'

'Great,' I said. 'That's great.'

Make the most of the facilities in your free time.

When I'd first arrived, she had flinched at my touch. I remembered it.

Sebastian had touched her, on that first day, when she'd flinched away from me. He often patted her on the head. So, now I came to think of it, did Irina. I thought of Sebastian, knocking on the closed door to Alex's room. 'Alex, honey, it's Mel, remember Mel?' She'd opened the door; *he* had reached out his hand, to touch the top of her head, just like I had done the day before; she had let him. She hadn't noticed his hand on her head, it hadn't bothered her. Sebastian was part of the furniture, he wasn't a force to be reckoned with, he was neutral, his touch carried no charge. He was staff.

I moved away from her so that our upper arms were no longer touching.

The sea spread out and away, grey today, flat and endless. There was nothing but the grey of it, the heavy and repeating grey, even when I closed my eyes. I sat still and just let myself feel it, the need to be held, by something.

Did I already know, on some subterranean level, that I would never see my mother again? *How did it go with Anton?? Spill the juicy details!!* I didn't reply to her texts, she went back to England and a few months later, at three o'clock on a Tuesday morning on the road home from Dartmouth, she drove her car into a tree. How might I have reacted if I had heard the news that day, in the nadir of my life, sitting on that rock with Alex? You stupid bitch, is what I might have thought. Splat. *You stupid fucking bitch.*

I looked at Alex's thin hands holding her phone.

All the times I've spent listening to you, sympathising with you, I thought. If you and your family were to give me just 1 per cent of your riches, I would be safe forever.

I thought of the future, of my whole life, I was filled with rage and I wanted to hurt her.

'There are some things I should tell you,' I said. 'About Tatiana, I mean.'

'About Tatiana?'

'Yeah …'

I shifted myself on the rock. I'd brought a light wrap with me. I pulled it around my shoulders. Summer was over, the air was getting cooler.

'Just some things that I overheard. She was never your friend. She was just using you, I'm afraid.'

I told her everything. 'She follows the money,' I finished up. 'That's all you need to know about Tatiana.'

The only agency I had in this world was in the way I chose to withhold or deploy information. I wanted to assert my scrap of power.

I don't care if there are consequences, I thought, in the very next second thinking, No that's not accurate: I *want* there to be consequences, I *want* there to be consequences.

We sat on the outcrop. It was hard to work out what she was feeling. Was she wounded, was she sad? She laid her phone face down beside her. A stand of seagrass waved in the wind. I looked at her skinny ankles and then her body shifted as she leaned, to heave at a large piece of loose rock.

She rolled it in jolts, scraping it across the path, to the edge of the outcrop. I followed her. She mustered all her strength, she plunged it over the edge and we both leaned over, to watch it break and smash.

PART THREE

The Maldives

20

They never did find anything criminal in Valentin's death.

There was a slew of news pieces in the days immediately afterwards. Over and over again I saw his round face, his short black hair and the gleaming crown of his head. I learned of the charges of fraud and embezzlement that had followed him from his home country, I learned of the inflammatory things he had said.

The French coroner found the cause of death to be consistent with hanging; he deemed it suicide, unsuspicious, the case was closed.

And probably that's how it was.

'Fuck, I can't believe you *met* that guy, that you were *at his house*,' friends said.

It was a thrill, to be linked to the whole thing in some way. I felt it gave me a sheen, something extra. But I was also very relieved when it began to die away, when the news stories shrivelled up. It was a relief that certain names were never so much as mentioned. Because that – that possibility – was outside the realm of what I was able to comprehend. To be brushed by the wing, the hint, was glamorous. The actuality would have been something else.

So, yes. Valentin hanged himself.

I did think, occasionally, of those hours in Anton's bedroom, of the dejection, the gun holster, the pleasure. I thought of his long lanky body, his sexy, bony fingers.

A note had been found when the authorities combed Valentin's place in the immediate aftermath of his death. It was a note asking for forgiveness and to be allowed back home. It was undelivered. There was something touching in the idea of a note. A handwritten note, like the ones you write when you are a kid, sitting in a chemistry lesson. You've been fighting, in the break just past you ignored each other, but now you're tired of it, you just want to make up. You write the note and ask the kid at the next desk to pass it along.

*

I already knew the job was in the offing when my agency contacted me because Alex herself had talked to me about it.

We had kept in contact, sporadically, in the three and a half years since that summer in Monaco. Very occasionally, we would write to each other on WhatsApp.

I'm taking my A levels in the summer, she wrote. *Mama wants a tutor to help me over February half-term. You know what she's like. If I have to have a tutor, I'd rather it was you.*

I'd told her I was up for it, that I still did the occasional tutoring job. *Tell your mum to contact the agency and set it up*, I wrote.

Cool, Alex replied. *It will be on our boat, in the Maldives.*

A few days later Alex WhatsApped me an image: it was of a painting. I enlarged it and looked closer. A still life, some items on a dark table: a golden goblet, grapes, a piece of cheese and a cheese knife, coins. It looked Flemish, seventeenth century.

Mama bought it yesterday at an auction, Alex wrote. *She's started to collect art seriously now.*

Did you ever do your internship at Christie's? I wrote back.

Yes. Last summer.

We're having a big event on the yacht, she said. *A big party*. I pressed her for more info. I wondered how she'd have time to study. *Don't worry*, she said. *You'll see when you get here.*

I had watched Alex's WhatsApp photos evolve over the years. I would notice them sometimes, the change, when I scrolled down through my chats. At first, she hadn't had a profile picture, it had just been that default outline of a human head. Then, a few months after the Monaco gig, I noticed one day that it had changed, to a kind of geometric image in pinks and whites and yellows, some sort of abstract painting, I'd supposed. When she had messaged me, after a year, to ask how I was and to talk about some book she'd just read, I saw that she had an actual picture of herself this time. Her hair was longer, her eyebrows had thickened, her face was thinner. She was wearing a black polo neck, she was sitting at a table, she was leaning her chin onto her hand. She had grown up. In the messages we exchanged just before I went out to join her in the Maldives her picture had changed once again. She had short hair now, very severe, very stylish. Her face was pale. I could just see the collar of a white shirt. She had a new expression, one I didn't remember and that I wouldn't have associated with her. It was one of confidence. Even – but I was only going on a picture, after all – of hardness.

*

There was an Ebola poster in Male airport.

It showed a man with a pink face, a bandage across his head and an expression of final and utter fatigue. His arms were outstretched and lines pointed to various parts of his body. IMPAIRED KIDNEY & LIVER FUNCTION, said the box pointing to his waist. The words INTENSE WEAKNESS hovered above him, pointing nowhere in particular. I stared at him, dazed from my 24-hour journey, which had included an eight-hour layover in the sepia-toned environs of Moscow airport. When I turned round I identified my envoy immediately, before I even noticed the sign hanging from his left hand with my name on it.

Tristan was first mate, he told me. His uniform was navy and showed his tall, healthy figure. His eyes were incredibly blue, his hair was brown but lightened by the sun.

'You must be knackered,' he said, in his Australian accent. He manoeuvred the tender away from the crowded Male jetty.

'So what's happening on their yacht?' I shouted over the noise of the boat. It bumped up and down over another speedboat's wake.

'Big party! This Friday. People are coming from everywhere. I've had to arrange transport for some of them to their resort. They've already started to arrive, they're being put up at the Mayaht. Have you been to the Maldives before?' he shouted.

'No, never,' I yelled back.

He slowed the boat and it became easier to hear him.

He pointed to a small atoll with palms standing on it like a cartoon of a desert island.

'They'll all be underwater in twenty years' time. Global warming ... There she is,' he said, pointing ahead of him.

So, there it was. Huge, black, gleaming, sitting on the sea.

'Wow,' I said. 'It's massive. I've never been on a super yacht before.'

'She's pretty sweet,' he said. 'I've worked on a few before but this one's pretty slick.'

He purred the tender closer, there was the smell of salt and petrol. I saw the name of the boat emblazoned on its side: QUEEN K.

We made our way to the landing area. Two other uniformed guys were standing there waiting to take our bags.

'If you haven't spent a lot of time on a boat before, it might take you a while to adapt,' Tristan said. 'Don't freak out if you feel a bit sick at first.'

'OK,' I said. I swayed, standing there on the wood of the landing dock.

'Mel.'

I looked up in the direction of the voice and saw Alex, standing on the main deck.

'*Hello*,' she said. She raised her eyebrows sardonically. 'You arrived in one piece, I see. Have Mel's bags been taken to the cabin?' she asked Tristan.

'Yes, miss,' he said, suddenly stiff, formal.

'Excellent.'

She was dressed all in white, a white shirt and white trousers. Her hair was starkly short, even shorter than it had been in her last WhatsApp photo.

I wobbled up the steps to her.

She stood waiting for me, still with that knowing smile playing over her lips. When I got to the top of the stairs she extended a slim arm towards me. I took her hand. She was wearing a watch with a rich black leather strap, but apart from that her wrists and fingers were bare. She leaned forward to kiss me on both cheeks and I smelled her crisp and fresh cologne.

*

Down inside the boat my nausea increased. I didn't know if it was a real, physical thing or if I was convincing myself of seasickness because of what Tristan had said. Alex wanted to show me the exhibition. 'And then you can go and collapse in the cabin, I promise,' she said. 'But you've got to see this first.'

She was leading me down a spiral staircase that went right through the centre of the boat, descending past a couple of landings. On the top landing a pair of sliding doors had opened, giving me a glimpse into what I'd guessed were the kitchen quarters. I'd seen a chef in his high hat and a few other people in uniform. On the next landing some uniformed women appeared carrying trays, bundles of towels, empty water pitchers. Alex greeted them, 'Natalie; Tania,' and they bowed their heads in return and called her 'miss', just like Tristan had done. The whole boat seemed to be a hive of activity but in all the various people we had passed I'd yet to see anyone I recognised.

'Here we go,' Alex said, once we got to the bottom of the staircase. She pressed a button next to a glass door. It occurred to me that we must be underwater by this point, deep down in the boat's hull, and the thought increased my nausea acutely.

The door slid open. 'Go on,' she said, and I went in.

'Wow ...'

'I told you my mum was collecting art.'

I was staring right at a Malevich. Modernist blocks of colour outlined the figure of a working woman from the Soviet era, holding a rake. She was without facial features, so expressed neither mordancy nor bemusement at her current location.

'That one's just on loan,' Alex said. 'She owns those.' She pointed towards some paintings further into the room. They were smaller, abstract. I didn't recognise them. I turned slowly round. The room was bright white. I found myself face to face with a Kandinsky. 'She owns that one too,' Alex said. The lights in the room were incredibly bright, the lines and shapes in the painting hectic. The boat gave another lurch. 'Oh, God ...' I said. I pushed past Alex and managed to get out of the room. I hung on to the wrought iron of the stairwell and looked about me. I clamped my teeth shut but my throat was bucking and convulsing, on a mission of its own. Just under the curve of the stairs I saw a bucket. I lurched onto my knees and was sick into it.

*

'I'm so sorry,' I said.

Alex had brought me up onto the main deck.

'You need fresh air,' she'd said.

'I think I'm just not used to the motion of being on a boat.'

She'd sat me down on a chair at a round table. I leaned forward and closed my eyes, took several breaths of the sea air, which was humid, balmy, hot. Not very refreshing, but better than being down there. When I opened my eyes I felt a little better. Looking around, I saw that the whole of the deck was covered with round tables and each table was surrounded by about ten chairs.

'Have some water,' Alex said.

'Thanks ... So, it's all coming along,' I said, indicating the tables. '*It certainly is.*'

There it was again: that sardonic, privately amused tone.

What a difference a few years can make when you are that age, I thought.

At the far end of the huge deck there were sliding glass doors leading to an indoor area. The doors kept opening and shutting, automatically, as uniformed staff came in and out, putting things on the tables, bringing out more chairs. I saw Sebastian – Sebastian! – come through the doors with a blonde, uniformed woman. They conferred for some seconds. Then they disappeared back inside the boat. Sebastian! I had a warm feeling. I'll hunt him out later, I thought.

'So, what's this event in aid of, exactly?' I asked Alex.

'It's for Mama to announce her new project. A launch party. I'll tell you all about it, but later.'

She glanced up at the uniformed people moving to and fro. One of them, a young man, was carrying an arrangement of mauve and golden orchids. He set the flowers down on the table next to us, which was covered with a white linen cloth. The other tables were still bare. He stood back, appearing to consider the effect of the mauve and golden orchids against the white of the cloth.

When he'd gone Alex stood and picked up the orchids. She set them down on our table, then sat back down in her seat.

Close up I could better see the orchids' design. The mauve and gold were not solid blocks of colour. They were leopard spots, over a background of cream.

'Beautiful, aren't they?' said Alex. 'They're Matsui Zygopetalum, grown by Andy Matsui himself, at the Matsui nursery in the Salinas Valley in California. They were cool-sealed and flown to Male.'

She was stroking a mauve petal gently between forefinger and thumb.

'The others are in cold storage. They won't be put on the tables till Friday, about two hours before the guests arrive. They only last a day. This one's just a test run.'

She looked at me with that odd smile. Her eyes widened. I looked back down at her fingers, to where she held the orchid. She had bent her thumb so that the nail broke through the petal, it was pressing down into the finger below.

*

I lay in one of the single beds in my cabin.

Lying down made the soft, rolling motion of the boat easier to endure.

I had showered in the ensuite bathroom, got all the stale travel dirt off me. The cabin was air-conditioned, cool. I had the duvet over me. The single bed was of a good size, it was more like a queen. It was fixed into the wall.

I looked across the cabin to where the other bed was, fixed into the opposite wall.

'I hope you don't mind,' Alex had said, 'that we'll be sharing a cabin. It's because there are so many people on the boat at the moment, there isn't much room.'

'Sure,' I said. 'Fine with me.'

Thinking: This boat is absolutely massive. There must be tons of spare cabins. Are you honestly telling me we have to share a cabin out of necessity?

But I didn't really mind either way. I was only on the boat for ten days. I'd earn some good money, and then I'd go back home.

I had yet to unpack. My toiletries were still in my washbag, my clothes were still in my suitcase. I recalled the ritualistic way in which I would once arrange my belongings when I first arrived on a tutoring job.

When I woke there was a tray on my bedside table. I lifted the silver dome. Baked chicken, cherry tomatoes. I had no idea what time it was. I ate a few bites and went back to sleep.

When I next opened my eyes, the tray had gone and Alex was there, in her bed.

'Hi,' she said. 'How's your jet lag?'

'I'll be fine by the morning.'

'That journey's a bitch.'

'Yeah,' I said. But I knew that she and her family always made the journey in their own jet, and their jet had beds on it. Actual bed*rooms* in fact, not just beds.

'I didn't know the motion of the boat would have such an effect on me,' I said. 'I think I'm getting used to it, though.'

She was wearing a high-necked, white nightgown. It looked stiff and well laundered. She was leaning against her pillows.

I turned onto my side, to face her.

'I hope you don't mind sharing a cabin with me,' she said.

'Not at all.'

'It's just ... I just ...' In her old-fashioned nightgown she looked like a child again. 'I thought it would be nice for us to have some time together, to talk.'

'Sure,' I said.

'So ...' she hesitated. 'How have you been?'

'Not bad.'

'Sebastian told me you moved to Vienna.'

'Yeah, that's right. About a year ago now.'

'Why?'

'I went to stay with an old school friend, I got some work teaching English in a kindergarten, and I just decided to stay. I like it there.'

'Isn't it kind of an old-fashioned place? Just Mozart and museums and stuff?'

'That's just the surface. That's what you see if you only drop in for a few days.'

'I don't think I could live somewhere like that. It would be too quiet for me. I want to live in a world city. Like New York or London or Moscow.'

'Do you, now.'

I looked at her smooth young face lying on the pillow, the plump lips – she'd just applied some sort of balm to them, they looked pink and glossy – and I felt a sudden overwhelming dislike.

'Yeah, don't you miss London?'

'No,' I said. 'I don't.'

'But there's so much fun stuff in London.'

Sometimes on my visits back to London I would drop into my old favourite places. Whitehall Gardens at the very tipping point of dusk when the trees loomed above the flower beds and the balustrades of the adjoining buildings leaned over the gardens like the terrace of some grand old Venetian hotel. A bar attached to the

Travelodge at the top of an unglamorous tower block near Portland Street, where the views were sweeping and decor pleasantly neglected, seemingly unchanged since the seventies. I liked the places that felt unselfconscious, that did not appear to be marketing themselves, that just ... were. A family-run Korean restaurant on Deptford High Street where the whole of the basement was a trompe l'oeil aquarium. Evensong in St Paul's Cathedral. The romantic grandeur of Abney Park Cemetery where roses wilted over Dickensian graves. The guys who burned incense and danced outside the corner shop at the beginning of Ferndale Road.

Sometimes I would take walks at dusk through the big terraced squares of Belgravia, the white houses empty and beautiful, owned by shell companies; I would wander on, to Knightsbridge, imagining the swinging sixties, long-haired male fashion designers in flares going to the Harrods pets department to pick out baby leopards, cheetahs, lions; I would see, outside the cafés and on the streets, in their personalised Lamborghinis, the offspring of billionaires, cruising around in the mellow twilight, the whole city open before them, theirs.

The profusion of green everywhere, sodden furling green in spring, dusty green in summer trailing blossoms, the deep Victorian romance of rhododendrons. On one visit back I went to Marylebone High Street to go to Oxfam Books, another of my favourite places, and when I came out onto the street a car pulled up, a blacked-out Jaguar like the one Kata had in Monaco, and three teenage girls got out. Plump sulky lips, very clean hair, expensive-looking clothes. They looked a lot like Alex. They stood in a group, holding their phones, they went into Daylesford, I saw them ordering smoothies. I imagined the homes that car had brought them from. Big, white and solid. Quiet, with peaceful gardens. I wondered what it would be like to be them, living in this city. Or to be anyone living in this city who had a home that was their own.

I had had a taste of it, when I had gone back to London after the job in Monaco. The place I'd seen on SpareRoom that I had thought looked nice *had* turned out to be nice. It was a house in

Brixton that belonged to a woman called Caroline and she was renting out two bedrooms for a year while she went to Frankfurt for a job. The other tenant was a woman called Lara, my age, a visual artist with a teaching post at Central Saint Martins. Caroline needed to come back now and then, she still had all her stuff in the house, and for this reason the rent was cheap by London standards for what we were getting. Upstairs, two bedrooms for sleeping, plus Caroline's room; downstairs, two rooms for living. We had become very close, Lara and I, and we had made a home together there. It had a small garden and Lara grew things in it and sometimes she snipped things from the garden and put them in glass vases and brought them into the house. We cooked together, watched films together, talked long into the night. I went on fewer overseas tutoring jobs, managing to find some regular jobs in London.

We were both a bit down the first time Caroline visited, tiptoeing around the space we had kidded ourselves was our own. We had moved some of Caroline's stuff around, but every time Caroline was due to return we consulted the photos we had taken on our phones and put her things back where they were supposed to be.

Caroline seemed nice. We had dinner together, all three of us out in the garden. We asked her about life in Frankfurt. She did something in marketing, for a design company. She probably earned the same as Lara and I did. I wondered how she had been able to buy this house, but a couple of weeks later when I was making space in one of the drawers in the kitchen I found an old letter to her from her dad and saw his workplace on the letterhead, some kind of boutique finance or hedge fund thing; his surname – Caroline's surname – was in the name of the company.

The gentle life Lara and I were living was Caroline's life, and we both did like Caroline, genuinely we liked her, we had a good time with her, that evening, sitting out in her garden having drinks in the long June light.

I knew that in a year Caroline would move back permanently and we'd have to get out but still, for a time, venturing out into the streets from the solidity of that home, I felt a measure of dignity and the whole city felt different to me.

We got a big white sheet and draped it over the sofa, which was a strident shade of burgundy, and Lara put some of her small sculptures around the sitting room.

The sitting room that we made ours; the sheet that made the white sofa.

It was in that sitting room that I got the call, early one morning, about my mum. It was on that sofa that Lara held me.

The missed calls on the phone I always left downstairs overnight to charge. The new call flashing through: Aunt Janet. The noise of my phone falling onto the floor. My sounds travelling through the ceiling because, moments later, bare feet on the wooden staircase: Lara, coming to me. To lift me from the floor and onto that sofa, to hold me as the light changed colour. It fell on us all that morning from the window, turning from thin to golden to bright. I saw it change even while my eyes were closed.

*

I was curious to know what Alex and her family had been up to in the last few years. What fresh emotional dramas had occurred, filling the wide open plains of lives devoid of material concerns.

I smiled. I made my voice gentle. 'So, tell me, sweetheart,' I said. 'About this party and everything. You said you'd tell me about it. Are you OK? What's on your mind?'

Thinking: Go on, give me another instalment of the soap opera, it does make good viewing. You can confide in me, just like you always did.

She looked at me, trusting, unselfconscious – why would she be self-conscious around someone like me? – just like she had been when she'd lain next to me in the bed in that room in Monaco.

She rolled over so she was lying on her back, looking up at the ceiling.

And then her lips were moving and she was telling it, the whole story, about what she had so elaborately set in motion. Where is my old sweet Alex, my puppy-like little girl? I was thinking, as she told me all about it, the malevolent thing that she had done.

21

The idea had first come to her on a cold sunny day in mid-February, almost exactly one year earlier.

She had asked Dmitri to drive her to Tate Britain to see an exhibition of the pre-Raphaelites. On their way there Dmitri said he had to stop to deliver something to her dad, who was about to have a business meeting in one of the private conference rooms at the Dorchester hotel.

Dmitri had drawn the car up in the parking bay in front of the Dorchester and Alex had lounged back in her seat, preparing to sit there and wait for him. Then, through the tint of the car's window, walking across the parking area and heading through the revolving doors of the hotel, she had seen Oliver.

Dmitri was already halfway across the parking area. Alex got out of the car and followed him. She followed him through the plush foyer and down a corridor, she hung back and watched him go through a door. When Dmitri re-emerged, some five minutes later, she asked him to wait for her in the car. If he was surprised to find her loitering there, he didn't let on.

Through the door Alex found a small anteroom furnished with two black leather chairs and a table covered with business magazines. She could hear the murmur of voices coming through a door on the other side of the anteroom, so she went over to listen.

She heard three voices: her dad's, Oliver's, and a man's voice she did not recognise. What were they talking about? She leaned closer. Something about gas pipelines, going across a border. Oliver was saying something about a company in Eleuthera, that was a name she knew, she'd been there, in the Bahamas the previous summer, it was where she'd learned to scuba dive.

After a few minutes Alex left the anteroom and waited in the hotel lobby.

When Oliver reappeared he was with a tall man who had bushy grey hair and was wearing a startlingly bright red tie. Alex watched them shake hands and the bushy-haired man leave. The bright red of his tie went well with the grey of his suit, she thought. He was better dressed than Oliver and her dad.

She got up from where she was sitting, on a cubed chair behind a huge decorative urn.

Oliver was affability itself. The surprise at seeing her showed in his eyes for no more than two, three seconds. 'Well, hello!'

It had only been a couple of years, but he'd visibly aged. His face had fattened.

They had chatted down the corridor and back through the lobby and once they were through the doors and out in the February cold she had asked, 'How's Tatiana?'

Alex already knew, through googling, that Oliver and Tatiana were officially a couple these days. Tatiana was still intermittently on *The Royal Borough*.

'Well,' said Oliver, 'she is well. Very well.'

'It's been so long since I've seen her,' Alex said. 'I haven't seen her since Monaco, and we had such a nice time together then. But I've been locked up in boarding school. What is she doing nowadays?'

'She is a force of nature,' Oliver said. 'I've never known anyone to work so hard.'

She had almost completed her undergraduate degree in History of Art at the Courtauld. She had juggled it with endless internships.

'I'm not very good at the names of these places,' he said. 'Gag—?'

207

'Gagosian.'

'That's the one.'

She'd even done a night course at Sotheby's. Something to do with Art and Finance in a Global Market.

And, in recent months, she'd started to consult here and there, in the capacity of *art adviser*.

'Interesting,' Alex said.

But she had already known that, too.

Two brothers, famous property developers, had erected an apartment building on the edge of Hyde Park. It was the city's most expensive real estate. When she had googled Tatiana's name, a couple of months before running into Oliver, it had brought up a feature about the opening of this apartment block and she had seen a picture of Tatiana, at the event to celebrate the opening, standing between the brothers. A lot of the buyers had wanted the apartments fully furnished, including wall decoration, and Tatiana had acted as the brothers' adviser, on behalf of their clients, when it came to buying art to put on the walls.

Tatiana had looked confident, imperious, standing between the billionaire brothers. It was hard to believe she was only in her early twenties.

'It would be great to catch up with Tatiana,' Alex said to Oliver, as they said goodbye outside the Dorchester. 'Please tell her to get in touch. Here, I'll give you my number.'

And then she'd walked across the parking bay to where she could see Dmitri, watching her, waiting for her in the car.

*

About three weeks earlier Alex had been sitting in the living room of the London house with her mum and Igor.

It was a Sunday morning and her mum and Igor were leafing through the newspaper supplements.

She had heard her mum give a long sigh. 'Look at this,' she said.

She was staring down at the magazine in her hand. She sighed again and passed it to Igor.

It was a double-spread photograph: a young, beautiful woman, dark-haired, immaculately dressed in a white dress, standing on a raised podium, addressing what appeared to be a rapt audience. At the edges of the picture were huge red and white balls that looked like giant mushrooms.

Igor turned the page.

It had been an event to mark the fifth anniversary of the opening of this woman's contemporary art foundation, in Moscow. Everyone who was anyone had been there.

Hollywood stars, society doyennes, fashion heavyweights, superstar artists and architects, European royals, titans of industry – there they stood, in evening dress, their faces turned towards the young woman on the podium, listening to her speak.

She was of Russian descent, this woman; she had been born and brought up in Moscow, she had been educated in the UK and had attended an Ivy League university on the east coast of America. She was mainly based in London, nowadays. She was married to someone almost as rich as Alex's dad. She was known to be highly cultivated; she went everywhere, she knew everyone. The dinner parties at her Grade 2-listed Holland Park mansion were legendary. Kata had never been to one.

*

Her mother's desire to take her place among the uppermost echelons of society had never faltered. She had tried and tried, done everything she could think of.

There had been minor victories, little inroads. Like the time she'd gone to that charity Christmas party, arranged by a young woman she'd met a few times in Moscow. Ilona was a supermodel who had married an English aristocrat. Her origins were Siberian and poverty-stricken; every year she invited celebrity friends and designers to a Christmas party where they could bid on handcrafted items, handbags in the shape of ice floes, Swarovski-donated crystal snow globes, to raise money for poor Siberian children. 'I had to wear fur when I was a little girl, it was so cold!' the model told her guests. 'Now, I would only wear fake fur.'

Alex's mother had hoped meeting the model might translate into a closer friendship, that she'd be invited to dinner at the home the model shared with her distinguished husband. But it hadn't happened.

She heard of a man who had lived in the UK for many years but had made his money from a Russian-based fashion empire. He had bought a historic and beautiful stately home somewhere in Norfolk, the crème de la crème went to his shooting parties. He and his wife had been featured in *Tatler*. From what Kata could gather, his wife was *best friends* with the editor of *Tatler*.

'If I had married someone like this man, instead of someone like Ivan ...' Alex heard her say to Olga, as the two of them sat disconsolate one evening over crispy duck from Hakkasan. She often said such things.

She did have some successes. She began to attend regular coffee mornings with other wealthy women of around her age, women whose husbands were steel magnates, CEOs of chemical giants, had invented indispensable domestic appliances, had banking networks and telecommunications empires. She went to launch parties for jewellery collections, to the openings of shops around Sloane Square; she went to Wimbledon, to the Audi Polo Challenge, she went to charity fundraisers in private homes the size of embassies.

But still.

She would hear her mum complain to Igor, Olga and Sergei, as they all lay on their sofas, late at night after a film, unwilling as yet to rouse themselves.

When would the day come, she would say to them, when she no longer had to jostle? For invitations, for introductions. Why was it so difficult? When would the day come when she could finally ascend? Would it ever happen, would she ever achieve that ultimate goal: when she could sit back, secure in the oncoming clamour? The day when the world, finally, would come to *her*.

Three days after running into Oliver, Alex's phone rang.

'*Hello!*' she said, when she heard the familiar voice. 'Yes, it was so great, running into Oliver. How *are* you? Tell me everything you've been up to. Oliver told me a bit; it sounds so interesting. I'd be fascinated to know more.'

After she put the phone down she had walked downstairs to find Igor and her mum. They were in the kitchen, looking through a lever-arch folder of laminated takeout menus that Magda, the London housekeeper, had put together.

She had sat down on a high stool at the marble island.

'Do you remember,' she said, 'that article you were looking at a few weeks ago, the one about the anniversary of the art foundation in Moscow?'

A shadow crossed Kata's face. 'Yes,' she said.

'Well,' Alex continued, 'I've been doing some thinking and you know, Mama, there's no reason why you shouldn't have something like that. I'm really serious. Why not? A foundation, a museum. Think about it. All you need is one: money to invest; and two: the right team of people to do it for you. That would really put you on the map.'

'Why did we never think of this before?' Igor said.

Her mum was looking from Igor to Alex with a mixture of uncertainty and the first tentative signs of excitement.

She frowned and for a moment the excitement ebbed.

'Do you think Ivan would agree?' she asked.

Igor waved away this question. 'One thing at a time,' he said.

'And you know what,' Alex said, 'if you did want to look into this idea, I know exactly the person you should talk to.'

22

I was to eat my meals in the staff mess while I was on the boat. Natalie, the head stewardess, had told me how to get there. Through the kitchen quarters, down some stairs at the back.

I went through the busy kitchen, found the little staircase. At the bottom of the stairs was a large, low-ceilinged, comfy room. There was a table fixed into the floor, surrounded by a cushioned bench. Sebastian was sitting at the table.

When he saw me he stood up, opened his arms wide and we hugged one another.

'We meet again,' I said.

'Welcome to the madness, honey.'

He looked older, as I'm sure did I. He looked tired.

'It's so good to see you, Sebastian.'

'You too, honey. So good. We gotta find some time to catch up properly. But you've come at a crazy time.'

Above the table there was a single porthole; I could see the pale silver of the sky. It was 7.30 a.m.

There was a pad of paper and a pen where he'd been sitting, an open laptop, a large diary planner.

'Preparations?' I asked.

'Yeah. Never-ending. Kata is stressing like I've never seen. I'm glad she's gone ashore for a couple of days. She's giving me a nervous breakdown.'

We gathered breakfast and coffee and I examined him when we sat back down. He looked chronically tired, as opposed to someone who's had a few hectic days, a few nights of no sleep. His skin looked thin and fragile.

'Vienna!' he said. 'I'm loving your Insta stories. It all looks so olde worlde and chic. And your boyfriend is hot. I wish I was in one place long enough to meet someone.'

'Would you ever consider that, Sebastian?' I asked. 'Doing something else, I mean. Something that would allow you to be in one place for a while. Something where you aren't at the endless beck and call of these people.'

Immediately, I saw him close down. His expression went blank. He stood up from the table, even though he was only halfway through his Nespresso. 'I wish I could have a deep and meaningful convo with you, babe, but I've got way too much to do.'

'OK,' I said. 'Sorry.'

I stared down at the tabletop.

A bright blue copy of C. H. Wright's *Survival at Sea*.

I sat in silence for about a minute, listening to him typing stuff into his laptop. I tried to think of something else to say. I was unwilling to leave on this note.

'It does all seem a bit hectic. Is it really so important, this party?'

'Honey,' he said, without looking up, 'it's the biggest day of her life.'

*

Lessons with Alex were to take place at the very top of the boat, in the room her dad used as a gym when he was on board. It had a running machine, a cross-trainer, weights. The machines had been moved to the side, and a table and two chairs brought in. The walls were glass, we had a 360-degree view of the ocean. The room was high above the main deck.

We were combing *Hamlet*, organising quotes for her to memorise for her English Literature A level exam. 'It's hot in here,' she said.

She stood and picked up a remote that had been resting on one of the machines, pressed a button on it. Black metal blinds came down from the ceiling, blotting out each of the glass windows. She pressed a switch by the door and some lights came on.

'Shall we put the air con on? Not too cold, twenty degrees or something.'

'Yes,' I said. 'Let's.'

She sat back down and opened her copy of *Hamlet* again as the air began to cool. She copied out two more quotes, then laid the book face down and began to talk.

*

For the reunion with Tatiana, her mum had booked a private room for breakfast in a Mayfair hotel. They had gone, the three of them: Kata, Alex and Igor. There was an open fire. The room was half-conservatory, full of green plants with white flowers tumbling off surfaces. The table was covered in silver coffee and tea pots, tiers of pastries and jams and berries, freshly squeezed juices. It was early March and a sharp bite was in the air.

Her mum had seemed nervous, fluttering her fingers towards the breakfast offerings without actually taking anything.

Igor, on the other hand, was full of excitement. 'Finally, I get to meet the famous Tatiana!'

When she arrived the cold of the wind was still in her long blonde hair. She was very smartly dressed. She was holding a briefcase.

'Kata! Alex! I'm so happy to see you both again! So, Kata,' she began, after the requisite amount of gushing small talk had flowed around the table, 'Alex tells me that you are interested in starting to collect art, or something along those lines?'

'Yes ...' Kata said. She looked to Igor. He reached out a hand and gave her shoulder an encouraging squeeze.

'Kata has fabulous taste,' he said to Tatiana.

'I don't doubt it.'

Had Kata been to this museum, to that museum, to this gallery?

Tatiana would show her around. That would be a fun way to start. A bit later, soon really, they could start to think about acquisitions. But it was important first to give Kata an overview. Was she free the day after tomorrow? Would morning suit her?

When Kata got up to go to the bathroom after her second cup of hibiscus tea, Igor had taken the opportunity to talk discreetly to Tatiana about her retainer, her fee.

*

Kata, along with Igor, and sometimes Sergei and Olga, began to see Tatiana two to three times a week. In the mornings Tatiana took them round museums and galleries. In the evenings she took them to private views. The weeks went by and she introduced them to dealers, she took them to dinners, to a gala. More weeks passed and slowly she began to make their presence known. This was an essential step, she told them, before they began to buy anything. You couldn't get everything at auction, and the dealers wouldn't sell to just anyone. They had to know you were serious.

Alex went along, from time to time. An institution had arranged a collectors' tour of some young artists' studios down in southeast London. The car drove them through endless streets where the houses were tiny and plastic bags flapped in front of junky-looking shops. She watched Tatiana at her mum's side, very protective, very solicitous, murmuring explanations in her ear, guiding her, prompting her, introducing her.

In July, Tatiana got Kata and Igor invitations to an exclusive 'happening' organised by a Swiss curator and an elusive and iconic architect. A select group of about two hundred members of the art world Who's Who gathered in Oslo and boarded a convoy of helicopters; they were taken to a glacier where they were the first people in the world to see the unveiling of an ice sculpture. A group of masked figures skated up to the ice sculpture and destroyed it with pickaxes; the reaction of the elite coterie of witnesses was filmed and shown at a biennale.

Occasionally, Alex joined them on their outings. Mostly though, she left Tatiana and her mother together.

She left Tatiana to do her thing, to work her magic. You have a gift, she would sometimes think, observing how Tatiana was with her mother. You can see exactly what it is a person most wants. She remembered the weeks in Monaco. How Tatiana had made her mum feel so included, so much a part of things, taking her here, taking her there. Yes, she thought, looking at Tatiana. You can identify a person's biggest weakness, the need that imprisons them, and then you can satisfy that need, to your own advantage. It's very clever of you, but it's also clever of me, to know that about you. You didn't notice me, watching you, did you? None of you ever did. But I have been. I have been watching you all.

*

All potential avenues were being considered. Acquisition, patronage, sponsorship, donation.

Tatiana said the idea of an art foundation in Moscow was wonderful, and what would be even better would be if the foundation were to have a charitable side. Well, first of all, it could in itself be a charity of sorts, a privately funded collection, a gift to the nation, but also it would be great if it could have a wing or a department that *raised awareness* about something. They brainstormed what it could be. Something to do with children was always good. 'Is there something that particularly afflicts children in Russia today?' Tatiana asked. 'Some disease? Leukaemia!'

They were getting there! They were very excited!

They sat in the living room eating Heston Blumenthal takeout from the Mandarin Oriental.

Alex observed their excitement. It was early December, a light snow spotting the windowpanes.

If Kata decided to go ahead with this idea, Tatiana said, then they should have an event to announce her intentions to the art world. The most important people, gathered in one location, because of her. And then they could get to work on actually making the thing happen. What about if they had the event on the yacht? That would be something! That would stand out!

'And so, here we are,' I said, gesturing at the blacked-out blinds, beyond and beneath which lay the expanse of the main deck, covered in its round tables, staff moving perpetually among them, tweaking, arranging.

'Yes,' said Alex. 'Here we are.'

A chill had gone through me when she had spoken of Tatiana's 'gift'.

I looked at the weights bench. I pictured Ivan lying on it, his sandy hair and impassive face. I imagined his muscles straining as he lifted the weights, his face remaining expressionless.

'And what does your dad make of it all?' I asked Alex.

'Well,' she said. 'That is the *thing*.'

That strange note had come into her voice again.

'What?' I asked.

She shook her head and laughed, she looked down and picked up her copy of *Hamlet*, still shaking her head and laughing slightly as she underlined something with her pencil.

'That,' she repeated, 'is *the whole point*.'

23

One morning, very early on, just a couple of weeks after her mum first started going about with Tatiana, Alex had gone upstairs and knocked on her bedroom door.

Her mum was lying face-up on a massage bed. A woman in a white uniform was sweeping an electrical device in upward strokes from Kata's jawline to her temple.

'Hi, Mama,' Alex said.

The woman lifted the electrical device off Kata's face so that she was able to answer. 'Hi, Chook,' she said.

'So, Papa's coming?'

'Tonight,' Kata said.

Her face was covered in something glistening, some kind of lubricant that allowed the wand to move smoothly.

'How long will he stay for?'

'Just for a few days. Four days, I think.'

'And you'll go out for dinner tonight?'

'Yes.'

'Mama,' Alex said, 'this is just my opinion, but I don't think you should mention to Papa yet your plan for an art foundation.'

'But why?' Kata asked. The wand moved in small circles over her forehead.

'Just because,' Alex said. 'Knowing what he is like ... In my opinion, you should gather all your information first. Wait until later. That way it will be harder for him to say no.'

'Do you think he might say no?' Kata asked.

'I do. You know how he is. About culture and things. Because he doesn't understand it. It's almost like he's, I don't know ... *suspicious* of it.'

She knew exactly what it was that she needed to say.

'Threatened by it, almost. It makes him insecure all that stuff, doesn't it? He might be rude to people if you involve him. Can you imagine him, with those art world people? I don't know, maybe I'm wrong ...'

She watched her mum's face harden. 'Ouch! Be careful!' she snapped at the facialist. A strand of her hair had been pulled by the wand. She batted the wand away and the facialist stepped back two paces.

'If I were you, I would really keep it to yourself for the moment,' Alex said. 'Seriously. It's your best chance.'

*

When her dad had been and gone Alex had waited for the right moment, making sure all of them were there: her mum, Igor, Sergei, Olga and of course Tatiana. They were having dinner together in the dining room, a sushi feast from Nobu.

She'd looked up the table to where Igor was pouring her mum a glass of champagne.

'Are you going to bring Dad into this?' she asked.

Igor, Olga and Sergei all turned to look at her, and so did Tatiana. Olga held her chopsticks in mid-air. Rice festooned with rare eggs; a couple of the orange-coloured eggs fell off.

Kata frowned. 'You said not to.'

'Yes,' Alex said. 'But if you are going to start buying pieces now ... Maybe tell him they are just for the house, or tell him it's a hobby that will also be a good investment. You know how Papa likes to put his money in things over here, to keep it safe.'

She saw her mum purse her lips and stare into the middle

219

distance, embarrassed to have such things mentioned in front of a relative stranger, Tatiana.

'Surely Ivan will have to be informed of this?' Tatiana asked. 'I mean, right now we're just in the planning stages, but once we actually get going I don't see how it would be possible to keep it from him.'

'Yes, at some point we will have to tell him, of course, but I think we should wait until later, there's no need to tell him right now. Mama understands why.'

'Alex is right,' Igor said. 'Later. There will be time later.'

After dinner they had settled in the living room and Alex had been patient. She was sure there would be a point in the evening when she'd be able to get Tatiana alone. The chance might occur naturally; if it did not, she would engineer it.

Half an hour later Tatiana got up from the couch and asked, 'Should I ask Magda to make us tea?'

'Magda has gone to collect from the late-night dry-cleaners,' Igor said.

'Then I'll make it,' Tatiana said.

Alex waited until she'd been out of the room about thirty seconds, then followed her.

She leaned against the marble island and watched Tatiana, watched her slim back as she reached up to a cupboard for the large Fortnum and Mason box that contained an assortment of herbal teas.

'Hello,' she said, taking pleasure in seeing Tatiana, who had not realised she was there, flinch. Her arms raised, the sharp-edged box quivering above her.

'So,' Alex said, when Tatiana had put down the box and turned to face her, 'Mama is going to do all this without telling Papa.'

'That's what you've told her to do,' Tatiana said. 'I'm not part of the family and I don't want to interfere but I have to say, I don't understand why you want her to do that, and I don't see how it's possible for him not to find out.'

'It isn't possible for him not to find out.'

'OK, you've lost me.'

'I want him to find out. I want him to know that Mama is keeping something from him.'

'Well, that's about the craziest thing I've ever heard. Why would you want to do that?'

'I have my reasons. It's too complicated to explain to you.'

'You are putting me in a very delicate position, Alex. What am I supposed to do with this information?'

'You can choose what you do with it. You can tell Mama what I just told you, or you can tell Papa, or you can tell no one.'

'Jesus.'

She poured boiling water into the large aluminium flask.

'If Papa sees Mama doing all this without telling him, he will be very angry with her. You know, with my papa, the most important thing is trust.'

'OK, this is beyond my job description,' Tatiana said. 'We are entering crazy town now. I think it's best we forget we ever had this conversation.'

She left the kitchen, her slender arms supporting the tray.

When Alex rejoined them in the sitting room the conversation was pattering between the grey modular sofas in its usual way. She took her place in her habitual armchair, cream bouclé fashioned like a cloud. Pitter patter. 'Oh and Igor, you were right, the sommelier at Le Gavroche really is ...' Tatiana so at ease, so at home. Perhaps the conversation, just minutes before in the kitchen, had never in fact taken place. Maybe it's all in my head, Alex thought. Maybe, it's just all in my head ...

Whatever its reality, it was evident, in the days and weeks following, that Tatiana had relayed none of it to Kata.

'The question, though, is whether she has told my dad.'

Alex's face was shiny and sticky under the bright lights and my face felt hot and sticky too, despite the air con.

'After all, he's a more valuable prize than my mama. He's the source of the money, and he's more powerful. In fact, Mama is the only person who doesn't seem to realise how powerful he really is.'

'My God, Alex,' I said. 'I've never heard anything like this. What do you think she's going to do? What do you think is going to happen? Why would you do that?'

She shrugged. She looked at me in that new, hard way.

'Who knows?' she said. 'And why not?'

She brought up an arm, danced her hand elegantly in the air before her.

'They always made me feel like I didn't exist.'

'And when you don't exist ...' – she shrugged – 'it doesn't matter what you do.'

24

Kata first met Daniela Shevchenko at Miami Art Basel.

Tatiana had arrived at the London house to travel with Kata to the airport. Kata was still upstairs getting ready, so Alex had waited with Tatiana in the kitchen. Tatiana leaned against the countertop, beneath the cupboard containing the Fortnum and Mason box of teas, just where she had been standing when Alex had let her know exactly what she could do if she wanted to drive a wedge between her mother and father.

They had stood together in the kitchen many times since, alone and with others, and Tatiana had never mentioned what had been said there, and neither had Alex. Sometimes Alex thought Tatiana might simply have disregarded what she had told her; sometimes this thought made her feel relieved. Other times, she looked at her mum, sailing past her down the stairs, or past her in the corridor, head raised, oblivious to anything but her own desires, and she remembered all the ways her mother had negated her in pursuit of her own ends. In such moments she wished Tatiana had taken what she had given her and found a way to use the information to her own cruel advantage.

'Such a shame you aren't coming with us, Lex!'

'Yeah,' Alex replied. 'School, you know.'

'But it's the Christmas holidays.'

'I know, but I have loads of coursework to do.'

'Here she comes!'

The sound of high heels on the stairs. Kata was wearing a black suit and spike heels. Leah, her new assistant, was behind her, holding her passport and a black coat to go over Kata's outfit. She helped her into the coat. It was rustling and complicated, black swirls and cut outs hanging all over the place.

'Bye-bye, Chook.' She stroked Alex's cheek. One of the swirls of her coat caught on the curlicue of a Louis IX console on her way out. Alex watched her hands tremble as she briefly attempted to disentangle it before standing up and allowing Leah to complete the job.

When she returned from Miami, all her nervous apprehension had gone.

Alex was working in the study when the car drew up. She saw her mother get out without even waiting for the driver to open the door. She watched her take the steps with what could almost, but not quite, be described as a bound. She could predict the tone in which her name would be called as soon as her mother entered the house and sure enough, a few seconds later, there it was: 'Lexi! Lexi chook!' She got up, they settled in the sitting room, Leah brought them tea.

Daniela Shevchenko!

Kata had longed to be in her orbit for some time.

Really, she was such an admirer, of both Daniela and her husband Vyktor!

'Look, Lex, here she is.'

She did a Google image search. Alex saw a bland-looking blonde woman, around her mother's age. She seemed to favour tailoring. She was never not wearing a suit jacket, it seemed. Her mother lingered over a photo that showed Daniela with her husband, who was shaking hands with the Duke of Edinburgh against a backdrop of wood panelling. Kata clicked on the image.

Vyktor Shevchenko welcomed into the University of Cambridge's Guild of Benefactors by HRH the Duke of Edinburgh after his £4 million donation towards a formal Ukrainian Studies course. 'This gift ensures that Cambridge will be a dynamic home for the study of Ukraine for generations to come,' said Professor ...

A further photograph showed the Shevchenkos in the company of a Conservative MP. *The British Ukrainian Society secures a parliamentary debate* ...

'What was someone like her doing at a Miami art fair?' Alex asked.

'She is very respected for her collection!' Kata said. 'She bought a Maurizio Cattelan for their house in Geneva! And also look.'

Another news piece: *Daniela Shevchenko instrumental in returning masterpieces of Ukrainian decorative arts to the Ukrainian Folk Museum in Kiev* ...

She had been seated next to Daniela at *the* dinner of the fair and they had got on so well! Candlelight flickering on sculptures, swaying palms, the sound of the ocean ... She had such an air of gravitas, Daniela, such an effortless way of commanding respect. She was so cultured, so intelligent. 'She's like those women, you know, Lex, in Paris back then—'

'The Salonnières,' Alex said.

'Yes, the ladies with the grand salons, she's like one of them, but now, and in fact she is having one of her dinners, next week, at her London house, and she's asked me to go! Really, she's being so helpful, she's said she's very happy to help me think over any ideas I have for my foundation.'

'That all sounds great, Mama,' Alex said. 'I can see why she appeals to you, but isn't there something you're overlooking?'

The news alerts were flashing daily onto her phone. There was no way of ignoring what was happening in Mrs Shevchenko's homeland: the protests that had swept the country for over a month, the revolutionary scale of the movement, the pressure on the Russian-aligned president.

'Is it not bad for Papa for you to be seen with Daniela and her husband?'

'But I already considered that, I'm not as stupid as you think. Papa already knows Vyktor, in fact they have done business together many times, so why would he mind? He's had many meetings with him, even in Moscow. I always wanted him to let us get to know Vyktor and Daniela better, but you know what he's like: business, business, business, and then, when he has time off, barbecues and video games and nothing else.'

Alex had recognised Vyktor from the very first photograph.

The grey bushy hair. He was even wearing the same bright red tie.

'He might have done business with him in the past, but aren't things different now?' said Alex.

'I asked Tatiana what she thought about it and she said it was fine.'

'What would—' Alex began, and then stopped.

Had she actually been about to say: 'What would Tatiana know?'

She shook herself, touched her hand to the sofa. Velvet.

That was the whole point about Tatiana. Her knowingness.

She felt the usual fear.

She looked up at her mother and felt the usual vindication.

This time, however, something else came in their wake. A fatalism. An indifference.

*

Miami had been a success. That's where they'd got the Kandinsky. Tatiana had really prepared the ground for them in the preceding months. People knew they were players, or were going to be, and were willing to sell to them. Tatiana took every opportunity to spread the news of the project in development. They had started buying for it, she said, and they would be looking to buy much, much more. They had got the real VIP treatment. They went to all the big dinners.

They should capitalise on their post-fair visibility, Tatiana said, and try to hold their event as soon as possible. They should gather everyone who counted on the yacht to announce their grand vision: an art foundation in Moscow that also helped out underprivileged kids. The party should nod towards both those aspects, Tatiana said. There should be an exhibition of works, a little taster of things to come, plus some awareness-raising. It could be drinks followed by a sit-down dinner. When the guests first sat down there could be a slideshow about the children, and an expert could speak. Just for ten minutes or something.

A team of event planners were dispatched to the yacht, undergoing its annual maintenance in Monaco. The team came back with a 20:1 model of the boat and Tatiana hired a co-curator for the party.

They already had a few big pieces, bought at the fair and at auction in recent weeks. It would be easy enough for Tatiana to rustle up some accompanying, lesser known but more contemporary works. Maybe from some up-and-coming artists with Russian heritage? It was good to stick to a country or a theme. 'More *cohesive*,' Tatiana said.

They needed one more standout piece, though, something really iconic.

'I know,' Tatiana said. 'How about we ask Daniela?'

*

When the invitation was sent to the printers Kata decided it was time to tell Ivan.

'It's perfect timing, in fact,' she said. 'I can tell him when we're in Moscow for New Year and Christmas.'

They landed on 26 December. The lights from their house made the snow look blue.

Alex knelt on the snow as Kira, old and stiff now, came out to greet her. 'Hello, old sweet thing,' she said, kissing the dog on her head. Her fur was pungent and slightly oily. She saw her dad watching from an upstairs window. He had not come out onto the snow to greet them.

She wanted to study his reaction as Kata told him in the den after dinner, but at the same time she could hardly bear to watch.

She was sitting on her hands, she dug them into the soft flesh of her buttocks as she listened to her mother's bright and artificial tones.

'Oh, by the way, darling, I'm thinking of having a little party towards the end of February, on the boat, just for some of the people I've got to know doing my art things … I've been thinking of setting up a little thing in Moscow, to display some of the paintings I've been buying, to show people. It will mean I have to spend more time here. I think it's important we spend more time together, don't you? But please, my love, there is no need for you to come to the event, it will be very boring for you. Much better you don't come and I'll fly straight to Moscow afterwards.'

When will he say something? Alex found herself thinking, her fingers clutching, her buttocks beginning to numb. She looked up.

Impossible to tell anything. Kira beside him now. His hand on Kira's head, where her own hand had been.

Papa, she thought.

He let Kata finish talking.

'And is there anyone involved I should know about?'

There it was.

She saw her mother look at her, wanting to know what she made of this. But she didn't know. She didn't know.

'Only Tatiana,' Kata said. 'But you know her, she was with us some years ago in Monaco.'

'Yes,' Ivan said. 'I know her.'

The even strokes of his hand across the sleeping dog's head.

'But anyone else, Kata?'

'No,' Kata said. 'I'm not sure what you mean. Just art world people.'

'Just art world people.'

He looked down at Kira. He was stroking her ears. He spread his fingers to gently encircle the whole of the old dog's skull.

'OK, Kata,' he said.

Alex was unable to reply a couple of days later when Kata turned to her and said, 'Well! I think that all went fine! Nothing to worry about!' They were in the back of the car that was taking them to the airfield. She stared at her mother's made-up face, her glossy lips, the grey cashmere swathing her solid form from throat to ankle, and she marvelled that a slab of such single-minded obliviousness could exist in the world, and that the slab happened to be her own mother.

'Good news!' Tatiana said, on their arrival back in London.

Daniela was willing to lend them a Malevich. The astronomical insurance bill wasn't a problem.

25

Kata arrived on board the day before the party.

Alex and I were at the end of our morning lesson. I'd gone out onto the tiny deck area surrounding the gym to get a breath of fresh air while she finished making notes on the Mao years. I held on to the rail and looked down and saw a person in a vast black hat being helped off the tender. Igor, Sergei and Olga were with her.

'Your mum's here,' I said to Alex.

'Oh,' she said. 'OK, I better finish for today then, I need to go down and help her. Come and say hello. She'll want to ask you how our lessons are going.'

Kata removed the hat once she was in the shade. 'Welcome, Melanie,' she said. 'I am sorry for the chaos. I hope you and Alex are managing to find some peaceful time to work.'

I reassured her we were.

'And how have you been, Melanie? You are well?'

'Oh, yes, thank you.'

She seemed much nicer than I remembered.

'I hope you will join us for the dinner tomorrow. We have made a place for you. Not on a table with Alex, I'm afraid. I'm keeping her with me.' She looked at Alex, her gaze filled with what looked like genuine pride. 'But you are on a table with some young people, I hope you will enjoy yourself.'

'Well, thank you.'

'It is our pleasure.'

'This girl,' said Igor, putting his arm around Alex. The years didn't seem to have touched him. He was resplendent in navy-blue deck shoes, brilliant white chinos and an equally brilliant panama hat. 'She's been such a help to her mama, even though she has her exams to study for.'

'I like to help,' Alex said. 'It's possible to study in the morning. I don't need the whole day.'

'She does very well in her studies,' Olga said. 'Hello.' She stepped forward to shake my hand. Her long hair was shorter, it was now a bob, it looked quite chic.

'Melanie, hello,' said Sergei, kissing me on each cheek. He looked immaculate, as he always had done. He exuded a fresh and pleasing scent.

'You have to see the orchids,' said Alex. 'We put the cool-sealed boxes in the storage room but there are a few samples on display downstairs. I can't wait for you to see them. They are so beautiful.'

'I would love that, my darling chook. Thank you for looking after everything while I was gone.'

'We have been on the Fayudel resort,' she said to me. 'We wanted some peace before the madness.'

'Makes sense,' I said.

'OK! Let's go, my girl.'

Alex took her mum's hand and led her off downstairs.

*

In my last weeks in London before moving to Vienna I dated two guys at the same time. One was a couple of years younger than me. He was peaceful and kind, he had a beautifully shaped nose and his skin felt soft and healthy; he was broke, he was a music promoter, he lived in a peeling room in a big flatshare in Finsbury Park. The other guy was late thirties, old Etonian, a fund manager, owned a massive house in Stockwell. He wore a beaded belt he'd bought on safari in Kenya. When I told him I'd never been skiing he repeated my statement in slightly aggressive wonder. 'You've never been skiing??' One night when I suggested he wrap his scarf around his head to protect it from the winter cold he said, 'No thanks, I don't want to look like a *refugee*.' But his ruling-class air was seductive. Waiters, barmen, cinema attendants treated him – and me, by extension – with deference. The knowledge that, were you to be taken permanently under his wing, you might have to contend with his private unpleasantnesses and peccadillos but you would be spared, in return, all wider concerns. I entertained fantasies of being his wife and in those fantasies I saw myself magisterially gentle and filled with infinite largesse towards the precarious of the world, of whom I was no longer one. When I looked down at his balding head between my legs I was filled with sadness and longing for the beautiful Finsbury Park boy, with his skin on my skin, right and simple as two simple animals, but I thought we would be children together, flailing on a stormy little raft, and it couldn't work, it couldn't sustain itself. It was a moot point anyway, because shortly afterwards I left for Vienna, and I never saw either one of them again.

I met Jakob four months after arriving in Vienna. He was sitting in Ellie and Kristof's kitchen pouring coffee from a stovetop espresso maker into a small white cup, his blond hair falling in a curve over his forehead, his blue eyes very tender, even though he'd never seen me before. 'Hi,' he said, looking at me standing there in the kitchen doorway. 'Mel?'

A few days later he came and found me in Café Bräunerhof. It was my favourite café, the one where Thomas Bernhard used to sit and read the newspapers in their wooden holders. I'd been going there for two months and the waiters had finally warmed to me. I loved how imperious the waiters were in Vienna. Many of them had held their posts for twenty years or more, with pensions and paid holidays; the café was their space not mine, it was on me, as newcomer, to learn their ways in order to *earn* their warmth, they had not been extorted, by their bosses, into a fawning servility. Jakob came and found me and drove me up to the vineyards above the city. After drinks we sat for a while in the dusty vines and he pointed out a lizard, a tiny thing, bright orange and blue. We sat together and watched it. When the lizard darted off I looked at Jakob, and I thought, You are beautiful and tender and magical and I like being in your presence, and I want to kiss you just for those reasons, I don't *need* you for anything but I want you, I want to be close to you and feel your skin on mine, and so we kissed and we lay and held each other there in the vines and then we went back to the big white bed in my barely furnished apartment and ever since that night it's been simple between us, it's just been simple. We are together.

The apartment is two rooms: a large room for living and a smaller room for sleeping. Next to the front door there's a kitchen area, with a shower in it and across from that a tiny WC. It's rent-capped and costs 650 euros a month. I earn 1,500 euros a month as a teaching assistant in a kindergarten and I top that up with some adult night classes and the occasional tutoring gig. I signed a five-year lease on the apartment with the option to extend to ten years. If you sign three five-year leases in a row on the same apartment the contract defaults to something called *unbefristet* – unlimited – which means the rental lease is yours, indefinitely, for as long as you want it.

Maybe because I am a foreigner, an outsider, I see it all through rose-tinted glasses, but it does seem like a dream to me, and the texture of the dream is gentle, dignified and kind. In the hot seasons I go to the municipal swimming pools and in the cold seasons to the municipal steam rooms and saunas. In the sauna I get to know other women from my district, we sit naked together. When I first started going they instructed me on the ritual of the *Aufguss*: never leave the sauna in the five minutes after the oil has been poured on the coals. You'll let the hot air out and the people in the sauna will shout at you.

I think back sometimes to my life on that rainy island where the Hunger Games prevailed. When by necessity one's way of being grew from the principle that to find happiness and security you had to get *up*, you had to get *out*. The lie that makes the structure, the structure that turns living into 'hustle', the hustle that takes living from us all.

I bought a wooden bed frame from Ikea and painted it white. A comfortable mattress. Soft sheets. The bed where Jakob and I make love. The sounds from the inner courtyard coming in at dawn, the light curtains blowing in, blowing out. The bed that holds me, the apartment that holds me, the life that holds me, the state that holds me, the photograph of my mother that I put by the side of my bed. She was just a kid when she had me, she was just a kid when my father died. Throughout his long illness she went every day to the hospital to sit by his bed. It was forty minutes away, she did that every day for months, it took him a year and a half to die. She had told me, sitting in front of that Italian café, that his friends had ignored her even at his funeral. 'When I met him, he was everything I'd ever dreamed of,' she said. When she met him she was twenty-two. When he died, holding her hand in a hospital bed in Plymouth, she was twenty-five.

The life that holds me and, in holding me, allows me compassion. Maybe you did the best you could, Mum. I'm sorry I judged you so harshly.

*

I came up from the cabin and on the landing area at the top of the stairs I paused, I stood very still and listened, because I'd heard an odd sound.

I heard it again. It seemed to be coming from my left, where there was an open door.

It was a keening noise.

A sob, followed by a murmur, and this time I could make out the word: '*Mama.*'

I walked on into the room and saw Alex, sitting by the window. '*Mama.*'

Through the window I saw a speedboat receding across the ocean, leaving its widening wake.

I went towards her. I noticed how thin her back was. Her posture was rounded. I could see her shoulder blades pressing against the sumptuous white fabric of her shirt. When I reached her I put my hand on her back and she felt bony and weak and unfit for the world, a prehistoric hatchling, a sad and stunted bird.

She was sitting on a bench, so I knelt down and held her from behind. I put my arms around her. I wanted to hold her. I brought up the sleeve of my shirt to wipe the tears that were pooling around her eyes.

The boat had gone, disappeared over the horizon.

'I *love* my mum.'

She whispered it, but she was vehement. 'I *love* her.'

'I know you do,' I said. 'I know you do.'

'And now something horrible is going to happen to her, and it's because of me.'

'What is going to happen to her? And are you sure it's going to happen? We are none of us as powerful as we think we are.'

'I think it will happen. I think it will happen.'

'What? What will happen?'

I moved my hands to hold her upper arms. I leaned forward and around her, to look at her face. I wanted her to look at me, but she kept her gaze through the window, where the boat carrying her mother had been.

'She always treated me like I didn't exist.'

She got up and walked into the middle of the cabin, where there was a huge bed.

'This cabin will be the cloakroom at the party,' she said. 'This is Mama and Papa's cabin when they are on board.'

'I know,' I said. 'It's the master cabin.'

She got onto the bed, crawled into the middle of it and curled up into a ball.

'I used to lie in between them,' she said, looking at me. She put one thin arm out to her left, another thin arm out to her right. She lay there, thin limbs outstretched into nothing.

26

The mauve and golden orchids were brought from the cold for their one day of glory. They bloomed on the white linen table-cloths, at the centre of the circular tables, surrounded by silver cutlery and long-stemmed glasses. A red carpet was rolled out on the landing dock, flanked by waist-high glass lanterns filled with candles. A flotilla of small speedboats would bring the guests from the Mayaht jetty to the yacht.

The staff had changed into their uniforms for the night: black trousers, pressed white shirts, black bow ties. They were in the kitchen, having their final prep with Sebastian. The curator and her assistant had already arrived and were doing a final check on things downstairs.

The DJ booth had been set up in a corner, near a stage and screen.

I wandered between the tables, glancing at the names on the stiff, propped-up name cards: Martina Santo Brasaccio. Hugo Pierre. Olympia de Pavlos. Prince Casimir of Luxembourg. My short meander through the place cards of some four to five tables took in minor European royalty, the creative director of a fashion magazine notorious for his exuberant polyamory, an international party girl whose aristocratic mother had killed herself by drinking weedkiller, a Condé Nast director known for his social connections and bonhomie, the director of a multi-billion-dollar

French luxury goods brand who was also a heavyweight collector. Kata had done well.

Right up next to the podium was her table, slightly larger than the others, seating twelve. Alex was on here, as was Tatiana; Igor had made the cut, Olga and Sergei had not. I circled it. Who had the honour, then? The director of a cultural institution in London famed for its summer party. A celebrity curator known for his vampiric obsession with youth culture. An aged, formerly subversive rock star who now lived in a stately home and led the local hunt. The Monégasque royals, the jewel in the crown of her evening, the head of the house of Grimaldi and his wife. And seated just to the other side of the prince, Kata's new best friend, Daniela Shevchenko.

I wasn't seated anywhere. One of the guests had brought along a plus-one at the last minute. 'Sorry, honey,' said Sebastian. 'Still, you can go to the drinks.'

*

Tatiana came on board at five o'clock.

The curator's young assistant was chatting with me and Sebastian on the side deck when he got the call – 'Hi, Tatiana,' he said, 'yes, I'll let her know, see you in a minute' – and went off to get his boss. Sebastian finished his cigarette and threw it into the sea before returning to his duties and I sidled down to the back of the boat to watch Tatiana arrive.

She was still beautiful. Her hair was slicked back and her strapless dress was a tight, silver sheath that came down to just beneath her knees. She knew how to wear it, how to move in it. She was supple, even in her high, spiked heels, even as she negotiated the yacht's landing area, climbed the narrow stairs to the deck: she moved *in* the dress. She held herself straight, chin high; I saw the shape of her breasts under the silver skin of her dress and I thought that no other guest coming this evening, none of the famous names, could possibly match her physical perfection.

237

Her lips were moving; she was wearing a headset. As she got closer I heard her saying, 'I'm on the boat now, I'm going down to check in with Evangeline. Yes, bring KoKo over. Why isn't he already here? We want music about half an hour after the guests arrive.'

While she was speaking, she called a waiter over. 'One moment,' she said into the headset. 'Take this downstairs,' she said to the waiter, handing him a folder and some laminated tags. 'To Evangeline!' she snapped, when he looked confused. 'Yes, hello?' she said into her headpiece. 'No, I've got to go, Kata's arriving.'

She removed the headset and walked back towards the landing dock and I heard the purr of a boat and the unmistakable voice of Igor, crying out 'TATEEYA-NA!' She stood there, straight and tall, waiting for them to come up from the dock.

It was an intimidating spectacle, the combination of hard beauty and absolute efficiency. There was a slight breeze but her hair remained slicked back, in place.

A sudden pressure in the small of my back made me jump; it was Alex. 'You look nice,' she said.

'Thanks,' I said. 'You too.'

I meant it. Her face was without make-up, her features were strong.

'Are you feeling OK?' I asked her.

I'd taken her up from the master cabin the day before and put her to bed early. Her eyes looked slightly puffy from the excess of sleep – fourteen hours – but on the whole her youth absorbed it.

'How are you doing?' I asked. 'Do you want to, should we ...' I didn't know what I wanted to suggest. 'Your mum ...' I said.

She laughed and looked to where the others were moving into the interior of the yacht and gathering around the tables. 'Oh, so Tatiana's arrived,' she said. There was no trace of the child in her now. 'Well, let's go and join them,' she said. 'Let's *get this show on the road*.'

*

Kata was clad entirely in black jet. Her dress was a column of black jet with black lace appliqué covering her collarbone and shoulders. Her shoes were black jet. Black stuff sparkled in her ears and on her wrists but I assumed this was not black jet, that it was a substance of higher financial value. She seemed more relaxed, more full of life, more genuinely happy than I remembered ever having seen her.

'You are looking very "cool" my girl,' she said to Alex. 'Not that your mama knows of such things. Melanie, hello, you are looking nice. Come, everyone, let's start our own celebration before the guests arrive and we have to be formal. Sebastian! Bring us two bottles of the champagne and please, come join us too!'

Sebastian popped one of the bottles, Igor popped the other, the bottles were beaded in cold bubbles. We lifted our glasses to one another. I caught Sebastian's eye, his face was one huge smile and mine was too, the DJ had arrived a little while before and at that moment he pumped out a tune for us, some euphoric cheesy beat I'd never heard before but it did the trick.

'And you asked if I would ever do anything else,' Sebastian said, moving closer to me. 'Well, look around you. How could I ever leave this? How could I ever do anything else, now?'

I didn't know what to say, so I said, 'Cheers!' I raised my glass to Sebastian, and then Igor, then Alex, then Sergei, who looked very smart in his suit, it was a beautiful shade of blue. The music drifted out over the ocean; we raised our glasses above the mauve and gold, the tangled beauty of the orchids.

Kata, Igor and Alex danced in a funny little conga. Kata deliberately bumped a hip into Alex and they both laughed.

Sebastian, Sergei and I drifted off to the side. They lit cigarettes. I did not, being within sight of Alex and Kata. The first glass of champagne was making me light, tipsy, ecstatic. The three of us leaned back against the rails to watch the others. They were all still dancing around except for Tatiana, who had moved slightly to one side and was talking into her headset again. She talked into it a bit more then removed it and gave it to one of the young waiters hovering nearby, appeared to give him some

239

instruction. He disappeared to put it somewhere. She had a quick word with one of the waitresses, who nodded and walked away with renewed purpose, she moved towards the dancing circle of the others and retrieved her glass of champagne from the table. I watched her as she began to dance with them, her dance moves were flawless, appropriate, exactly what was required, not stiff at all or awkward, but with no sense of abandonment. I had a sudden flash, a glimpse, of Tatiana's days, her diligent, self-optimising regimen. I saw her waking at dawn to drink a cup of hot water with a slice of lemon, do some yoga stretches, reflect on the day's goals and visualise the day's wins, I pictured her in the gym by seven and blow-dried and ready for action by nine, immaculate, maximised, ready to fully actualise her potential. All this art consulting stuff brought her into contact with some of the world's richest and most influential people, because they hung around the art world like flies on shit, the endless functions that went along with it a great source of recreation for them, guaranteeing as they always did similarly glamorous attendees who were more often than not well dressed and good-looking, aesthetically pleasing locations, nice table decorations, well-curated food, a sense of being with it, in a 'scene'.

The fashion industry offered them something similar; the two often overlapped.

I wondered to what extent all the contacts Tatiana seemed to have cultivated over the years, all the social capital she'd amassed with her sublime appearance and her imperturbable confidence, her discipline – I wondered how much of that had translated itself into actual financial capital, into cold, hard cash. How much did one earn, being an 'art consultant'? To someone like Tatiana, for the world she moved in, nothing, probably, nothing; it was all a means to an end, a long hustle that would have to pay off some day into something permanent and massive, something that could not be argued with, something that would give her ultimate position and leverage, she had made a life that would bring such opportunities within her sphere and she would have to identify one such opportunity, work it in the way she knew how. For the Tatianas of the world, nothing less than billions would do. I felt sick, wondering what was to come. KoKo's euphoric beat distorted in my ears, a slow robotic howl. I held on to the rail at the side of the boat.

Igor, colourful cummerbund stretched across his round belly, was doing a sort of comic shimmy.

'Igor,' Sergei said, 'is the most trivial man I have ever met. But he makes me very happy.' Sebastian smiled. 'And what else is there?' he said. 'To happiness.' He raised his glass.

'Here they are!' I heard Igor cry, and I followed his gaze down the boat. A man carrying a large video camera was emerging over the lip of the steps, followed by a boom operator. A woman brought up the rear, wearing a headset, pointing in the direction of the dancing group.

'Oh my God,' said Sebastian. 'How do I look?'

'Who are they?' I asked him.

'It's the *Royal Borough* crew. I don't know why I'm stressing about how I look. It's not like they're gonna film *us*. But we might show up in the frame!'

'I didn't know Tatiana was still on that.'

'I think she's just back in it for this season. They're gonna film the party.'

Kata clasped her hands together when she saw Tristan, immaculately uniformed as ever, escorting a blonde woman across the deck. I recognised her from googling before Kata said her name: 'Daniela!' Kata had forced her hands back down to her sides, suppressing any visible signs of transport of delight, as was her way. She was measured as she kissed Daniela on each cheek. Daniela was not in a suit jacket in this heat, but her dress maintained the tailored theme in honour of the missing jacket.

I saw her lips moving as she talked to Kata, unable to hear what she was saying above KoKo's relentless beats. She was gesturing at the tables, the flowers, at the resplendence and the glitter, the whole dazzling display. I wondered where her husband Vyktor was today of all days, as Russian flags were raised above buildings in a peninsula in their home country, as armoured personnel carriers rolled in convoy through cities on the shores of the Black Sea.

I looked across the deck, above the tables bearing silverware and fluted glasses and orchids, searching for any sign of that in Daniela's eyes, or in Kata's. I saw Kata stand next to Daniela and both of them smile stiffly into the lens of the video camera that had suddenly swung right in front of them, saw the cameraman raise his hand in a thumbs-up. At the checkpoints blocking passage into Sevastopol it would be cold, the cold of late February when the ground has been petrified for too long, but here it was so mellow, so balmy, too warm for Daniela's suit jacket, too warm for anything but chilled champagne.

Tatiana made a gesture to KoKo the DJ; in the silence that followed, she glanced at the film crew, making sure they were in position, getting it, and then she stepped towards Kata and raised her glass.

'To Kata,' she said. 'To your great success. This is only the beginning.'

Igor whooped. We all raised our glasses. 'To Kata!'

Kata's face was suffused with a pink glow. She waited for us to quieten down. 'Thank you,' she said. Then she raised her own glass. She tried not to look in the direction of the cameras. 'To Tatiana,' she said. 'Who has been my adviser and now, I hope, I feel, is my good friend. None of this would have been possible without you.'

27

I found a good spot to watch the guests as they arrived. I watched boat after boat moor at the landing dock, idle there while uniformed staff helped the occupants onto the red carpet, then speed off again to collect the next group.

They came and they came and they came. Many of them were beautiful. Those who weren't strictly beautiful radiated something else. I saw the woman who directed the London institution famous for its summer party – the hottest ticket in town – come up the stairs. Within seconds, she was surrounded, her cheeks were kissed, she was ushered into some group. She looked in her late fifties. She was wearing a dress that was obviously designer but of a shape that seemed stiff, indifferent to her body. She wore it inattentively, her hair was scraped back in a way that seemed equally inattentive, she wore no make-up.

Some young people came on board, aggressively dressed, heads topped with baseball caps. Despite their defiant clothing they seemed a little unsure of themselves and stuck together. I assumed this was the 'young artists' contingent, maybe the authors of the lesser-known works in the show, and this was their first truly heavyweight art world bash. Some otherworldly female creatures came up the steps after them, dressed in total contrast: basic femme, begowned, long blown-out hair. As they came closer it became clear that parts of their anatomy had been surgically enhanced: lips on that one, nose on that one. I assumed they were models but not high fashion, possibly Victoria's Secret.

Oliver seemed a little out of his element when he arrived. His usual confident bluster was in abeyance; as he stepped off his boat he appeared surprisingly tentative. In that moment there was something of the country bumpkin, provincial, about him, compared to this glamorous, jet-setting bunch. But maybe I'd just imagined that, because he wasn't long off the tender before his name was called, before people shook his hand, men in pastel suits with pomaded hair, even the woman who organised the summer party, and he was chatting away, a picture of ease.

*

The noise of them was deafening. They covered the vast deck as they mingled between the tables. KoKo the DJ was funking his head to his own beats. Guests went up and down the spiral stairs that led to the show. I'd had three glasses of champagne by now. I didn't know a single person and I wasn't a part of this party in any way, but I went among them and looked. At one point I stood at the edge of the deck, looking out over the railing. Alex came and stood beside me.

'Your mum's done well,' I said.

I leaned forward a little over the boat's edge. We were beyond the reef and the water was very dark. I could see the top of the K of the boat's name. Alex was leaning with me. 'Papa bought it for Mama for their tenth wedding anniversary,' she said. 'When I was eight.'

She lifted her hand and when she brought it back down again the champagne flute she was holding, which had been full, was empty. Her face was utterly bereft.

'Alex!' I said, but before I could continue she rolled her eyes and that hard, sardonic look came over her once again. 'I am *going*,' she said, 'to get another glass of *champagne*,' and she threw her empty glass into the sea.

Half an hour later, KoKo the DJ was announcing: 'Ladies and gentlemen! If you'd like to take your seats, dinner is served!'

I stayed on deck, at the edge, as they all sat down. I looked across to Kata's table. Ah, she was ensconced between her royals. Prince Albert really does look like a bumblebee, I thought, he's got such a fat, round head. But where was Alex? She wasn't at her place, at the table. Oh, there she was, approaching it from the other side of the deck, or trying to at least – she was swaying, crazily, she swayed right into another table, two of the people on it had to hold her upright, she pushed their arms off her and continued on her way but then she tripped again and this time she actually fell onto the floor. I stepped forward and as I did so I saw Sebastian approaching swiftly from the direction Alex had come from; he bent and helped her up, he put an arm around her waist and led her back off to the other side of the boat. A few people at tables nearby had seen it but they didn't seem concerned. For the most part everyone at the tables seemed to be having a whale of a time, just chatting and drinking and sparkling and twinkling. Nothing would spoil their evening – they were on a super yacht! In the Maldives!

I tracked Alex and Sebastian down to the small staff deck, beyond the kitchens. Alex was sitting on the floor, with Sebastian next to her. Her eyes were closed and she was holding a cup of black coffee. 'Have another sip, honey,' Sebastian said gently. There was a glass of water next to her and a chunk of bread on a side plate.

Sebastian looked up at me and shook his head. 'I'll see you in a little bit, honey,' he said, softly. 'She just needs a bit of time out.'

When Alex heard Sebastian, she opened her eyes and looked up. She struggled to focus. 'Oh, hey, Mel,' she said and smiled weakly before closing her eyes again.

*

At the after-dinner speeches a woman was speaking into a microphone on the stage while on the screen behind her images flashed up of thin children with huge, sad eyes, huddled together, dressed in rags. The previously convivial room had quietened down into an appropriately pensive hush. The woman gestured towards Kata and the boat broke into applause. Kata acknowledged the applause by bowing her head and keeping it bowed for a long time. Images filled the screen again. A digital rendering of a vast, modern cube; the walls of the cube came apart and moved all over the screen and we were zooming inside, to see partition walls with paintings hanging on them, sculptures and installation rooms full of flickering lightscapes and people wandering through the rooms, pointing and gasping in awe, and small children all ragged and uncertain-looking being led in, then sitting cross-legged on the floor and drawing stuff with crayons and suddenly they are beaming and happy and we know: their future is assured, they are going to be *just fine*, they are saved, everyone here tonight has saved them!

Dessert had been whole poached pears, upright, covered in a dark chocolate and Louis Royer cognac sauce.

'There's plenty extra,' Sebastian had said earlier. 'Come and join us in the mess, we're gonna have our own feast,' but I hadn't, I'd stayed put, out here, on the side of the deck on my little perch, watching it all.

Towards the end of the main course I'd seen Alex re-emerge, she had come across the boat to her mother's table, steady on her feet now, sober. She had sat down and as she did I saw Kata beam with delight and immediately introduce her royal companions – 'My beautiful daughter,' I could imagine her saying. 'My pride and joy.'

The images on the big screen disappeared and it went white again; the woman's speech had come to an end. Applause broke out once more all over the boat. 'Thank you, thank you,' the woman was saying, 'for being here tonight, at the start of this journey, and now, finally, before the dancing begins' – she gestured towards KoKo the DJ, who had a black goatee and was wearing a black fedora hat – 'please will you join me in a round of applause in welcoming to the stage the woman herself, I'm in awe of her generosity ...'

Kata gathered herself up and made her way to the stage. The long black snout of the video camera followed her. As she passed Alex she reached down a hand and Alex reached up hers. They squeezed each other. Kata climbed the few stairs to the stage, the overhead lights bounced and glittered off the jet of her outfit. When she got to the microphone she turned around.

'Thank you,' she said. Her voice was breathless, tremulous, shaking with emotion. 'Thank you all, so, so much, for coming ...'

I glanced down through the railings, out to sea, and saw the speedboat approaching.

28

I followed the railings down to the rear of the boat in time to see them disembark. I stood at the end of the deck, looking down at the landing dock.

When Ivan stepped from the speedboat into the lights of the dock, I saw he was dressed casually, in jeans, T-shirt and trainers. Vova was holding something in his hand that looked like a laminate folder or pouch. Anton had what looked like a small overnight case. Once they were all on the boat they stood for some moments, in a circle. Ivan looked at his watch and Vova got out his phone, but then there was the sound of a door opening and Vova put his phone away. Tap, tap, tap, on the wood of the landing dock. High heels. I saw the top of her golden head as it passed beneath the railings.

She went to the circle of men. She talked and they nodded. I saw her take the laminate folder from Vova, examine its contents, then give it back to him. She pointed towards the doorway she had come through, the staff door on the landing dock that led into the engine room and on into the crew mess. The men exchanged a few more words with their boss and then left, and they were alone together, Ivan and Tatiana.

I looked down at them, her blonde head, his dark head, close together. Were they touching? Not at that moment. I waited for them to touch. I wanted to see it. Her slim body in its silver sheath of a dress. She was taller than him, in her high heels. I waited to see his big hand come down to the small of her back, to take residence just above the swell of her buttocks, on the silver skein of her dress. But then she was retreating, to the staff door Anton and Vova had gone through, and he was walking towards the stairs that led up to the main deck, where I was.

I moved back to the very edge of the boat, the opposite side from where the steps would deliver him. I waited and then watched as he reached the deck and paused, to look ahead of him, to take it all in, the whole extravagant scene.

He was not conspicuous. His casual attire marked him out from the other guests, but he could easily have been some non-uniformed lackey, about his business, seeing to something; some kind of sub-engineer who doubled as a plumber, off to check on a blockage in one of the bathroom sinks. He began to walk up the side of the boat and I mirrored his progress, the tables of revellers between us.

Kata was still up on the stage, talking. She was thanking a list of individuals. 'Lucien de Prouvée, for all of your advice ...' She gestured towards him, the silver-haired owner of an auction house; he bowed his head in response.

Ivan stopped about ten metres from the stage. He leaned back against the railings, crossed his arms over his chest and watched her.

There was movement from one of the tables. It was Alex, standing, staring in the direction of her dad but then turning to walk the opposite way, towards me, head down and moving swiftly; she came out from the light and bustle of the tables to join me in the shadows, where I sat, on the lip of the deck.

'Oh ...' she said. Her breathing was quick and ragged. She fumbled for my forearm and when she found it she squeezed it with both of her hands. She looked at her mum, still up on the stage, and then to her dad, leaning against the railings, watching her.

Tatiana came out of the doors that led into the kitchen area, on Ivan's side of the boat. She resumed her seat.

I didn't want to tell Alex that I had seen her dad and Tatiana together. It all felt so horrible, as if some malevolent force was gathering around Kata, and I was remembering Alex at the window of the cabin, saying, 'Mama, Mama.' I didn't want her to know anything, because maybe nothing would really happen. But the very fact that Ivan was here and Tatiana had known he was coming meant that something was going to happen.

There was a sudden sharp pain in my side as Alex jerked her elbow into me. 'Ow!' I said, and she was leaning against me, lolling as if drunk, her lips were to my ear and she was whispering, in a strange voice that made me shudder: 'I wonder when she told him! I wonder how she did it!'

Kata was thanking person after person. We watched him watch her, thanking so many people, all these people, everyone except him.

All the layers she wore to protect herself, the pouting hauteur, the raised chin, the slowness of gesture, had fallen away. She stood in naked happiness. Seen and accepted at last.

Ivan began to walk towards her.

The stage was reached by means of three steps on its left-hand side. I suppose you could jump onto it, if you were agile, but the measured way to access it was to climb up the three steps. Ivan climbed up the three steps. When Kata saw him, she stopped speaking. The hand holding the microphone stayed where it was. He took the microphone from her. She stayed where she was on the stage, mouth open, hand open where the microphone had been.

'Hello, hello,' he said into the microphone, as if to test it. 'Good evening.'

There were some murmurs here and there from the watching occupants of the round tables, but they quietened within a few seconds. They sat looking at him, waiting to hear what he had to say. Just another speaker, another after-dinner speech.

'I am the owner of this boat,' he said. 'Everything you have enjoyed over the last few days has been paid for by me. The paintings you saw downstairs have been paid for by me. The meal you have just eaten was paid for by me.'

He cleared his throat and reached up a hand to scratch his beard. He had a light, sandy-coloured beard, short and neat.

'Get off my boat,' he said. 'Now. I've given instructions to Mayaht, they are sending over your taxis. Please form a queue.' He pointed in the direction of the landing dock.

No one responded. The guests sat where they were. There was complete silence.

The TV camera swivelled steadily, back and forth.

'Get off,' he said. 'Stand up and form a queue over there. Come on, get up, over there, go on, go and queue, six to a boat, I think.

'Get off,' he said again, when no one moved, when they just sat there, staring at him. He didn't say it angrily, or aggressively. He was mild. He rubbed his neat sandy beard again. 'Get off.'

The people at a couple of the tables in the middle began to stand. I saw them exchanging glances, the women gathering up their handbags. This seemed to break the general paralysis because the other tables began to do the same, and then, instead of silence, there was a swell of murmurs, the sound of many voices.

Kata had not moved. Her arm was still only halfway down, where it had been when Ivan took the microphone from her. She was watching them all get up, start to leave. The whole party breaking up, over. More and more people stood to go. Her head and eyes moved in the direction of each new table as the occupants rose. Her left hand rose, and then both her arms were reaching, it seemed to me they were reaching to plead, to pull all the leaving people back, but she must have known the futility of the gesture because a few seconds later both arms sank limply, to hang defeated by her side.

*

Within seconds, the noise was deafening. They were all standing now, leaving their tables, milling in the direction of the landing dock. I saw many of them turn their heads to look back at Kata, raised and in full sight of everyone, motionless on the stage. None of them went up to her. They just looked at her and talked among themselves. I heard the sound of laughter coming from different places in the crowd, swelling from here and there, and I saw people raising their phones to take photos of her. I'd seen some of them filming Ivan's speech. They're going to have the party of their lives when they get back to Mayaht, I thought. I saw one of the young artists contingent pour himself out a last glass of champagne and down it before moving away from his table, grinning and laughing and chatting with the people next to him. There really were a lot of people, their numbers were more evident when they were standing than when they had been sitting.

It took a long time for them to go. Six to a boat. It seemed to me they inched their way down towards the landing dock, never ceasing in their noise, their chatter. I even saw one of them, a guy, beckon a waiter, ask him something; the waiter looked hesitant and shook his head; I saw the guy insist; the waiter looked around him, walked off towards a table near the edge of the boat and brought the man the bottle of champagne that had been sitting on it, and three glasses.

I saw Daniela rise to leave with everyone else, reaching for her pale leather clutch before she was approached and apprehended by Vova. She returned her clutch to the table. With Vova's hand on her shoulder, she sat back down.

29

Alex stared straight ahead. She turned to me. 'Hmm?' she said, even though I hadn't said anything.

Sergei had gone up onto the podium, he was next to Kata, holding her. He was rubbing her back, he pulled her to him and kissed the side of her head.

Igor and Olga were mute and staring. They stared at Ivan as he came to take a seat at the main table, next to Tatiana. She leaned towards him and said something in an undertone, to which he nodded. He said a few words in reply. The proximity of their heads, bowed towards one another. Oliver was watching her, from across the table. I tried to read his response. Tatiana, Ivan. I thought I did detect some discomfort, but it was hard to tell with a man like Oliver. Tatiana said to Vova, at the opposite end of the table beside a silent Daniela: 'Vova, the documents?'

Vova stood to hand Tatiana the laminate folder. He sat back down and started doing something on his phone. From the way he was moving his finger around, it looked like he was playing a game.

'Come and sit down,' Ivan said. He said it to Kata and Sergei, still up there on the stage.

I moved closer, to a nearby table, passing behind Vova and Daniela as I went. I saw that Vova was in fact playing a game. It looked like a recent iteration of Tetris. 'Shit,' he said, as he moved a block into the wrong place.

Sergei was still holding on to Kata. He led her down off the stage and to the table.

'What you have done is very cruel, Ivan,' he said. He had moved his chair close to Kata's and he had his arm around her still. I loved him in that moment. Quiet, unobtrusive Sergei. Actually showing some compassion, some thought for a person other than himself.

Ivan pulled the sheaf of documents from the laminate folder and as he did so I looked up and beyond him for a moment and saw Alex, a few paces behind him, leaning against a post that had been decorated for the party with festive strips of white material, a sort of pale maypole.

'OK,' said Ivan. He examined the documents in his hand. He had put on some glasses. They were rimless, they sat a little way down his nose. 'Please,' he said, as he handed the documents to Igor. He was indicating that Igor should pass the documents down the table to Kata. Igor took the documents, glanced at the top leaf, hesitated. 'Please,' Ivan said again. Igor held them out to Kata. She didn't take them. Sergei did. 'You will need your lawyer to look over them,' Ivan said. 'And then he can contact my lawyer. The details are all there, there shouldn't be a problem.'

He seemed weary, he yawned, he rubbed his sandy beard.

'I have filed in Moscow already, that's where the case will be heard.'

Oliver's brow had furrowed, the air of discomfort around him increased. He lowered his eyes to stare rigidly at the tabletop. It occurred to me that he and Tatiana were the only people present who did not understand Russian.

'Maybe I could have overlooked the fact that you wanted to keep all this from me,' he said, waving his arm to indicate the tables, the glasses, the detritus of the night's festivities. 'Maybe I could have put up with you thinking of me as a pig from Ingushetia not good enough to mix with all your fancy new friends. Maybe. Maybe not. But Daniela, Kata?'

Kata's big staring eyes swivelled towards her new friend. Daniela had closed her eyes. I had not looked in her direction for a while. She was sitting very straight, in her well-cut dress, head bowed. She looked demure, composed, but for the closed eyes, the ashen face, the tendons in her arms raised from the clenching of her hands in her lap.

'Daniela?' Ivan said again. 'Do you have no conception, Kata, of what is happening at the moment?'

'But I thought,' Kata said. 'I thought ...'

'Thinking has never been your strength, dumb cunt,' he said.

A cry escaped Olga at the ugly words; she brought her hands up to her mouth in fear, as if to take back the sound, but Ivan didn't even look at her.

'They were playing both sides. Weren't you, Daniela? Waiting to see which way the wind would blow. Well, you know which way now, don't you, Daniela? In about' – he consulted his watch – 'five hours, that little peninsula will no longer have a parliament. We've been talking with Vyktor, Daniela. Just a little business meeting, let's say. We took him on a little boat trip from Kerch.' He laughed. 'She looks like she's about to shit herself,' he said, to the table at large.

'Relax,' he said. 'Now he knows how things are going, he's staying on the right side. Why wouldn't he? He's made enough money from us from that pipeline.'

A change was coming over Ivan's face. Bands of tension were hardening his cheeks. He was in the grip of something, and it was frightening to see.

'She was using you, Kata. It was useful for her to be seen with you, photographed with you. You thought it would keep the heat off you from our side, didn't you, Daniela? While you and your husband came to a decision at your leisure? To make money in a country you have to be on the winning side.

'It all comes down to money. When will you realise that, dumb cunt? You think I'm not good enough for any of the people you mix with, but the only reason any of them want to be close to you is to get close to my money.

'Did you think Tatiana was your great friend? Maybe you would be interested to know that both Tatiana and Oliver have been working for me for some time.'

Oliver and Tatiana, recognising their names if nothing else, exchanged glances.

'They are doing what the English do best. Making money from people who have more money. Useful parasites. Oliver's been doing some washing for me and Tatiana's been doing some spying. She told Oliver as soon as she started working for you exactly what your plans were and I paid her a very generous fee to keep an eye on you. It has been useful to keep Daniela close, but that doesn't change the fact that you kept it from me, Kata, and for all you knew it could have put me in a very bad position, but you don't care about the position I am put in, do you, bitch, and you don't know anything at all.'

He waited, after delivering this, but there was no response from Kata. I looked at her, sheathed in Sergei's kind and steady arms, looking towards her husband, her face still blank, as it had been since the moment Ivan had taken the microphone from her. When would the shock wear off? I wondered if she even heard what he was telling her.

He repeated himself: 'Your great friend Tatiana. Can you hear me, Kata? Hello? Is there anything in there? Your great friend Daniela. Yes, they really liked you so much, didn't they?

'Did you think anyone here tonight cared for you? You bought them, that's all. Everyone can be bought.'

Vova had laid his phone down to listen without exiting his game. The device squawked panicked bleeps as blocks and cubes and columns piled towards the top of the frame.

'Turn that piece of shit off,' Ivan said.

I thought of what Alex had told me, how those Moscow boys at the university had made him feel, how he'd squeezed the ball inside himself to revel in its pain, and I thought, He's squeezing the ball now, and in remembering that it was Alex who had told me those things, I remembered Alex herself, and it came full upon me, that he was saying all this, enacting this humiliation, all in front of her, his daughter, his own child.

I looked to find her. She was still there, leaning against her post.

I heard the sound of a howl, a loud and senseless noise, and I saw the noise was coming from Kata's mouth.

So here it was, finally, some kind of reaction, a voice to her pain but as I turned back one last time – I'm coming, Alex – I saw it was not Ivan she was looking at, as she howled her betrayal. She was looking at her dear friends, at Tatiana and then at Daniela, the girls, the ones she thought had welcomed and accepted her at last.

I went to Alex and raised her from the floor, to take her away from it all.

None of them noticed us go.

*

Alex went straight to her bedside cabinet. She got a foil packet and cracked out one pill, two pills, three. 'Wait, Alex, wait,' I said, I held down her arm and examined the packet – Zolpidem, 7 mg – 'that's too high a dosage to take three, Alex, please don't take three.' She went limp, I released her arm and as soon as she was freed she scooped up all three pills and put them in her mouth. 'I've taken three before,' she said, her voice thick and distorted by the pills sitting on her tongue, pushing me away as I went towards her. She picked up the glass of water on her bedside cabinet and swallowed. She got into her bed without undressing and pulled the duvet over her. 'Please,' I heard her say. 'Turn out the lights.'

The hump of her body on the bed, covered by the duvet. I picked up the foil packet and hid it under my pillow and then I switched off the light on her bedside table. I switched off the light on mine.

It seemed dark at first. But the lights from the boat's exterior crept round the edges of the blind and after a while a dim yellowish tint infused the dark and made visible the beds, the cupboards, the cabinets, the walls.

I got onto my bed. I just lay there.

There was a great, clanging shudder. The whole bed seemed to dip right down and then rise, to sway back and forth before juddering into a more settled position. Someone must have given instructions to the captain: we were moving. I shifted and pulled the duvet over me.

We were moving through the ocean, clouds of diesel smoke spewing into the atmosphere behind us.

To think that I had imagined anything erotic between Ivan and Tatiana. I recalled Tatiana's demeanour at the table as she had witnessed Kata's howl. She had not looked triumphant. Nor had she expressed regret or tried to comfort Kata. She had looked at the slim watch on her wrist. Today's job done, she probably felt it was time she went to bed, to get her requisite hours of sleep, sleep not as an epicurean pleasure but as a necessity to optimise her for the next day's tasks. Oliver had looked uncomfortable, the kind of English man who cannot bear a scene.

No, there was nothing bodily. There was blood, there were bodies, but they were out of sight and far away, in a different time zone and a different climate.

All libidinal energy had been channelled into something else. An endless hunger, eating insensately on.

On and on. What could ever halt this boundless growth?

What rupture?

And if not rupture, what small gesture? Done by one, and then another. Millions of tiny gestures that, together, might bring about some new reality, a collective expansion of consciousness. I felt heavy and swooning, as if I had taken some of Alex's sleeping pills.

The boat was moving relentlessly forward, churning its gallons, and elsewhere the ocean was burning, and continents were burning and we had almost run out of places to burn.

I felt the boat move me through space even though my body was not moving. I heard Alex's loud narcotic breathing. She had flung off the duvet, she lay on her back, mouth open.

I lay a long time, until there was another jolt, and a dying away of sound: the boat was stopping.

And then, sometime later, a loud knocking, knock, knock, knock, on the cabin door.

30

The door opened to Sebastian. 'Come out,' he whispered.

He looked at Alex's bed. The duvet had slid down, she was on her back, asleep. 'Shh,' Sebastian said. Light was shining in from the corridor. I got out of bed. Sebastian went into the bathroom, then opened the cupboards in the bedroom. When he joined me out in the corridor I asked, 'What's going on?'

In a low voice he said, 'Kata's disappeared.'

'Disappeared?' I repeated, stupidly. 'What do you mean? How could she disappear?'

'About fifteen minutes ago Tristan went to take them back to Fayudel on the tender. Olga and the guys were still on the deck, they said Kata had gone to the bathroom. Tristan went to look but couldn't find her. Now we're all looking.'

I checked his phone and saw that it was just after 1 a.m. 'There are lots of places she could be,' I said. 'The boat's huge.' Sebastian nodded. 'We're looking. Come on,' he said, and started walking down the corridor away from the cabin, towards the central stairwell.

'Where do you want me to look?' I asked, as I followed him up the stairs.

'I don't know. Everywhere. Just look everywhere. Even places that seem stupid. She's had a lot to drink, according to the guys. She's probably passed out somewhere weird.'

'OK.'

We reached the top of the stairs and he kept going, towards the front of the boat. 'Just give me one minute,' I called after him. 'I'm going to grab a coffee.'

The huge kitchens were still full of people, the boat's full-time chef, two extra chefs who'd been hired for the event and their battalion of sous chefs; they were washing up, rubbing down surfaces. I weaved my way through them and headed down the steps to the staff mess. I went to the Nespresso machine. As the machine whirred into action I heard footsteps on the stairs behind me and when I turned around I saw that it was Anton.

'Hi,' I mumbled, whipping my head back round to face the coffee machine.

'Hello,' he said, and came to stand right next to me, so close I could smell him; he still wore the same cologne. I saw his bony hands tap on the countertop.

'Would you like a coffee?' I asked him.

'Please,' he replied. I handed him the first coffee and started to make another for myself. He leaned back against the counter, took a small swig of his coffee. My heart had skipped around when I'd turned and seen it was him coming down the stairs.

'I heard the guys can't find Kata,' I said. 'I'm just going to drink this and then I'll help them look.' I poured some cold water from the water cooler into my coffee so that I could drink it quicker. I downed half the cup.

He hadn't responded to my statement. He leaned against the counter, staring into his coffee. He drank it, then put the cup down.

'For the last half-hour I have looked for her,' he said. He shook his head. 'She has gone.'

I stood where I was. He met my eyes. He looked frightened.

'What do you mean, *gone*? The boat's massive.' I spread my arms out wide. 'It's huge! There are loads of places she could be!'

He shook his head.

He walked over to the table and lowered himself onto the bench. He leaned back and closed his eyes.

'So, you're not even going to look?'

'I have looked.'

My coffee was finished, I had drunk it all, I was alive with it.

'Well, I am going to,' I said. 'I am going to look.'

'Good luck.'

I went up the stairs and back through the kitchens. Out in the atrium I paused. I went down the central stairs to the floor I knew contained the most guest cabins, to the rear of the boat.

I opened the first door. I saw two twin beds, unmade, large bottles of mineral water half drunk on the cabinet between them, a suitcase with clothes spilling out. I stepped further into the room, I looked in the bathroom, I opened cupboards. I went back out into the corridor and approached the next door. The same scene met me again and did so for the next few cabins. Senior members of the party crew must have been housed down here. A large pair of headphones on a bed in one cabin marked it as KoKo's. Where was KoKo the DJ? Was he searching as well? When I'd looked in every cabin, I went back up the corridor towards the stairs.

I went up and out, onto the outer strip of deck that ran all the way along the side of the boat. There was an identical deck below. Looking down I saw Natalie, the chief stewardess, also searching.

The water near the boat was lit up by lights. Beyond that, dark water, all the water of all the oceans.

Seventy per cent of the earth's surface.

I went down the stairs to the landing dock and through the small door into the engine room. The boat was stationary but there was still such a rattling and clanging down here, such a high killing noise and so many pipes interlacing and interlocking, so much metal, such a vast machine. The main engine room led to smaller engine rooms, I looked in these too.

At the prow of the boat was the exhibition room. I tried the door but it was locked, presumably because of the valuables within. I rattled the door several times and pushed, and it occurred to me that of course Kata would have access to this room, that maybe she'd locked herself inside. In a lull between my rattling and pushing I heard footsteps on the other side of the locked door coming closer. I waited for the door to open but it was only Natalie.

There was a stretch of corridor beyond the internal stairwell and through there were the staff cabins. It was cramped and warrenlike down here. I checked inside the first cabin, a small room with a bunk bed. There were staff moving back and forth through the rooms. Through an open door I saw Tristan, the first mate, brushing his teeth in a bathroom with his smart uniform unbuttoned at the neck and looking bleary-eyed, and I wasn't sure if he was starting or finishing a shift. I knew there was no point in looking down here as there were so many people around; if there was anything to see they'd have seen it.

I went back to my cabin, mine and Alex's. I opened the door and stood there on the threshold. She was still in bed; asleep, by the sound of her breathing. Still on her back, in the same position as before.

There were so many stairs in this boat. It must plunge down so far beneath the sea. I walked up some stairs again. Here was the master suite that had been turned into a cloakroom for the party; here the window alcove where I'd come upon Alex, sitting and watching the speedboat carrying her mother, watching it cut away across the sea.

I had stood exactly here, just inside the door, watching her watching it, the boat that was going away.

'*Mama.*'

When would Alex wake up? Would we let her sleep through until morning?

Maybe by the time she woke up we would have found her mum.

Just across the hall, the vast space where the party had taken place was empty. I wondered where Olga and Igor and Sergei were, where Oliver and Tatiana had gone. The table they'd been sitting at with Kata had not yet been cleared, it still held plates from the dinner, glasses, the orchids now dead. I sat down at the table in Kata's place.

She sat here during her party looking back and forth in girlish expectation. Nervous and skittish. Tremulous. Trying to hide her desires behind an aspect of impassivity, big lips pressed down, but not succeeding in hiding them. Never succeeding, not remotely. She could appear mannered and posed, a monolith of affectation and greed. At the same time, she was wide open, so open as to make you cry for her, want to cover her, want to shield her. It was that nakedness. The helplessness, wearing her hopes for all to see and squash. Hostage. This is not where any of us would have wanted things to end up. I kept my gaze on the tabletop because it was as if Kata was still up there, on the stage. If you could pity her, you could pity everyone. When she stood up on that stage, all she had wanted was to be loved.

*

Once again, it was Sebastian who jolted me from reverie. 'There you are!' He'd banged through the door leading from the centre of the boat. 'Is Alex with you?'

'No. She's sleeping.'

'She isn't sleeping,' he said. 'She's not in the cabin, I just checked. I thought she must be with you.'

We looked at each other, mouths open slightly, unable for a moment to comprehend the situation we found ourselves in. This was becoming nightmarish. This was becoming farce. I stood up. 'OK,' I said. 'There are lots of places she could be. Maybe she went to the kitchens to get a snack. There are lots of places she could be,' I said again, repeating the words I'd said about Kata, they echoed back to me, and I suddenly wondered if I was even awake, maybe I was still down there in the cabin, this all had the repetitive nonsensical logic of a dream.

Sebastian was shaking his head. 'I've looked there,' he began, and then broke off, as if aware of his repetition too. He stood in silence for some seconds. 'OK,' he said, 'fuck it, let's look again then.' I followed him across the deck and down the steps, plodding behind him, grinding down into the stairs at each step. My legs were heavy, the coffee was wearing off, I was a centre of gravity, so heavy I would sink this whole boat to the bottom of the sea, I could feel it sinking with each step I took.

The same army of chefs and helpers were in the kitchen, doing the same things, scrubbing, soaking. Down and through we went again, opening cabin doors, down through the interlacing engine rooms with their networks of pipes and winking electrical points, the heavy grinding noise of machinery. Along corridors inside the boat, along decks that ran down its sides. We went into the navigation room and asked the captain if he'd seen anything. 'No, mate,' he said, and we saw him exchange a glance with Tristan, back on shift. 'You've got to be fucking joking,' he said. He was already working with the coastguard, the huge security lights around the edge of the boat were blazing outwards and illuminating the sea in a circumference of some fifty metres. He shook his head, looking back at Tristan. As we left I heard the words 'fucking shambles'.

I followed Sebastian down more steps, along the side of the boat and then into the central atrium and towards the master cabin. Instead of going into the master cabin he stopped in the small hallway and opened a door to the left. 'Oh! Is that not a cupboard? I always thought it was a cupboard!' Clearly it wasn't a cupboard because now we were in another, slimmer corridor and descending yet more steps. 'But I never knew about this place!' I said. 'Maybe Kata's down here!'

'No, I checked,' he said, and then he held up a hand to indicate that I should be quiet.

I couldn't hear anything. I shook my head at him but he raised a finger, cocked his head and then it came, floating up from below: a thin sing-song.

We rushed down the steps and there, sitting at the bottom, was Alex.

Sebastian turned back to look at me and said, 'Thank God,' and started laughing. I was laughing too, I wanted to reach out my hand and touch Sebastian, hug him.

Alex sat in the small atrium at the bottom of the stairs with her back against a door.

'Sebastian,' I said, 'Sebastian,' I reached out my hand to grab his elbow and point, 'Look,' but he'd seen it too, because he was kneeling on the floor next to Alex and saying, very gently, 'Oh, Alex, sweetheart, what have you done to yourself?'

She had pulled her trousers up to her knees and her naked shins were covered in blood.

'Huh?' she said, looking down at herself. Then she looked up again and jerked her head towards the door behind her.

'Hey,' she said, 'they are fucking in there.' She laughed. 'They are *fucking* in there,' she said.

Sebastian looked at me, then he turned back to Alex and I heard him shushing her: 'Shh, Shh.'

'Tatiana and Papa. They are fucking in there.'

'Tatiana left the boat hours ago, darling,' Sebastian said. 'I saw her go with Oliver, she went on the tender.'

'"I did it,' she said. 'They are fucking in there, my dad is fucking Tatiana.'

Without making the conscious decision to do it I found I was opening the doors that led off this tiny corridor, this corridor I hadn't known existed. There were three doors, minus the one Alex was leaning against; I opened them and dumbly took in neat, empty cabins, made-up, queen-sized beds. I checked in each of their ensuites: nothing. When I came out of the last one, Sebastian was still sitting with Alex but he was looking back and up, to the top of the stairs we had come down. I followed his gaze and saw that Anton was standing there. Alex looked up at him too and repeated what she had said to us: 'They are fucking in there and I did it,' and she jerked her head again, in the exact same way as before, behind her, indicating the door she was leaning against.

Anton began coming down the stairs.

'Hey,' I said, 'hey, hey, wait—'

'It's OK, Mel,' Sebastian said. 'Mel,' he repeated, 'it's OK.'

Anton reached us at the bottom of the stairs and in one fluid motion he bent and gently picked Alex up. In the space where her body had been we saw the slim, soaked kitchen knife.

From within Anton's arms, Alex pointed back at the door and jerked her head again, this time without saying anything.

'We will take her to the hospital at Male,' Anton said. 'It's the closest place, it will take us half an hour in the tender. Come on.' He turned in the direction of the stairs.

'Has anyone checked in there?' I said. 'In there.' I pointed at the door Alex had been leaning against. 'For Kata!'

No one said anything.

'Ivan is in there.'

'But has anyone actually checked? It's the only place on the whole boat that hasn't been checked, isn't it?'

'Where else could she be?'

Anton looked at me and sighed.

'They might be in there, together,' I said.

Alex jerked her head again. '*Fucking*,' she said, but softer this time.

'Who is going to look in there?' I asked.

Still none of us moved. Anton looked towards the door. He made a half-move towards it and then stopped. Sebastian and I were watching him. He knew we were watching him, he made a half-move again, as if to lower Alex onto one of the stairs so that he would be free to go and look in the cabin, but then he stopped, stood still, and I realised that he was too scared to go in.

Sebastian spoke. 'I'll go, I'll go,' he said. He spoke quickly. I wanted to hold both Sebastian and Anton to me. I wanted to stand in a ring with them and hold their hands. Neither Sebastian nor I wanted Anton to see us witnessing his fear. It was OK for us to think of Anton and Ivan as equals, buddies. We wanted him to know that it was OK for us.

'I'll do it,' said Sebastian.

'Thank you,' Anton said. He began to move away and up the stairs with Alex. I wanted to go with them but of course I wanted to see inside the room more. I had to see inside the room, and so I stayed where I was, as Sebastian stepped forward and opened the door.

It was dark in there. He held the door ajar and knocked, tentatively. 'Excuse me ...' he said. Our ears were full of the word Alex had been repeating, my heart was beating, beating, to be entering the inner sanctum like this, '... but we *have* to check,' Sebastian whispered, and we did have to, he knocked on the door properly, loudly, this time, and then he actually stepped right into the room and switched on the light.

There was a big bulge in the bed. There were scattered clothes on the floor. Sebastian was moving towards the bed when the bulge of duvet shifted and moved and Ivan sat up from within it, his face dazed and bleary, it was clear he was waking from sleep. He looked confused, the duvet slid further down. He was alone in the bed.

Ivan said something in Russian, his eyes came into focus, he looked at us both, he took in who it was, who we were, it took a few seconds for him to emerge from sleep, to comprehend the situation: that we two lackeys had actually come into the cabin where he was sleeping and disturbed him. His chest was naked and hairless.

The fury came. 'What the *fuck*,' he began, but Sebastian was ignoring him, walking across the cabin to the door of the ensuite, the sole remaining place on the boat: he opened it, he looked, he stood back so the bathroom was visible to me: empty. He turned to me. 'She has ... gone,' he said. He shook his head. He spread his arms, palms up, helpless. 'She has gone,' he repeated, and then I knew: that we could not do it, we could not give Alex back her mum.

'Who has gone?' It was Ivan speaking. 'Who has gone?'

Sebastian came to me at the door and we looked back at him. He had pulled himself up and was now sitting on the edge of the bed with his legs sprawling onto the floor. He wasn't even covered anymore by the duvet, he was naked, scrambling.

'Who has gone?' Ivan said again. 'Kata. Do you mean Kata? Do you mean Kata?'

There was no fury anymore. His eyes were wide, he reached out a hand towards us.

267

'Please,' he said, 'what do you mean?' He said her name again, he stretched out his arms to us. It was hard to look at him.

'Kata.'

*

Out on the deck Anton turned to us, still with Alex in his arms. 'Should we put something over her legs?' he asked. 'To protect them while she is in the boat.'

'I'll get Tristan,' Sebastian said. 'I'll tell him to bring the first aid kit, there must be surgical spirit and gauze.' He moved off. 'I'll meet you on the landing dock,' he said.

We carried Alex down there.

'I don't know if we should put antiseptic on them,' I said, indicating the worst of the cuts. I was imagining the pain. 'Maybe it should wait till she's in hospital.'

We got her into the tender and sat there, waiting for Sebastian and Tristan to come. Anton held Alex across his lap, she leaned into him. I remembered that this was someone she had known all her life.

'I am going to give you a little brandy now, to make you sleepy,' he said. Still holding her with one big arm, he retrieved a small silver bottle from the pocket of his jeans.

'OK,' she said. He put the bottle to her lips. She took three small sips.

The searchlights still blazed out. Because the immediate vicinity of the boat was so bright it was hard for our eyes to adjust to what lay beyond it. I couldn't see the sea past the arc of the lights but I imagined it, stretching away, no land in sight. The lights made a racket, a loud vibrating hum. The motion of the water knocked the tender in a steady beat against the dock. I looked down at Alex and saw her lips were moving and I leaned closer to hear what she was saying. I heard Anton saying, 'Shh, little one.' She was lying horizontally across his lap but she wasn't looking up at him. She was staring into space and mumbling. I leaned closer again to hear. I heard her repeat the word, 'Chukotka. Chukotka.'

I wanted her to be there, in that place, where the snow stretched away from the windows as far as the eye could see and inside everything was warm and bright and cosy. I wondered if she was back in her Brett the Hitman Hart costume or if she was lying between them in a warm bed, half-asleep, waiting for morning to arrive.

There was the noise of running on the steps down to the landing dock. Sebastian was back, followed by Tristan. They got into the boat with us. Tristan went straight to the driver's seat and started the engine.

I put my hand on Alex, gently, resting it at her side and Sebastian held his hand to her too and we were moving, slowly at first and then faster. I looked back to see the searchlights extinguish and we were on a sea that was now totally dark, the lights of Male just starting to appear in the far distance.

Acknowledgements

Thank you to my incredible agent, Katie Greenstreet. Huge thank you to my editor Luke Brown, copyeditor Robina Pelham-Burn, proofreader Anne Rieley and to Robert Greer, Mila Melia-Kapoor, Emily Frisella, Mehar Anaokar, Steve Panton, Jack Murphy and the rest of the team at Profile. Thank you to photographer Rafaela Proell.

For love, friendship, support, feedback on drafts or a combination of the above, thank you to Carlotta Bach, Anna Barfuss, Nicola Barr, Lara Behrens, Sophia Brown, Bella von Bohlen, Chris Chapman, Sadie Chapman, Charlie Collins, Sheena Cowell, Ed Davey, Gregor Donaldson, Keren Dunn, Melanie Ebenhoch, Jean Farish, Arianna Fleur, Melissa Franklin, Inga Fraser, Francesca Gavin, Keiran Goddard, Yuki Higashino, Zoe Hood, Nick Hughes, Alexander Jameson, Andrew Jameson, Elisabeth Kihlstrom, Dean Kissick, Krzysztof Kaczmarek, Sam Kriss, Kristina Marberger, Lara Orawski, Lukas Posch, Hannah Ross, Titania Seidl, Annie Sheppard, Natasha Stallard, Bernhard Staudinger, Emma Stonex, Pawel Szostak, Anton Tweedale, Jane Whitfield, Barbara Zeman.

Special thank you to my second family, Ellie, Jakob, Frida and Esme. Jenny: thank you for everything.

Most of all – and how could I ever thank you enough – thank you Mum and Dad.

In loving memory, Grandpa Sir, Grandpa Philip, Grandma Toni and Oliver.